'Mags, you're fairly new as a cell member. But one thing I can tell you right now: Fight is the most effective thing that ever happened to the women's movement . . . Fight is not a democratic assembly, it's a guerrilla army fighting for half the world's population.'

FIGHT stood for Feminist International Guerrillas. They claimed that they would 'hurl down phallic tyranny' but the popular media thought they were acting 'for havoc and terror'.

Margaret Stubbs is young and tough, and a valued cadet of FIGHT. But she is a human being as well, and it is in the light of her character that FIGHT, its overall strategy and detailed terrorist planning, is shown here.

FIGHT includes some of the most terrifying women ever to congregate in a fictional setting. They operate through organisations, plans and disciplines designed for women to rule the world.

It is a story of great violence. Margaret is plunged into a world of militant women of whom some are supreme commanders and some mere infantry: a community of terrorists hell-bent on confrontation with the male world and its established ramparts of civil and military law.

The story ranges from London to New York and then to a guerrilla camp – referred to as 'The Convent' – on an isolated mountain in Mexico. This is where most of the action takes place, including some heart-stopping air combat.

David Boggis has tackled this vast and controversial subject with knowledge, spirit, and exciting detail. The result is challenging and absorbing.

by the same author

KILLER INSTINCT
A TIME TO BETRAY

THE WOMAN THEY SENT TO FIGHT

David Boggis

Macmillan London

ISBN 0 333 35937 2

First published 1983 by
MACMILLAN LONDON LIMITED
London and Basingstoke
Associated companies in Auckland, Dallas,
Delhi, Dublin, Hong Kong, Johannesburg,
Lagos, Manzini, Melbourne, Nairobi,
New York, Singapore, Tokyo, Washington
and Zaria

Typset in Great Britain by
WILMASET
Birkenhead, Merseyside

Printed in Great Britain by
THE ANCHOR PRESS LTD
Tiptree, Colchester

Bound in Great Britain by
WM BRENDON & SON LTD
Tiptree, Colchester

to Heather and Wendy

CALLING

CHAPTER 1

Take out the traffic and the people and you can hear London breathing. It was creepy, Margaret Stubbs thought with her eyes ranging intently through the lamplit chiaroscuro, waiting, counting down seconds. Four o-two. Four o-three. Nothing broke the silence. Only the cold tipple of the ceaseless February rain and lub-dub, lub-dub of her heart, crashing like marching feet through the deserted office building.

Four o-four. Four o-five. Come on, come *on*, you must be finished by now.

Her eyes jumped. But no, nothing had moved. Just imagination.

Fingers, keep them still. Imagination could play whatever practical jokes it liked when you were watching for the law at four in the morning in a Fenchurch Street office block while someone planted a bomb. What a way, Margaret Stubbs thought. What a way to start a service to humanity.

Then through the shadows Lorraine was there, snub-nosed, aggressive, a glint of outside light on gold curls, a wide-hipped contrast with Margaret's lanky frame. 'Piece of cake. We've got nine minutes, let's go.'

The rain was an undisguised blessing. It would keep night workers indoors and make an excuse to run in the street. The Porsche was across Lime Street. Starting it took some coaxing and Margaret was still blipping the throttle when the heavy thump of the explosion reached them.

'Shit,' Lorraine muttered, and glared at her watch. Early.

Margaret pulled her scarf another half-inch up her nose and let the Porsche into Leadenhall Street. Getaway routine: well mannered driving west through the City and across to the M40, then hammer all the way to Oxford and hand the car over to the cell tasked with hiding it. Margaret slowed for the Bishopsgate junction with the wipers planing through the layer of rain.

A police panda car crossed the junction, going north.

Lorraine held her breath. Margaret let the Porsche roll. The panda car's brakelights went on and it wheeled round and came back for them. Margaret halted.

Through her teeth Lorraine hissed: 'Go on! Go on!'

Margaret said nothing. She let the panda driver halt across their front, open his door and get out.

Then she slammed the Porsche backwards round with the pendulum of the rear engine's weight swinging the front sideways on the rain-slicked asphalt and was halfway back up Leadenhall Street before the policeman had his Pocketfone out. With a dab on the brakes she went right. Exhaust rasped shrilly off close-set walls and suddenly they were travelling.

Lorraine shouted: 'You want nav?'

'I know where I'm going.'

A right and a left. Floodlights ahead. As they braked, Lorraine saw they were at the Tower. Margaret peered out, edging forward for a turn west.

Headlamps blurred in a cloud of spray crossing Tower Bridge at 80 were a police Rover. Too late, Margaret cut the lights. The Rover vanished to the north but they could hear its tyres. Margaret could almost feel the brutal skid as it braked.

East, then. She put the lights back on, all six this time, and thrust the Porsche past the bridge mouth, then down beside it on the cobbles. But the Rover was after them. Margaret shoved.

Group 2 competitions treatment on a Porsche 911S gives you maybe 240 brake horse, the impact resistance of an excavator bucket and the roadholding of a scalded cat. Then all you want is the nerve to use it.

Margaret was doing less than 70 when she reached the first dock bridge but it was still a clear jump with the crash ringing through their heads as the sump shield bottomed on the cobbles and in the mirror she saw the policeman leave the road likewise only when the Rover landed it slewed into the high dock wall before continuing. They could have done with helmets, but helmets only got you noticed. A very rapid right-hander now and Margaret hung out the back end for it, straightened for the next dock bridge, screamed airborne over it with the policeman following and probably loving it, smashed back on to rainswept asphalt. And saw the turn tighten up, going left.

Circle and bar, *London Transport Wapping*, the Porsche askew on the wet and very quick, check the mirror. They'd pulled out a few yards from the Rover, not much, they'd just have to hope. She went hard down through the gears, Lorraine white-knuckled on the grab handle, *handbrake*, and she put the Porsche broadside on opposite lock to slow down. She slotted it into the side street she'd known about.

And was in luck. A lorry was unloading, a yard gate open beside its tailboard, and quick as the thought Margaret swung the Porsche round it, into the yard. She halted.

Rain peckled on the roof and for a sickening moment reverse wouldn't engage.

A man, dazzled in the spotlights, shouted: '*Oi!*' The Rover growled past out of sight. Margaret turned the Porsche deftly and swung out on the road.

Headlights blazed at them from a second police car wrenching round the lorry.

Instinct is quicker than reason: your instinct is to hit what's parked rather than what's coming at you, and before the policeman could reason that he'd got the Porsche bottled up in a cul-de-sac, he'd hit the parked lorry and Margaret had gone up the kerb. She scraped between the wall and the now crunched police car, squeezed out again, and drove west.

Back past Wapping station, speed needle flickering on to 90, then hard braking. Lorraine hadn't expected it.

A footpath ran between the houses to the right. Margaret went down to first gear and sidelights. She'd taken the bumpers off yesterday, she knew the Porsche just had room, and this time no one had seen them.

Lorraine let out her breath. They emerged into a barely lit back street. Still no one was about, and as the Porsche bumped down the kerb Margaret selected headlights and changed up cautiously. A right and a left. A cul-de-sac. Lorraine was staring, tense, incredulous. Again they climbed up the kerb and this time as Margaret sneaked through the gap Lorraine saw they were entering a recreation ground. Swings and roundabouts; goal-posts; tall, severe, council-style buildings. Margaret selected one of the buildings and drove up beside it. A library, Lorraine

11

realised; it fronted on to a wide street. They hadn't found this just by luck; this was painstaking, thoroughly detailed recceing.

Margaret drove warily west from Stepney to St Paul's and down Ludgate Hill. Already London was growing busy, already there were crowds round the fire engines round the building they'd hit. And the police knew the Porsche's number.

But it wasn't going to lead them to the Oxford cell. Off Farringdon Road, Margaret drove up the hill among the hustling news vans, doubled through a couple of alleys, and slipped down a ramp into an underground garage that said *Strictly Private*, with the name of a big newspaper group. It was deserted. In a space labelled *E. B. Munday* Margaret parked.

'This chap Munday's on St Lucia till Friday week. I rang his secretary.'

Lorraine pulled her scarf down from her snub nose. 'Jesus Christ, you've done your homework on this one!'

Margaret was having a job with her lower lip. She concealed it: this was no time to get childish; this or any other. She settled her glasses on her nose. 'We'd better not waste time.'

'I'll phone Oxford.'

They leaned into the back. On the narrow rear seat they had shopping bags with innocent raincoats instead of their dark anoraks, and skirts instead of their dark jeans. Lorraine didn't like skirts, but too bad, this was an operation. Hindered by the steering wheel, Margaret kicked off her boots, pulled on the skirt, and pulled down her jeans. Lorraine was cramming her discarded clothing into the shopping bag as Margaret wriggled into the raincoat.

'I'll find that phone box,' Lorraine muttered. It was understood that they left separately.

Margaret stuffed her dark clothing down in the bag, still wearing gloves. The car was finished, but they didn't need to leave anything for the lab people to find and analyse for hair samples and fingernail fragments. In the mirror Lorraine was moving cat-like up the ramp, a chunky, medium-height figure with a gleam of streetlighting in gold hair. Margaret twisted the mirror.

She saw her own face, oval, bespectacled, dark chestnut hair swept back to go under the headscarf. And pale now under the Andean tan.

Her lips were under control again and she moved them in a prayer of thankful relief.

Lorraine had gone. Using the shadow, Margaret left the underground car park and began moving deep into the maze of courtyards and back alleys behind Fleet Street.

* * *

In the beginning was the fear, and the fear was behind her and in front of her, above her and below and all around her. Someone or something was hunting her, a formless Minotaur in this labyrinth that she'd entered without knowing where or when and without knowing which door to go through to get out, knowing only that behind the corner she'd just turned came the fear, and it was getting closer. Starting to stumble, starting to panic, she snatched open the door. And there the girl was, all bloody with the knife wounds yawning and her hair half ripped out and her mouth agape and her eyes staring in mindless terror. The scream echoed in Margaret's brain.

'Margaret. Margaret.'

With a jolt she sat up. Blood was pounding in her head, her pulse rate going like the Porsche's pistons. Renata was on the edge of the couch, leaning forward, worry etched into her pale, acne-speckled face. 'It's all right, Margaret.'

With difficulty, Margaret grasped where she really was. The women's common room at Buckingham College, the one they let the medical students use as well as the other undergraduates like Renata. A dream, that was all it had been. But the Porsche hadn't been a dream.

'I feel terrible.'

'D'you want to miss this afternoon's lectures?' Renata said in her thin, piping voice with its echoes of the gaunt terraces of Huddersfield.

'No.' If anything would give the game away, that would. She couldn't seem to take sleepless nights any more. It wasn't lectures this afternoon, anyway, it was lab work.

'What was it?' Renata murmured. 'Julie?'

Margaret nodded. It was months now since she'd found Julie O'Dell's body but the nightmare had never let up. Human dissection she could handle, she wouldn't have got into her

13

second year of medical studies otherwise; but that had been something very different. Finding Julie that way was what had made Margaret determined to join Fight.

Fight would have claimed responsibility for the bombing by now. Feminist International Guerrillas, they called themselves; 'to hurl down tyranny' was their own version of the ending, but the tabloids called it 'for havoc and terror', and that was one of the printable variations. The key to Fight's philosophy was that male-dominated governments and industries were driving the world ever closer to destruction and that until women took power – not merely a share in it – the entire race was in increasing danger of annihilation. The trouble was that men never would give up the power they held, at any level from presidential office to marriage bed. Fight accepted that. And thus the paradox: that the women in Fight's secret cells stood compelled to adopt the very tactics of the masculine tyranny that for all society's sake they had to overthrow. That they must declare men their enemy, combat them on their own terms. And beat them.

Julie O'Dell had been on the fringe of Fight. She'd started at Buckingham at the same time as Margaret; they'd been close friends. She'd died hideously, knifed by some nutcase who thought feminists were out to castrate him. Or so the police said, not that *they'd* put much effort into finding the murderer.

Margaret Stubbs had, starting by making quiet inquiries about how to join Fight.

Fight had contacted her. In the person of limp-haired, sardonic Renata Vernon, economics student, dissatisfied ex-Communist for whom Marx was too moderate, and now Fight guerrilla.

'Come on,' Renata said, and patted Margaret's knee. 'Let's get a cup of tea.'

*   *   *

Rush-hour people were cascading down the steps to the Tube station in the whirling darkness of Marylebone Road. Passing the news-vendor, Margaret slowed her pace, tempted by the bill: *Angry women claim blast*, but she didn't normally buy an evening paper and wasn't going to attract attention by changing her routine. She allowed the torrent of people to carry her out of the rain and down to the platform, grubby, shadowy, Victorian. Her eyes flicked over the headlines as she waited. The stop press panel said: *Car found*. Then she was surging aboard the train.

She hadn't expected a seat and didn't get one. Weariness weighed heavy on her and only the press of the people round her and the gravity shift as the train accelerated kept her upright. A man in a camelhair coat stood against her, very smart, neatly trimmed sideburns, five o'clock shadow but not too much of it, her own height, five eleven. And no, she didn't recognise him, it was just that he looked like a film star, Robert Redford or someone. Trying to catch her eye, too, and she looked away purposely, disdainfully, no I *don't* like strange men picking me up and particularly not pushing their bodies against mine just because the train's crowded. Her arms, pinned to her sides. If he moved his hand like that once more . . .

Station lights, deceleration. Margaret braced herself. In the edge of her eye she saw the man in the camelhair coat step on to the platform, the cocky swing of his strong shoulders as he strode away, and she spared a moment's hatred for his arrogance.

There was a seat now, but Margaret let it go to a fat black woman laden with shopping. She hung on the strap as the train crashed away. She felt drained, despondent. And bitter, bitter, bitter.

CHAPTER 2

The old, wide-rim Toyota Celica was the most beat-up thing on
four wheels that Margaret Stubbs had seen since she left the far
provinces of Peru. Judging by the cockpit clutter of tripmeter,
fuse box, maplight stalk, it was the one Renata Vernon used for
rallying. Renata was driving south now, into Clapham; she'd
collected Margaret at Charing Cross.

'How many Valentines d'y' get?'

One, Margaret remembered, but it wasn't a question Renata
expected answered. It was Wednesday, two days since the bomb.
In Balham in a grid of back streets they got out and walked two
blocks through the rain past the curtains glowing multicoloured
from the tellies. Margaret's parents hadn't even a black-and-
white, but it wasn't the cash: they thought television was
'worldly'. Odd that that no longer went for radio, or newspapers.
Renata vanished inside a door in a faceless Victorian terrace.

The hallway was in darkness. On the threshold, fear grabbed
Margaret and she knew this was her nightmare, come alive, and a
knife or a cosh anywhere among these shadows might do for her
what someone had done for Julie O'Dell. Dear Jesus, forgive
me. She walked through.

Lorraine Easson was waiting upstairs with Mary Abbott, Mary
sitting motionless as always with her neat, white hair and her
calm, Mona Lisa face. She was the last person you'd think of as a
Fight urban-guerrilla cell commander, Margaret invariably
thought.

Margaret made the tea; she was the junior person in the cell.
They didn't waste time with chit-chat: the sooner they were out
of here, the safer. Mary said, velvety yet direct: 'The explosion
was early and we lost the Porsche.'

Defiantly Lorraine jerked her tight, gold curls. 'Faulty timer.

16

That's all it could've been. Didn't show up under test.'

Mary just watched, still, impassive, waiting till Lorraine started to shift, guiltily. Then she fixed the calm, brown eyes on Margaret. 'How did we lose the Porsche?'

'A police car spotted us and got suspicious.'

'How did you know it was suspicious?'

'You can tell.' Margaret was defensive. 'The way a driver . . .'

Mary pursed her lips. 'You can tell?'

'We were buggered from the time the pig saw us,' Lorraine said harshly. 'Margaret did the only thing. The pigs already knew about the explosion – if we'd tried going on, we'd've been busted in sod-all flat.' You wouldn't have thought, listening to her, that she was a university lecturer with an MA in social history. 'We got out by bloody good driving based on a bloody good advance recce.' She gave Margaret an approving nod.

Enviously, Renata lit a cigarette. Normally she got the specialist driving jobs.

Mary, implacable, said: 'We *still* lost the Porsche. Do you *know* how much that cost to acquire and prepare?'

'Listen.' Lorraine flung out a hand. 'We got a real publicity coup, radio, the box, *everything*. That's what counts. We're driving the idea home, hit by hit: one, that women aren't just good for universal nannies or a Friday-night screw; two, that the phallic jackboot is doomed!'

Renata crossed her legs again, huddled in a corner on the lino flooring, and brushed ash off her knee. Margaret sat miserably under the criticism. The small room was yellow-lit, with the February fog filtering in where the window fitted badly, and her chair was hard, wonky with one short leg. Lorraine sat on a broken television set, knees wide apart like a boxer between rounds, but for all her big talk she was scared of Mary, too. Fight taught you to be scared of your cell commander, scared of her power.

'*And* the brass,' Renata said, practical. 'They spent three million quid putting yon computer in there, and now look at it. That'll go down a treat at t' annual meeting. "Oh, no, our chairman sees no reason to alter his staffing policies as regards promoting women." ' She spat a laugh.

Calm in the sole armchair, Mary fixed her eyes on Margaret's. 'How did you feel?'

'I agree with Renata. Property's our best target if we want the best publicity. We only harm ourselves if we hurt people, even men. But . . .'

Mary's old brown eyes were clear, sharper than Margaret's short-sighted ones. 'Go on, Margaret.'

'Correct me if I'm wrong, but it all seems a bit haphazard. We bomb a hostile company here, raid a bank there: how does it all fit together? We're heading for disaster if we're merely floundering about with no special strategy.'

'Of course we've got a strategy!' Lorraine gestured angrily. 'What this whole thing is about is jolting the average, ordinary, downtrodden, browbeaten, psyched-out, male-tyrannised woman in the street into realising that she *has* got control over her own and humanity's future – it isn't all just up to faceless fools in male-run ministries.'

'Hearts and minds,' Margaret murmured.

'You can sneer!' Lorraine snarled. Margaret hadn't been sneering, but she didn't dare say so now. 'Wanda Zelaszny says it again and again: until women realise they *can* defeat phallic tyranny, they'll never even try.'

Zelaszny, Margaret remembered. The hidden guru of Fight. The American social anthropologist whose theories about ancient matriarchies had caused worldwide controversy, years earlier. And who was now underground somewhere, leading Fight.

'Fight's three-point programme is a strategy,' Renata said, gesturing limply with her cigarette, eyes wide as if astonished at having to state the obvious. 'You look at what Zelaszny says. The world is at risk from the male-run nuclear powers. At the same time, women everywhere are suffering tyranny by men. Only the restoration of the ancient matriarchies will end phallic tyranny and save the world from destruction. And only women can restore them.'

Margaret had read that, herself, in Zelaszny's books: the theory of the matriarchies. Zelaszny had convinced a lot of people – not just women – that an older, wiser world civilisation had been governed exclusively by females. And then been swept aside by the ignorant brutality of phallic power.

Fight's programme was clear, from Zelaszny's political writing. Women had to restore the matriarchy, but first they had to weaken male power – in government, in the economy, in the home – to the point at which a concerted uprising by women would destroy it; and at the same time they had to convince uncommitted women that they could succeed against men. Terrorist attacks would serve two of those purposes: to weaken phallic power and to convince women that it could be done. Revolution was a different matter. Revolution would require a cadre of trained, battle-hardened women.

The thing was, Fight had them. They were at the same place as Zelaszny was, Fight's world headquarters. Wherever that was. Margaret watched the others: Lorraine, snub-nosed, sullen in her jeans and rollneck and closely clipped nails; Renata, pale, flat-chested, sneering past her cigarette as if scorning her own feeling of insignificance; and Mary, white-haired, clear-eyed, very still in her heavy grey skirt, and wiser and more feminine than any of them.

But then, Mary was the only one of them who'd met Wanda Zelaszny, and to judge from the way she reacted, it had been like meeting a messiah.

'You are all right,' Mary said. 'Dents in big companies' balance sheets will make *them* realise we're serious; our success in difficult operations will give more women the confidence to be ready for uprising, when it comes; and the fact that our methods are humane will bring those male elements that can be used at all round to our support.'

The methods hadn't always been humane, though, and weren't always, now.

'Men are by nature predisposed to competition, destruction, death – the Thanatos principle. Women are by nature predisposed to survival, their own and their children's. With nuclear weapons, designed and positioned by men, poised to destroy our world, humanity has reached the end of a phase of history in which women have been able to afford to rely for survival upon men. Women must take the power to disarm the world and rule it in peace. If men resist that, men must be overthrown, as the tyrants they are.' Mary paused. It was virtually a quote from Zelaszny, Margaret realised; but Mary didn't believe it any the less for that. You could always see a light in Mary's eye, a reflection of confidence or faith, when she talked about Zelaszny. She said: 'It won't be easy.'

19

Renata crushed out her cigarette.

'We'll break now,' Mary said. 'Margaret, when is your next flying training?'

'Saturday, weather permitting.' She'd stood, smoothing her skirt in unconscious reflex; aware of Lorraine, shrugging down the old rollneck, and Renata, shoving her arms into her bulky rally jacket.

'Renata will need you on Sunday,' Mary said. 'We must replace the Porsche. We've got two write-offs that can be welded together. The car will be needed operationally by another cell.' She looked at Renata. 'Will you take Lorraine? Margaret, come with me.'

Margaret felt the tension again, felt rather than saw the quick turn of Lorraine's head and the flash of strange anger in her steel-blue eyes. She'd noticed before how a guerrilla's status within the cell correlated with the amount of time granted her alone with the cell commander.

Lorraine left with Renata and then Margaret went out apprehensively with Mary. Drizzle brought the fog close around them and narrowed the greys and blacks of the street to a damp globule of consciousness with the implausibility of a studio set. Streetlamps gleamed shiftily and the pavements glistened, slick as treachery. Mary unlocked the Cavalier. It was newish, unremarkable. The right sort of car for a grandmother with a gay son, and a daughter hiding in a battered-wives' refuge; a grandmother who'd broken her career to raise a family and been refused a job when she'd tried to bring her talents back to work; who'd divorced her husband of twenty years because most of the time had been torment.

'Don't take that criticism too much to heart.' Mary slid the car into traffic. 'I know you were unlucky, but we have to analyse, to see how to do better next time.' Lights changed; she went through the gears. 'It was very shrewd of you to ask about strategy. You're a deep thinker.'

Margaret tightened up inside, then remembered Lorraine and Renata weren't there to get jealous. She tried not to look at Mary with her sensible coat and demure skirt and the scarf at her throat.

'Don't worry about that operation, Margaret. I've been asked to write a special report about your particular role in it, because our leadership feels that, for a cell member of your age and your junior standing in the movement, you've performed exceptionally well. And don't worry about strategy. Fight has a master plan that's been prepared at a level much higher than ours. We have plans laid, on an international scale. There's something coming up, I can't say when. But when it does, the whole world will take notice of us.'

CHAPTER 3

Somewhere downstairs you could hear the metallic whine of a high-speed drill, and a confident voice, *no, really, this won't hurt a bit.* Richard Caine had to hand it to his chief, he knew how to pick a secure rendezvous. The surgery was a rabbit warren, all the staff had been screened, and the patients were always far too preoccupied with the insides of their mouths to notice who came and went.

'Humane bollocks,' Caine said. 'It wasn't humane in Glasgow when that submachinegun squad killed four blokes coming out of the pubs. Or those two they kneecapped for alleged wife-battering.'

'The wives were undoubtedly battered.'

Patchy afternoon light from the attic window caught the typescript report, lying on the medical trolley between the two men that was serving as a coffee table. Robin Barrington Yorke peered at Caine over his glasses, professorish in his shiny dark jacket, at his side the heavy stick he'd used for walking since he came out of hospital in 1941. Caine with his camelhair coat flung over the chair, the dove-grey tailored suit and navy pinstriped shirt and film-star panache, was a vivid contrast.

It didn't make Caine inefficient as a Defence Intelligence operations director, though.

'Right, but I mean, okay, that isn't an excuse.'

'Indeed not.' Barrington Yorke waited.

'We've got three million quids' worth of "humane" damage,' Caine said, 'we've got this hot-rod Porsche *in our hands*, and the most we can get out of Rahab is vague mutterings about a cell that might or might not exist in Oxford. I think you *ought* to do as I recommend there.' He gestured at his report. 'Get the steering committee off its butt and get some proper surveillance on

Fight's agitprop. DCI McKnight already knows all the names. *I* know, I know, so far we can't touch them because all these bloody cows in agitprop keep their dainty little arses on the right side of the law and scream free speech and phallic tyranny as soon as anyone looks through their books to see how many statutes they're inciting people to break. But they're the cover for the underground cell structure, they're the tail that wags the bitch. Virtually the one useful thing we *have* got from Rahab is the contact system between the agitprop activists and the cells. Given proper coverage, we could catch every contact and blow every single cell.'

'In the UK.' Barrington Yorke blinked. 'And what about France, or West Germany, or the United States?'

'They have the same option. The structure's uniform internationally.'

'It won't work.' Barrington Yorke folded bony hands together; sparrows hopped scratchily on the tiles just above. 'Detective Chief Inspector McKnight hasn't the staff resources. Even supposing she had, you might break two or three cells, but Fight would very quickly realise what we were doing, and all the other cells would submerge untraceably.' Barrington Yorke believed in never underestimating an opponent. Eve McKnight would have agreed. She was leader of the CID team investigating Fight – the politics of its agitprop wing and the acts of terrorism by its secret cells. She'd been chosen partly because she was a woman, mostly because she was a gifted police officer. But Scotland Yard hadn't been authorised to run covert agents inside Fight; DI had. 'Bear in mind the sheer numbers we're talking about,' Barrington Yorke told Caine. 'At least three cells are operating in London, probably two in Glasgow, probably this one in Oxford, apart from activities we've identified in Sheffield, Leeds, Belfast, Cambridge, Brighton, Birmingham. There might easily be as many again that have yet to come to our notice. We're talking in terms of perhaps a hundred undercover Fight guerrillas in the UK alone.'

Caine's film-star eyes glittered, angry, impatient.

'What is more,' Barrington Yorke said, shifting in the borrowed, waiting-room chair to ease his back, 'you'd be running Rahab into danger, and I am not having that.'

'Let me be the judge . . .'

'You're impatient with Rahab, you want results. So do we all, so does Rahab. But don't force her pace.' Barrington Yorke slipped his glasses a little down his nose and gave Caine the look that so enraged the younger man. 'Rahab is the best agent anyone has ever had inside Fight, anywhere in the world. Our allies would not thank us for exposing her. Don't forget what happened in the States. The FBI put twenty or twenty-five women officers into Fight's agitprop wing, spread up and down the country. Only sixteen lasted longer than a fortnight, none of them penetrated to the cell structure, and every one of them was eventually flushed.' He paused. 'Not only that – Fight murdered three of them.'

'I know what happened in the States.' Caine knew the FBI's experience with Fight. They'd picked him to direct Rahab because he knew America, despite Barrington Yorke's belief that a woman would have run Rahab better.

He'd risen to the task, though, Barrington Yorke had to admit; in more senses than one. Rahab was a gifted young woman who was perfectly capable of parrying unwanted attentions by her director; yet Barrington Yorke had had misgivings about Caine's calculated tactic of seeking an emotional involvement; and he knew there was more than plain professional technique in it when Caine exchanged messages by means of brush contact with an attractive female.

Apropos of little, Caine grumbled: 'What gets me is what all these women want to go in for violent behaviour for in the first place. I never seem to get knifed in the ribs by the ones I meet when *I* pick up a sixty-quid lunch bill for two. Do *you* know any women who can honestly say they're dissatisfied, or discriminated against?'

'The women's movement has become polarised. There was a time when it was popularly thought outrageous for women to campaign against the nuclear family and when organisations such as the Society for Cutting Up Men – which never amounted to much in the end, anyway – were thought to represent simply the extremist fringe of a movement that apparently threatened the structure of society – or at least, Western society. The movement won some battles. The fact that laws were enacted in numerous Western countries guaranteeing women equality in certain necessary spheres was an indication that the community as a

24

whole believed that women had a right to the objectives they sought.

'Then, more recently, a large part of the movement changed its direction. The emphasis came to be placed on the *importance* of the family, a recognition that people weren't fulfilled by jobs alone.' Caine was kicking himself; this lecture was the last thing he'd wanted. 'It came to oppose any thinking that placed males and females in opposed and warring camps, and instead to plead for co-operation between men and women working jointly for equality.

'And thus arose the polarisation. Many radical feminists watched that happening and saw it as a betrayal of the movement. They really believed that the new laws had fallen far short of their objectives; moreover, many among them genuinely feared that males *might* exterminate the human race, by nuclear war.' Barrington Yorke looked over his glasses. 'Frankly, I wouldn't care to argue against the feminists on that issue.

'So there existed a powerful groundswell, albeit mainly in the developed nations, of discontented women, disillusioned with their own movement, and feeling an urgent need to change society. That was the groundswell that Zelaszny identified, addressed, and formed into what might yet become a tidal wave, with Zelaszny at its crest. All those malcontents were split up, unco-ordinated, until Zelaszny united them with her belief – it isn't a hypothesis, all those learned works about Mycenae and prehistoric Zimbabwe notwithstanding, not on the evidence she presents: it's a belief – in a vanished and latterly *covered-up* golden age of wise and just matriarchies. And now Zelaszny has filled those people with a messianic faith and a religious zeal for restoring her supposed matriarchies.'

Downstairs, a man with a mouthful of wadding was trying to explain something to the dentist. The sun had gone in, a drip of rain tapped at the window. Barrington Yorke rummaged in his briefcase, reflecting on Caine's choice of codename. Rahab was the biblical inside agent in the siege of Jericho, and a harlot; witty, for a wide-eyed, straitlaced zealot whose parents were former Protestant missionaries. Barrington Yorke handed over the report he had for Caine.

'Pasarell's just had this from CIA at Langley.' Special Agent-in-Charge Frank Pasarell was leading the FBI inquiry into Fight

25

and was based in New York. 'They've identified a chap in Havana called Vassily Andreyev who's been hobnobbing a lot lately with Gregorio Tabio, deputy head of Cuban counter-intelligence.'

'A.k.a. the bloke who does all the work,' Caine grunted, scanning the CIA abstract. 'I didn't know gun-running came under counter-intelligence.'

The CIA had a suspicion, which no one had yet disproved, that Cuba was smuggling arms abroad, some of which ended up in Fight guerrillas' hands. The sinister bit about that was that Cuba was widely held to be a nation that handled a lot of work for the Soviet Union that the Soviet Union didn't want to be caught doing.

'Now, Vassily Andreyev', Barrington Yorke said, 'is a lieutenant-general in the KGB.'

Caine raised his eyes. 'Yeah?'

'He's almost sixty. There's . . .'

'Inexperienced kids like that need the odd foreign posting to broaden the mind.'

It was true that the political power in the KGB lay largely with men rather older than Andreyev, and he was no youngster; yet Barrington Yorke kept having difficulty in concealing his dislike of Caine's brashness.

'The rumour going about Havana is that Andreyev is there to train Cuban counter-intelligence experts. Gregorio Tabio, I don't know if you know . . .'

'Black. Age forty-two. Illiterate till the age of eighteen. Wife, five kids, including one who's thought to be the brains of the sixth form.' Caine was reading it from the CIA report. 'Close associate of Fidel and Raúl Castro. Thought to be chiefly responsible for the arrests of . . . Jesus Christ, no wonder the Yanks don't like him much.' He'd come to a long list of US agents, nearly all Cuban nationals, whom Tabio had caught. 'A bloke like *that* doesn't need advice from Moscow, he ought to be training their lot. Recently begun . . .' Caine looked up. 'What the hell does he suddenly want to learn to fly for?'

'We don't know. But you're plainly right about his needing no training from Andreyev.'

Caine plonked the report on his neatly creased trouser leg and gave Barrington Yorke a direct look, frowning. 'And a lieutenant-general's a bit high-powered to be sent on a lousy gun-running kick. Is Andreyev supposed to have been tied up with that business last November in the Gulf of Thailand?'

Four months previously, a near-water trawler out of a port near Bangkok had vanished, out near the main shipping route south and west from Vietnam. It might have been taken as just one of those mysteries; but when the Thai authorities and the CIA got wind of what smelt like an unusual interest on the KGB's part, they started looking for the vessel properly. They'd found it, several fathoms down, lying on the coral with the sea-cocks open and the crew still on board. Machinegunned, to a man, butchered in cold blood before the boat had been scuttled.

'Well, that seems to be what the Americans are wondering,' Barrington Yorke replied.

'So they think that's connected with Fight, that Andreyev's now up to his eyebrows in trying to cover it up, and that Moscow, via its faithful old proxy, Cuba, is behind Fight.' Caine stared.

Barrington Yorke shook his head but said, 'Yes'. Caine realised he was indicating misgivings. 'So Pasarell suggests. But neither he nor the writer of that CIA report has supplied any convincing reason why Moscow would want to stir up feminist revolt. There are more women than men in the Soviet population, therefore any such attempt would lay the country open to insurrection by more than half its people. I should be very wary of jumping to conclusions.'

27

CHAPTER 4

Brakes off, undercarriage down and locked, propellor pitch fixed, flaps. 'Bravo Sierra, downwind for two five.' Gravel pits below, dinghy sails bellying, but this was the marker for the turn. Speed, under max flap, push the lever, retrim, throttle back, line up the black strip. 'Bravo Sierra, final.' And now for the interesting bit. *Slam* through the updraught off the spinney, nicely caught, throttles fully shut and use the nose to adjust speed, *bounce* into the low turbulence, and this is where a Piper Seneca 1 light twin is on its worst behaviour and Denham has a very narrow runway indeed.

Margaret Stubbs brought the Seneca sideways over the fence with the props hardly turning, then as the speed sighed away shoved it straight with a bootful of rudder. She felt the satisfying single *thud* as the mainwheels touched, together, and stayed down. Then she pushed on full throttle, raised the flaps, and went up like a lift as the February wind gusted and caught her square on the nose.

Normally she'd have been flying from Oxford and using something that was still under maker's warranty, but she knew the old Seneca's owner and she knew that, in weather like today's, the combination of Denham's tiny runway and an aeroplane that didn't like crosswinds would be the best sort of discipline going for a person bent on getting a commercial pilot's licence as well as a doctorate in medicine.

Margaret Stubbs had spent most of her life in the Andes of Peru. One of the most lasting impressions she'd brought back to England was of friends she'd known, dying when the earthquakes struck. Watching their pain and knowing there was no help. And, gradually, forming the determination that one day she wouldn't just be setting broken bones under an awning: she'd

28

be making sure the amputation cases got flown to hospital.

An Andean flying-doctor service, with herself as the flyer *and* the doctor. Just to make sure.

Because she had to make sure, she couldn't just present some government office with a good idea; it would never do more than gather dust. And to make sure, she had to do anything that was necessary to put the idea into practice, to overcome every obstacle. Her eyesight, for a start. Passable, just, for a private pilot's licence; not for commercial work.

But there were ways round that, too, she'd been told.

*   *   *

Gusty daylight was failing and the man next door was turtle-waxing his Datsun. 'Hullo, Margaret.'

'Hullo.' She ducked her chin a bit, avoiding his eye as she slammed the old Escort's door, her mother's car. He ought to know better, married with two kids.

He watched her, though, since he thought she hadn't noticed. The raincoat unbuttoned and catching in the wind that lifted the heavy chestnut hair off her slim shoulders; the preppy vee-neck, unconsciously suited to a preppy figure; the fluid, quick movements of the slender hips and the long legs in their supermarket blue jeans.

Ignoring him, she went into the shabby semi. In the front room, her father was talking to one of his flock, and her mother stepped into the kitchen to greet her. Predictably, comfortingly, the kettle was on the gas. Margaret smiled wryly at her mother. You spent the day flying and lying and came home to a nice cup of tea.

'Have you had a nice day?'

Yes, if you find it nice wearing out your thighs and shoulders flying crosswind circuits. 'Busy, thanks.'

'You're looking tired.'

Margaret turned. In the distortion of the uncurtained window her oval face was pale, her high cheekbones unusually prominent. Being tired was risky. You might risk letting your naïve and loving parents imagine that you were part of a guerrilla cell.

'It's the flying,' her mother said. 'It's too much, on top of all your studying. You should give yourself a break.'

29

So kind, Margaret thought guiltily, so slow to see evil. A woman who, like her husband, had given the best of her life to her mission, who'd come home with her skin ruined with ultra-violet and her cheeks hollowed with illnesses she'd ignored, and whose eyes still shone with a Sunday-School child's love of God. A saint who didn't even realise she'd become a martyr. Margaret smiled hauntedly and avoided her mother's eye. Deceiving her parents made another reason to hate herself. They were so good, so trusting; yet the only reason that they heard no lies was that they asked no questions. Mary Abbott would have asked questions. Yet sharper wit didn't necessarily make her a better person.

Margaret stood up and peeled off the raincoat, hung it up, and patted her mother's wrist. 'Must go and catch up with my reading.'

*   *   *

Never make a pickup near your home. The shabby semi was in Ruislip and so Margaret took the Tube as far as Wembley Park and Renata collected her there in the battered Celica.

'What time d'you get to bed this morning?'

'Four.'

Renata shook her limp hair. Working for Fight was one thing, but lose a day's studying to build up CPL hours and you had to sandwich the studying somehow between grabbing a bite and grabbing sleep. If you dared sleep when any moment that you closed your eyes you might see Julie O'Dell again, the way you'd found her.

Wind played skittles with crisp bags and old Coke tins. Renata parked in a broken-down council estate where the terraces backed on to neglected allotments. Lorraine was in a rusty shed by some garages, bulky in an ill fitting overall and wearing welding goggles. She grinned at them, flushed and smudged. She'd almost finished the panel-beating. Margaret put her raincoat over a bench and pulled on an overall.

The work took longer than she'd expected. They broke for lunch at gone two with the hammers still ringing in Margaret's brain. They'd each brought sandwiches and a Thermos. It wasn't until Margaret sat down that she realised how tired she was.

Fatigue was becoming her normal condition and she didn't like that; you were too wide open to mistakes, too prone to feeling guilty that your loving parents thought you were at the university Christian Union. Sunday was such a difficult day to explain away.

They started welding. Lorraine had some idea of how to go about it, Margaret none, but Renata knew what she was up to and she supervised them, her thin Huddersfield piping acid as a schoolmarm's above the hissing air.

At four they flopped back on the bench with the bodyshell welded up. It wasn't a professional job but it wasn't going to get professional scrutiny, and it would hang together at least as well as some of the cars Renata had seen brutally rallied.

Lorraine ripped the plastic on a six-pack of Heineken. 'Renata?'

'Oh . . . all right.'

'Maggie?'

Margaret smiled wryly. 'Thanks.' The corruption indicated trust, maybe friendship. She pulled the ring, sipped cautiously. Then, involuntarily, stood and peered searchingly through the grimy window.

'I wouldn't do that, Maggie,' Lorraine said.

Margaret turned away. She glanced at Lorraine but Lorraine was tipping back her lager without suspicion. Margaret still felt tense, though she'd seen nothing out there.

'Margaret,' Renata blinked, pale-eyed, 'how can you get a commercial pilot's licence when you're as shortsighted as you are?'

'I'm not that shortsighted. I can read the instruments without glasses. There's nothing to stop me training to CPL standard over here and getting the licence itself in Peru. I've got contacts there.'

'Or Mexico,' Lorraine said.

Margaret glanced at her. She wanted to ask why Mexico but she dreaded making Lorraine suspicious. In fact, she dreaded Lorraine.

Renata scrutinised the bodyshell. 'This wants trimmed.'

Margaret and Lorraine went over. 'Shit,' Lorraine muttered, 'I did that bit.'

She reached under her overall. Light flashed off a blade and Margaret flinched.

31

Lorraine grinned ferociously. 'All right, Maggie, it's only a knife.' She opened her palm.

It was a big sheath knife, its six-inch blade worn thin by whittling, and razor-sharp. The wooden hilt bore a single notch.

Lorraine bent away from Margaret's frozen gaze and took off the soft excess metal in a couple of scrapes. Margaret was feeling cold inside as she wondered who it was Lorraine had killed.

*   *   *

Thursday in Whitehall with the weekend on its way and the traffic raucous under windblown cloud. Richard Caine's cover was working at an Inland Revenue office and he had his mind on the girl he was meeting for lunch when, four paces out from the door, the masonry started chipping at nose level and he moved fast, he didn't want the next chips to be bone from his skull. Not one of the ex-Vietnam M3s like they'd used in Glasgow, he was thinking, the sounds and the ricochet velocities were all wrong; probably one of the Nato FALs they'd nicked in Norway. By then he was prone, half under a parked post van, his Mauser HSc cocked and levelled, though he knew he wasn't going to use it: he might hit anyone, and so might they have done. He glimpsed the car, the Escort Rahab had told them about, going like a tornado.

Where the hell did the silly bitches think they were, Prohibition Chicago?

He dusted off the camelhair coat and went back indoors, flushed, flinging the Robert Redford forelock out of his eyes and wondering what to start using for cover now.

*   *   *

The tension was wrong, Lorraine sensed it, glancing at Margaret through the darkness of her decrepit old Fiat as she found the turning off Shaftesbury Avenue. They'd been to the mixed judo workout at the university union. All Fight guerrillas were supposed to train.

'You ought to take a higher grading, Maggie.'

'I don't see . . .' Margaret had only ever taken a yellow.

'You're a menace to those kids who think you're a novice. You're worth a brown, maybe a black.'

No answer. Sod you, then, Lorraine thought, and shoehorned the Fiat into a kerbside gap in an ill lit alley. She led Margaret through a gate in a ten-foot corrugated-iron fence with a notice, *No Unauthorised Entry*. It was behind Leicester Square; they were putting in a new Tube line, the site a morass of clay, brick rubble, pumping gear, bulldozers. Right on the far side was the hidden way into the office block where the cell was meeting and in the deepest of the darkness Lorraine saw Margaret flatten herself, suddenly, back to the fencing.

'What the *hell's* wrong with you? You're acting like your cover's blown.'

Margaret breathed: 'Don't.' Lorraine chuckled and led Margaret inside, into the back bit where the work went on, away from the reception lounge with its fountains and indoor foliage.

'Just a brief report,' Mary Abbott said. She was sitting poised and still as always behind some manager's desk, Renata huddled in a swivel chair, smoking defensively. 'The Escort you built runs perfectly and the cell that used it sends congratulations. It was used in an operation against a senior Defence Intelligence agent who uses the name of Richard Caine.'

Lorraine lounged across the door. The cleaning women who'd let them in, Fight supporters, weren't in earshot. Margaret had sat on a filing cabinet and now she was bracing herself, breathing deeply. 'A hit?' Lorraine said hungrily.

'A warning.' In other words, they'd missed. Mary eyed Margaret. 'They recovered the car despite a police chase. Good planning paid off.'

So that was all, another rap on the knuckles over the Porsche. Margaret nodded and swallowed. Renata jerked her little feline chin complacently, the next driving job safely hers.

And then the tension went and they were free, talking theory again, Mary guiding, eyes alight with the messianic memory of her meeting with the great Zelaszny. Yes, there was a difference, Lorraine said, more and more ordinary women were showing greater selfconfidence, increasing independence, because of agitprop's words and the cells' successes. Not enough, though, in Renata's view: too many allowed men to ride roughshod over them. And Mary still calm, never letting anything escape her.

Renata was saying, 'What *does* happen about kids? I mean, y've got to have 'em, and yet screwing's the absolute *embodiment*

33

of male domination.'

'If that's your experience,' Mary said, 'it's a shame, but . . .'

'Christ!' Lorraine spat disgustedly. 'A shame? I never expected that sort of misguided attitude from you! You must've had a hell of an experience. What's your experience, Maggie?'

'I . . . wh . . .' Nothing else came out.

Mary, fleetingly, caught Margaret's eye. 'Lorraine, I'll put any questions I consider relevant. Meanwhile, remember who is your commander.' She stared Lorraine out; it didn't take long; the Zelaszny effect again, the utter confidence of being right. 'Two schools of thought exist,' Mary explained. 'One is as you and Renata evidently feel, that intercourse symbolises woman's domination by man; the other is that intercourse is acceptable with a suitably approved man and should be allowed for the sake of those women who get pleasure from it. There's room for both views.

'The key, in Wanda Zelaszny's theory, is that childbearing must be strictly voluntary, as it was in the ancient matriarchies.' Mary really believed the ancient matriarchies had existed. That quality of zeal hadn't come just from reading Zelaszny's books, it had come from meeting Zelaszny herself. Listening to Mary, Margaret had a vision of her as one of the ancient, wise, ruling mothers. With an innate, feminine wisdom that was entirely up-to-date. 'The volunteer mother can, according to her views, then be impregnated either from a sperm bank – assembled, again, using carefully approved men – or by traditional coitus. The important thing is to prevent any suggestion of possession of the child by its father – it must always belong, via the mother, to the Fight community. The easiest way to ensure that is by the sperm bank, and so that is the theoretically preferred method.'

'Men should get a taste of their own medicine,' Lorraine said. 'They've spent long enough using women as sexual playthings, it's high time . . .'

Margaret said, 'Don't *do* that!'

Mary and Renata turned. Lorraine was turning the sheath knife incessantly in her hands; they could see its single notch.

Mary said quietly, 'Put your toy away.'

*　　*　　*

34

Lorraine left with Mary, Margaret went alone to the Tube. She flopped shuddering into a corner of the carriage. She hadn't been blown. Tension shook itself loose from her, and the trembling took over her hands and calves, and she turned her face into the corner and let the chestnut hair fall down in a screen round her head to hide her from the sprinkling of other late-night passengers. But Julie was there every time she closed her eyes, and so was the unasked, unanswered question of why Fight had thought Richard Caine might be a DI agent.

CHAPTER 5

This time the secure RV was at a theatre, deserted by daylight. Richard Caine reached it across the cobbles of Covent Garden, groped his way through the shadowy tunnels behind the stage, and found Barrington Yorke in the dusty box where he'd said.

'No ill effects?' Barrington Yorke murmured.

Caine muttered coarsely. 'There'll be ill effects on Rahab if I get my hands round her snow-white neck. It's all very well knowing this car's up for an operation – here we all are wondering which bank's in for a snatch, and they use it on me. Now I can't get her to find out whether that really was just a warning or whether they'll be back for another try.'

He wasn't the best person to be running Rahab. Not for the first time, Barrington Yorke wished he could have had his own choice of director. 'Never forget that, close as you may be geographically to Rahab, she's as deep inside hostile territory as if she were inside the Kremlin. I will not have her endangered. Another thing. I gather she is aware that Lorraine Easson has killed.'

'Yeah, right,' Caine said. 'But, I mean, okay, her cover's intact. It's time that girl got her finger out.'

Barrington Yorke folded bony hands together and looked away from Caine. The box was dark and the silence of the empty theatre was eerie, if you were sensitive to atmosphere. 'I used to know a man who was a rally driver,' Barrington Yorke said. Caine groaned inwardly: here came one of Barrington Yorke's legendary, and unfailingly infuriating, analogies. 'He competed in the Monte Carlo, the RAC, all the big ones. He was very skilful and drove very fast, but he never won a rally. His cars would always break down under him because he drove them so hard.'

He that hath ears to hear, Caine thought, let him hear. He sat in sour silence in the shadows and waited.

Barrington Yorke turned to face him again, the stiff movement betraying the pain in his back. 'And has Rahab said anything about this young German girl, Giselle Stamm, whom the German authorities are interested in?'

'Not a thing,' Caine said baldly.

Barrington Yorke eyed Caine over his glasses. Giselle Stamm would be perhaps fourteen now. Her short life had been turbulent. Her mother, Sabina Stamm, was the daughter of a wartime Luftwaffe ace, a Nazi Party member, who'd shot down more than two hundred Allied aircraft; Sabina had been following in his footsteps – in career if not in politics – training as a pilot, when she'd dropped out and gone underground into what was then the Baader-Meinhof group in West Germany. Giselle's father had been a terrorist who'd rethought his politics and given himself up to the police, and who, when Sabina was eventually arrested, had taken Giselle, then two years old, and attempted to give her a home. Sabina had collected a long sentence: she'd shot a policeman. Then in the years she spent in jail she changed her ideas: from violent anti-capitalism to violent feminism.

So, naturally, the first move when she escaped was to kidnap Giselle so that her daughter could absorb Fight's philosophy of the future, could become a fighter against men's tyranny and not some docile unit in one of the great male world-systems hell-bent on destroying humanity. Together in hiding, in the cell structure or maybe somewhere even more secret. Almost two years ago, that had been.

'They are looking for Giselle Stamm,' Barrington Yorke said, 'for the sake of a pointer to her mother. Sabina Stamm is a very dangerous woman.'

'Right, okay. So are these two dropouts from the Italian Red Brigades, Giovanna and Cornelia Piotti; so's this Charlotte Rondeau, the marksmanship ace who shot that top detective in Montreal; so's Jo Colwell, this female hood who killed three blokes in Los Angeles. You want me to go on? Rahab's got a wanted list long enough to go round her bust about six times.'

The emotional involvement. Partly, Barrington Yorke reflected, it was a mistake in that not even Caine, for all his abrasive objectivity, could escape being affected; and there was nothing especially professional in pretending not to care if you thought you'd been snubbed. The old man in Peru who'd recommended Rahab in the first place, before Fight was ever heard of, had showed vastly more respect than Caine ever had for the young woman's gifts. A paradox: Caine had grown up in an age of emancipation, of sex equality guaranteed by law; yet the old Peruvian had grown up in a society of rigid *machismo*, where the man ruled the roost and the wife was a possession to be fought over.

'Sabina Stamm will be found close to Wanda Zelaszny. If Giselle Stamm can be found, her mother will be traced.'

'That's a job for Pasarell in the States,' Caine said.

'It's a job for all of us.' In the quiet of the theatre, Barrington Yorke eased his back again, with difficulty. He glanced at Caine. 'Have you ever read any of Zelaszny's work?'

'What?'

'It's perfectly legal. That's the meaning of a free community. I've read several of her books. You or I or any revolutionary-minded undergraduate may perfectly freely read the works of Marx, or Guevara, or Wanda Zelaszny, or Adolf Hitler. Hitler's a classic parallel. If people had read *Mein Kampf* properly and taken it seriously in the 1920s, global politics today would be entirely different. People *should* read Zelaszny's work, to see what her programme really proposes for our world. Many people would be surprised to read her conception of the imagined "ancient matriarchies". There's no nonsense about democratic consensus, for instance. A modern matriarchy would be run autocratically, with a supreme leader and an administrative council whereby considerable power would be concentrated in really very few hands. The zealots among the feminists all love this idea, of course. Strong leadership appeals to them, but above all there's this, really . . .' he groped a moment for the word '. . . *messianic* quality about Zelaszny's writing that at times manages to make the wildest absurdities appear deterministically inescapable, if only the faithful will believe. Which of course many do.' He told Caine: '*You* should read Zelaszny.'

'Any time I want intellectual ideology,' Caine said, 'I'll read Mickey Spillane.'

Barrington Yorke didn't seem to notice. 'Has Rahab said any more about that reference to Mexico?'

Caine said: 'That was just talk.'

CHAPTER 6

Heart rate quickening, Margaret Stubbs set down the phone. For a moment it was just her and the shadows of the hallway in the shabby Ruislip semi; the tap of her father's typewriter, sermon notes; the whirr of her mother's sewing machine.

Head round the door. 'That was someone from university. I might be back late.'

Wind whipped her face with cold rain in the yellow black streets. Thursday, March 8, mid evening, an odd time to be half paralysed with terror. Mary Abbott had never phoned her at home before.

The Cavalier hissed in fast to the kerb and Margaret got in and Mary drove away quickly to the roundabout for the M40. 'Is that your medical kit?'

'Mary, it's only diagnostic and it isn't even comprehensive for that.'

'It's better than nothing.' Wind rocked the Cavalier. Margaret saw the speed at 95 and knew it took a lot to get a white-haired grandmother driving like that.

'What's happened?'

Mary wouldn't say. She was into Oxfordshire before she turned off. Deep into the sodden black farmland with the leaves and twigs littering the lanes she turned off, the track muddy, grass in the middle in the headlights. Then from behind a barn someone came out and Mary braked. Boots, jeans, anorak; the figure bent to the window, a woman, youngish.

'Here, you're on private land, you know that?'

'That's all right,' Mary said. 'We're from the international well-wishers' club.'

'Get going,' the woman said, and Margaret thought: the things they pick for passwords.

Two hundred yards on, the farmyard was derelict, the flags slippery with rain and mud as they dashed across, into the one lighted room. The silence hit Margaret like a lash. Her first thought was that there'd been an earthquake: it was that, the last time she'd seen blood and white faces like this. Julie apart.

Lorraine Easson was standing chunky, snub-nosed and sullen by the door. Dark clothing, balaclava. An operation and it had gone wrong. A woman of maybe twenty-two was slumped against the wall, gripping a left wrist thickly wrapped with bandage. Another, olive-skinned, eyes scared, knelt by a fourth, grey-faced and semi-conscious on a camp bed. And there was blood on the blanket and on the prone woman's lips and running down the frame of the bed into a pool beside it and trailing right across the floor where they'd carried her.

Margaret knelt by the camp bed. 'I've got no drugs.'

'She's had morphine,' Lorraine said.

Pulse. Weakening, fibrillations. Bad. The guerrilla was small, tanned, mid thirties, her breathing leaky. The pink tint of the blood on her lips told Margaret she'd been hit in the lung but she raised the blanket anyway. Not one bullet but two. They'd deflected when they hit her, travelled obliquely through the rib cage and caused massive injuries.

'Where's the blood?'

They just stared at her. Margaret swung half round. 'Come on, where is it? Blood, for the transfusion! You can't have dragged me out here just for . . .'

The guerrilla's heart stopped. Desperate, Margaret tore open the bloodied shirt. In her mind there were sterile theatres, qualified surgeons, nurses, but behind her Mary was saying softly, *no, there isn't any*. Trying heart massage at a point like that was more magic than medicine, anyway.

Margaret leaned back. It wasn't quite midnight. 'She's dead.'

The youngster with the wounded wrist rolled her head, moaning faintly. Lorraine said, 'Shit'. An epitaph. The one with the scared eyes crossed herself and the reflex puzzled Margaret.

'You must be crazy!' Suddenly she was shouting. 'You break security, you drag me out here, you must have *seen* not even a *hospital* could have saved her! And then you expect *me* to work miracles!'

The one who'd crossed herself walked unsteadily outside.

They heard her being sick. Mary put a hand on Margaret's shoulder. 'You did everything you could. Now you should tend the living.'

Slowly Margaret nodded.

The youngster's wrist had stopped bleeding; but a bone had gone. Margaret splinted it. 'How did you do it?'

'Uh?'

Lorraine grunted: '*Comment c'est passé?*'

The guerrilla replied: Margaret didn't catch the French. This was a new one, then, bringing in Continental cells for UK ops. No wonder the security forces had such a job catching Fight.

Check under the eyelids, she'd had all the morphine she needed. 'Get her anti-tetanus as soon as possible, repeater in three weeks. And that one' – she nodded at the one who'd been sick, back in the door now, shivering – 'wants tranquillisers for at least a fortnight.'

She stood up. With Lorraine and Mary she went out into the rainy black night to bury the guerrilla they hadn't saved.

* * *

Mexico City is the world's largest conurbation, fourteen million souls, and it spreads horizontally rather than vertically like New York. But it has its tower blocks and one of them is the Múñoz Foundation Building, on Calle Tacuba, parallel with the Latin American Tower two blocks south, but less tall. At its foot, an Indian woman was selling nuts and peppers spread on a ragged cloth while two others waited for a different sort of client, and in its penthouse, as the Spanish manservant retired decorously, three women from the opposite end of the socioeconomic spectrum sat in conference.

One owned the building: doña Alma Múñoz de las Heras. She was Mexican born, vocal, opinionated, and the press regarded her as a harmless eccentric; but she had the Midas touch nevertheless, she ran a business empire that was expanding, world recession or not. Her eccentricity took the form of ankle-length Victorian dresses; a white vintage Rolls; riding side-saddle on her *hacienda* near Acapulco; refusing to set foot in an aeroplane, although her organisation ran one; and – although they'd never caught her at it – taking her relaxation on

41

mescalin trips.

The second was American, her stocky build contrasting with doña Alma's slenderness. Marlena Kuhr ran a US-based conglomerate that was bigger in diversity and turnover than doña Alma's, and they'd collaborated more than once on a billion-dollar project. Unlike doña Alma, who'd never married, Marlena Kuhr was divorced, twice. She wore Dior dresses, silk because she liked its touch, and her amiable, motherly air had often misled business rivals into thinking she couldn't make tough decisions, fast.

Although not exactly in fear of the third woman, Kuhr and doña Alma were certainly in awe of her. She was slight, beyond middle age, wearing glasses that made her look studious and a grey suit with the sort of crisp cut that suggested the decisiveness of a lawyer, although she wasn't one. She was Wanda Zelaszny.

Zelaszny glanced once at the closed-circuit television screen to make sure the manservant had gone from the passage, then nodded at Kuhr.

'You know Oxford, England?' Kuhr said.

Doña Alma said, 'No.'

'It has a big auto plant on the edge of town, BL – used to be called British Leyland. Operation was a payroll job, on the trans-border system. Easson from London Two wrote the tacplan, Lille One came over to crew it. Okay, it went to hell. Point is: Abbott and this new operative, Stubbs, pulled the chestnuts out the fire.'

Kuhr waited. She had a heavy, chubby face that looked as if it had been put together as modern sculpture from a few thousand penny-sized bits of bronze, and her eyes, with their talent for kindness and ruthlessness alike, now betrayed uncharacteristic deference. Zelaszny peered out through the south window but she couldn't see Pópocatepetl for industrial smog. She had the face of a hunting eagle and even when her distant eyes weren't on you, you still felt she was reading all your thoughts.

Doña Alma said: 'Stubbs's name came up before. She did well in the attack on that computer.'

'Spell it out,' Zelaszny murmured.

Kuhr said, '*I* guess we ought to take a look at Stubbs.'

Zelaszny tightened thin lips. She opened a briefcase and pulled out a wad of files.

42

Kuhr watched her critically. 'That's bad security, carrying those files around.' Doña Alma wouldn't have cared to criticise Zelaszny.

But Zelaszny only smiled at Kuhr, unnervingly with her eyes still hard. 'Abbott wasn't in this, for obvious reasons. Renata Vernon wasn't, either, since Lille One had their own hotshoe and Vernon doesn't have the aptitude for action work. Easson planned and led the heist, only she blew it. So along comes Stubbs – brainy, coolheaded, student medic, qualified pilot, highly motivated, upbringing in Peru . . .'

'I read the file,' Kuhr said.

'She's very young,' doña Alma said. 'Only twenty.'

'Sure.' Zelaszny nodded. 'But she has experience, she has talent. She's the one we want.'

Kuhr lit a black Sobranie. She put a lot of concentration into it. She brought her eyes back up to Zelaszny's. 'I don't like the Julie O'Dell bit. It's potentially explosive. I say we just take a look at her.'

With the conviction that always mesmerised other people, Zelaszny repeated: 'She's the one we want.'

CHAPTER 7

In the room over the East End sari warehouse Lorraine looked pugnacious in the usual rollneck and jeans, Renata simply muddled, in a faded purple ankle-length dress that clashed with her rally jacket. Mary Abbott, severe in a cream silk blouse and charcoal skirt, eyed Margaret critically as she stalked in, late, with aircraft lubricant on her supermarket jeans. The little Asian woman called Surekha who'd let her in closed the door quietly behind her. It was Saturday, March 10.

'What happened?'

'Ignition fault. I had to spend half an hour ground-testing before I could take off.' But Mary wasn't after explanations from Margaret.

Surekha came in timidly with a tray of tea, then vanished again. It was cosy in the small room, the warmth heavy from the radiators. Lorraine, blunt, defensive, told her story. The first shots, around the payroll van; the roadblock, the police rifles that they hadn't expected. This hadn't been Fight's first armed action, not by a long chalk. But what was different and, to much of the public, baffling about Fight was that it was the first feminist group prepared consistently to use guns, and organised enough to use them effectively.

Yet the reason wasn't far to seek, they'd told Margaret. Fight's women fought because, since tyranny began, enough women had wanted and needed to fight against it. What was new about Fight was that it was the first organisation to have got guns to its women and trained them to use them.

Mary watched Lorraine steadily. 'You abandoned the payroll. Your squad panicked. You lost one guerrilla dead and one wounded.'

Margaret squirmed. Lorraine said savagely, 'I got them all

out! The pigs never found us!' She hated Mary telling her off.

That was Zelaszny's strength: not simply that she'd filled so many radical feminists with her missionary zeal for reconquest of the seats of power she believed women in ancient times had held; but that she was organised enough to get her guerrillas shooting straight, organised enough to create the cadre of battle veterans who would lead the revolution when male authority had been weakened enough.

'They didn't find our base,' Margaret said. 'That's important credit . . .'

Mary shushed her with a palm. 'Can you explain why your squad panicked?' She stared at Lorraine. 'Could it be because you took too long opening up the van, too long deciding whether to pull out, too long deciding whether to start a full-scale gunfight?'

'That's a bloody lie! All right, we had trouble with the van. But you can't swing that one on me. And *you* try stopping some young kid banging off a gun out of plain nerves!'

'Be fair,' Margaret pleaded. 'Lorraine did everything she . . .'

'That's enough from you!' Mary's eyes met Margaret's, surprisingly angry, the Zelaszny effect coming out now in sheer aggression. On the BBC the other day some MP had been saying how surprised he was that so many women should be attracted to the programme of someone so extreme as Zelaszny. He'd quite missed the point: other feminist leaders had failed because they'd never been extreme enough. But now Margaret was challenging authority. You didn't do that. 'You'd better answer for yourself. What time did you get back on Thursday?'

'A quarter to three.'

'And there were questions?'

Margaret nodded. 'Also we missed some blood on my clothes. So I said someone I knew had cut their wrists but been saved, and I'd been called in to keep it unofficial.'

Mary eyed her sceptically. Renata, smugly, lit a cigarette. Lorraine wrinkled her nose. Mary shrugged. 'Well, Margaret's the only one who comes out of that with any credit. She made a brave effort to save one guerrilla's life, gave medical aid to another who was slightly hurt, turned out when she was called, and has apparently maintained security.'

'I did what I could,' Margaret said. 'The same as Lorraine.'

45

'No other Fight commander could have even gunned her way out of a corner like that,' Lorraine said through her teeth. 'Even allowing a technical failure, I've proved one thing: that women really are capable of handling a fight in a tight spot.'

She had her hands, white-knuckled, on the knife with the notch in.

Mary said dismissively, 'Now tell us something we didn't know.'

*   *   *

Voices rising in the dusty, grey reverence filled Margaret's ears like the sound of the Seneca's engines but, alike, left her mind free to function. The master plan. That big project Mary had mentioned. There'd been not a word about it since; the thought nagged her. *On the altar thine all must thou lay.* Yes, all. The rhythm carried her voice with its own momentum, the way her commitment to Fight carried her life. Lorraine would laugh, she thought, to see her here in her father's church, in a prim dress, and a cardigan to ward off the paraffin-scented cold, and her mother at one shoulder and a crony of her parents' at the other.

Evening service, the minutiae of the conventions faithfully observed. *And now we shall bow before God . . .* Deviation scared them so much: a guitar up the front perhaps for a youth service, never for serious worship; the suspicions a camelhair coat aroused when everyone dressed in grey raincoats. People like these would be the hardest to liberate because they dared not believe that if the trunk of their beliefs shed superfluous branches, others just as good would grow in their place. And if you lacked the courage or maybe the cruelty openly to invite their disapproval of your deviation, then you bowed your head while the preacher prayed and thought about what you'd just read up in Wanda Zelaszny's theory. Thought about how the honesty there really might hold out hope for ordinary people. Thought how persuasive her argument was, how inescapable her conclusion that not until women held the power in London, Washington, Moscow, Paris, the power they'd held in the ancient matriarchies that male historians had conveniently forgotten, not until then would the world live in peace.

And of course you believed the paradox: that before women

46

could set the world at peace they must set men at war. Because never in all history had a tyrant given up power without being forced to.

Singing again, her mother doing the descant, carried away. Margaret preferred to keep a low profile, if you could say that about the lankiest woman in church. Sometimes the boys looked at her. Only four boys in her age bracket attended regularly: one worked at the Jobcentre, one mended phones, the third sold insurance and the fourth was halfwitted. One day she might be in battle against those boys. *Every hour I need thee.* She got a glimpse of a man's face, not one of the four, but banished it; it looked too much like a film star. Another, quite different, man's face took its place. Deeply tanned, Spanish-looking, hair going to silver, with wise, knowing eyes.

She'd known Mario Roca in Peru. He'd taken her under his wing, maybe sensing the vulnerability of a young girl in a country not her own who was starting to attract looks from men who hadn't necessarily Roca's own honourable intentions. He'd taught her survival in the wild, he'd taught her self-defence, he'd started her on judo. And the main thing he'd taught her was that survival or death, winning or losing, wasn't decided by her environment or by her opponents but by her. In her own mind. *Believe* first that *you* will win. Neglect to, and you'll hand the advantage to your opponent.

Margaret was going to need that psychology on Monday night.

*   *   *

Monday night at the university union judo club, one of the week's three mixed sessions. Lorraine was there, Margaret saw as she limbered up, modesty preserved with a white T-shirt under the loose Japanese jacket; but Renata wasn't, Renata was off taking lessons in driving heavy lorries. Margaret had broken sweat, taking a hammering from a brown-belted man much heavier than her, when Lorraine bowed in challenge. The routine hand grips, the shuffling, circling; a fast hip attack from Lorraine. Not fast enough. They were on the mat, groping clumsily for a hold down, when Lorraine broke off, she'd had enough. Up again, and the hand grips.

Lorraine muttered, 'Suppose you've heard about that one

47

from the other night?'

'Renata said.' Margaret stepped wide as Lorraine lunged for an *o-soto* that she hadn't the reach for, countering with two fast attempts at *harai-goshi*, right then left.

'Stupid cow,' Lorraine said, adding sullenly: 'Not you.'

Renata had seen Margaret that morning in the college refectory. *That girl's dead. No, not the wounded one, the other one. Poured half a bottle of vodka on to a bottle of sleeping tablets. She was the silly bitch who started t' shooting.* Margaret remembered the shocked one who'd been sick. What sort of tranquillisers *had* they given the poor kid?

'How did it happen?'

'Christ knows,' Lorraine grunted. And they both attacked simultaneously, a rare happening in judo with its reliance on timing down to fractions of a second.

They snapped back out, feet spaced, defensive. Lorraine's face was red, lower lip thrust out. Every time they went on, Lorraine would convey superiority in judo skill and physical power. Margaret knew she shouldn't let her, it was the cardinal point that Mario Roca had laid down: you will win; never let them make you doubt it. But Lorraine had Margaret psyched, and knew it.

'Hardly your fault,' Margaret said.

'Shit,' Lorraine sneered, and went down into the deep defensive position with her bottom sticking out and her left hand gripping Margaret's belt instead of her wide sleeve.

It was an unmistakable challenge and Margaret didn't want to end up in another mêlée on the mat and she tried one of the most difficult attacks in judo and it almost worked. She doubled and spun, trying to convert it into a shoulder throw, down on her knee hard enough to friction-burn the skin, but Lorraine tried something complicated and they ended up on the mat just the same. But Margaret came out on top and she knew better than to follow up her advantage with a hold down, she hadn't the strength in her arms, so instead she crossed her hands on Lorraine's lapels and got the strangle on her, fast and firmly.

Lorraine jerked her stomach. Margaret didn't budge. Lorraine rolled, Margaret held her, Lorraine tried her legs. Margaret stayed out of reach, and knew the strangle was on, because Lorraine started digging her fingertips under her collar

48

to ease the pressure and dislodge Margaret's hands.

But she wasn't going to tap. Impatient suddenly, Margaret tightened up the grip, but Lorraine only bit her lip and refused to submit, one hand struggling to ease the pressure, the other trying alarmingly well to put a singlehanded strangle on to Margaret.

All around them, people were whirling, countering, breakfalling. Down on the mat, Margaret and Lorraine looked sculptured.

Then Lorraine yanked on Margaret's collar, simultaneously wrenching her own body, and the jolt gave her finger-room on her collar and she ran her hand down and broke Margaret's grip and was rolling after her, grasping for a strangle of her own, when the coach called: 'Change!'

They bowed. Margaret was shaking. When they straightened, Lorraine's eyes were the colour of the knife with the notch in its hilt.

It was a relief to Margaret to be challenged by a green-belted boy with a shock of fair hair. He was heavier than her, stocky, quick on his feet, but after a lot of manoeuvring Margaret got him with a classic leg throw. He was a good loser. When the coach called, 'Change,' and they bowed, he gave Margaret a cheerful grin and gripped her arm.

'Thanks, great stuff! How come you're wearing that yellow belt? You should be green or blue.'

'Well . . .'

'Come for a drink afterwards and tell me about it.'

She smiled. 'Love to, but I've got so much work on . . .'

Some other time, he said, and looked so disappointed when she stalled, it made her sad.

Showering, afterwards, Margaret moved in a wistful dream, longing away the loneliness, wanting to be wanted. Other people had other people, it was unfair that Margaret had no one closer than a coded phone call away. Yet the duty remained. To Julie O'Dell's memory and that of the guerrilla who'd died and the other who'd killed herself, and to the lives of those guerrillas and their potential antagonists who still had breath. Towelling her face, Margaret scrubbed angrily at the few small tears of self-pity that had mixed with the water from the shower.

'What's that thing?' Lorraine muttered unexpectedly across the changing room as Margaret started getting dressed.

49

Margaret blinked myopically. But Lorraine could see perfectly well what it was, a bra. 'For heaven's sake, Lorraine.' She put her glasses on, to give herself confidence.

Lorraine felt guilty, she realised, about the suicide. Mary was the only person who got any sort of respect from Lorraine, and at the last cell conference Mary had given Lorraine a slap on the wrists, Margaret a pat on the head. So Lorraine reacted with the mindless jealousy of a thwarted child.

More than ever Margaret hated the bickering, the trifling irritation that stretched existing tension to the limit of tolerance. She hated all fighting. Its violence frightened her, and that made her think of sex, and so frightened her all the more; and still she didn't know why her mind should equate sex with violence, so alarmingly. Judo was more controlled. Judo was all right now and then for exercise, although Margaret knew better ways of keeping fit. But when she'd left Peru, and Mario Roca with his wise, kind eyes and his quiet-voiced lessons in backstreet self-defence, she'd believed she could relax and be at peace. She'd felt only bitterness when she'd found herself still fighting.

CHAPTER 8

Traffic on the Thames Embankment moved fluidly in mid-evening, apart from the boy racer who thought he knew better than the rules. Caine's secure RV tonight to meet Barrington Yorke was the back of a taxi that in fact belonged to the DI car pool.

'The one who was killed was called Michèle Duvillard,' Caine said. 'Telephonist, employed at one time by CGT.' Confédération Générale du Travail, one of the biggest French trade unions. 'Living apparently normally except she was on the run from her husband. Lille One's commander. Brouzet identified her from the teeth casts we took when we found the grave.'

Brouzet was Caine's opposite number in France. He'd been in London that day to compare notes.

'The one who suicided was called Brigitte Coulon. Shop assistant, not brilliantly educated. Brouzet's traced the remaining two women in Lille One, but they're inactive now, naturally, with the cell being pulled out. That policy, as of course I pointed out, is a bit of info for which we're indebted to Rahab.'

'What action does Brouzet propose?' Barrington Yorke braced himself as the taxi took a bend.

'I've persuaded him to sit tight and watch.' For once, there was actually some truth in that. Brouzet had wanted action, which was no more nor less than Caine expected from a red-blooded security man who was fed up with seeing terrorists having it all their own way. Brouzet had wanted to arrest the survivors of the cell but Caine had persuaded him that that would have hazarded Rahab. That had been Barrington Yorke's argument.

The taxi halted, tourists crossing the zebra in Parliament Square.

'Presumably', Barrington Yorke said, 'the attempted wages

51

robbery was nothing to do with the "big coup" that we've heard about from Rahab.'

'Yeah, right. I checked that out. She has heard a very few further mutterings about this "coup", but that wasn't it. I can't get her to dig out any details. She can't, either, get any confirmation or otherwise about whether this Soviet thing in the Gulf of Thailand has a bearing. And of course I'm still waiting for confirmation of the Soviet involvement in Fight. They're too smart to have left receipts for Kalashnikovs lying around.'

'We haven't actually identified any Kalashnikovs in Fight's use.' The taxi turned left, crossing the Thames. Barrington Yorke had gone thoughtful. 'We've identified American M3 submachineguns, Belgian FAL rifles, but no Soviet equipment.'

'No, right, but, I mean, they wouldn't exactly want to advertise the fact. Those M3s were captured in Vietnam. The Soviets got them off the Vietnamese, handed them down to the Cubans, and the Cubans handed them down to this lot. Or so the CIA suggests.'

Barrington Yorke could never feel comfortable with the use of 'Soviets' to refer to the Soviet Union's citizens or authorities. It was like calling a person a 'committee'. 'The FALs came from Nato arms dumps raided in Norway.'

'And we still can't say conclusively Andreyev never had a hand in that. He *is* still in Cuba?' Caine glanced across, interrogatively.

'Oh, indeed, yes, sunning himself yesterday on Varadero beach. And still in close touch with Gregorio Tabio.'

'The counter-intelligence ace who is presumably still brushing up his flying for no reason the CIA can figure out yet.'

'Indeed,' Barrington Yorke muttered to himself. The taxi started jockeying for lane with a container lorry. The lorry lost.

'Okay,' Caine said, 'I'll get Rahab on to the weapons.'

'Mention them to Rahab by all means but don't make her feel she's under pressure.'

Caine gave his chief a sidelong glance. 'Rahab's okay. She won't make mistakes.'

'Any amateur makes mistakes. Rahab is an amateur. That is her greatest strength but it's also her gravest weakness.'

52

CHAPTER 9

Time had been when the lofty Mayfair flat had been smart and sought-after. The tenant was a widow, a person who'd been involved for years with Fight's agitprop, and she'd put the place at the cell's disposal. Thursday, March 15, Lorraine dressed as usual, Renata in a long cotton dress too light for the weather, eyeing Mary Abbott like a child who'd been naughty and knew she had a ticking-off coming.

'Lille One has been closed and has gone underground,' Mary said, motionless on the chair with her impeccably styled white hair and her knees neatly together in their trim, maroon slacks. 'As you know, any cell with 50 per cent casualties is automatically closed. I can't tell you what's happening to the two survivors – doubtless they'll be reactivated in due course.'

Renata concentrated on shaking loose a cigarette.

Margaret said hotly: 'Who gave that girl those tablets?'

'They weren't the tranquillisers you suggested,' Mary said. 'They were hypnotics given to her earlier by her GP.'

'Someone should have known, someone should have stopped her. Anyone could see she was in shock, it didn't take me to tell you.'

Smoke uncoiled from Renata's cigarette. Its bitterness mingled with the flat's smells of sour milk, cat food and gas. Draughts whispered somewhere but Mary's voice was colder. 'I'm not interested in that aspect. I'm concerned, and so are the highest levels of Fight command, that our security may have been broken as a result of one bungled operation.'

Lorraine snapped: 'You aren't swinging . . .'

'Be quiet,' Mary said, and again in surprise Margaret watched the way Lorraine clenched her teeth shut, cowed by the reflection of Zelaszny in her commander's eyes. Mary said, 'I

53

cannot over-emphasise the importance of security. I'm blaming no one. I'm simply pointing to general principles.'

'I'll tell you a general principle some of us don't seem to be aware of,' Lorraine said. 'The integrity of the Fight movement comes before whims of personal taste. Security comes before home comforts.'

Renata glanced nervously at Margaret. Mary murmured, 'Who are you talking about?'

'I'm talking about one of our members. I . . .'

'All right,' Mary blazed, 'name her!'

Lorraine jerked her gold curls at Margaret. 'There's the woman who's putting the lot of us at risk for the sake of an easy life, living with her parents. Sooner or later they're going to want to know what she's up to when she's away on Fight business. And it's . . .'

'Margaret's perfectly entitled to be the judge of that,' Mary said.

'There's more to it, if you'd just let me finish! She doesn't live like a dedicated guerrilla, in a commune like Renata or me, she doesn't act like one and she doesn't even dress like one. She . . .'

Mary said, 'What exactly are you accusing Margaret of?'

Spying, Margaret's brain echoed. You didn't need proof for a thing like that, not in a guerrilla network. Just suspicion, and they'd take her into an alley and Lorraine would get out the knife and someone would find her looking like Julie O'Dell. Please God, no. She sat there rigid with her face like blotting paper under the Andean tan, and Renata indifferent, cigarette poised, fingers plucking her dress, Mary motionless, clear-eyed, all-seeing.

'Failing to live like a guerrilla.' Lorraine bent one finger.

Mary snorted. 'And your evidence for that is that she lives at home? What do you say, Margaret?'

'I . . .' The knot in her stomach, the block in her throat.

'She hasn't even got an answer!' Lorraine jeered triumphantly.

'Be *quiet*!' Mary said, unmistakably angry. 'Margaret, if you'd rather speak later, you may.' Margaret nodded mutely. 'What else?'

Lorraine said, 'Failing to act like a guerrilla.' She bent a second finger.

'Meaning what?'

'Lifestyle. Wanda Zelaszny said social conformism is incompatible with the life of a true guerrilla.'

Mary frowned. 'Social conformism?'

'This pathetic little show of religion. Encouraging men.'

'Religion?' Mary's eyes were hard, fixed on Lorraine's. 'That is not only an indispensable means of allaying suspicions when you live in a home where your parents are former church missionaries – and who also would be the last people to betray their daughter to the police, even if they began to suspect that she might be involved with a secret organisation. It is also the best cover any one of us has got.' She raised her chin. 'And what do you mean by "encouraging men"?'

'She can't even go to judo training without trying to pick one up.'

Even in her dread Margaret glimpsed again the boy's innocent grin, his shock of hair. She'd never even learnt his name.

'And you don't think she should?'

'Of course she shouldn't, it's inconsistent with a true guerrilla's lifestyle.'

Ash fell from Renata's cigarette; glass jars clinked downstairs as their hostess put things away; in the street, a van three-point turned.

'Why "of course"?' Mary asked. 'Tell me where Wanda Zelaszny has ever said the guerrilla must partition her life wholly from all male contact? How do you suppose our fight can ever be understood without reference to and familiarity with men and their ways of behaviour? Why, even in the convent there are men.'

Convent, what on earth was the convent? Maybe something in Zelaszny's theory that Margaret had missed, despite her meticulous study.

'Now what else?' Lorraine hesitated, white with fury, and Mary prompted: 'Her dress? Was that it?'

'Yes, it was! Any true guerrilla dresses like a fighter, but *she*' – she was too incensed now to name Margaret – 'dresses like some pea-brained office dolly. Bras, skirts . . .'

'That is the way I often dress.' Mary kept a straight face. 'Are you accusing me, too?' She paused. 'Let's have an end to this nonsense. I will listen to any genuine complaint against any cell member. But petty squabbling of this nature merely threatens to reduce us to the level of unliberated housewives with no real philosophy to fill their minds.'

Lorraine breathed, 'Why, you . . .'

'Yes?'

Lorraine fizzed at her. Softly Mary said, 'Any insubordination in this cell will be punished.'

Feigning boredom, Renata crushed out her cigarette.

Mary said: 'This cell is to prepare itself for an operation some time during the next three weeks. I shall expect it to function as a team, not as disparate and rival parts.'

Margaret didn't look at Lorraine. Next time she went on an operation under Lorraine's command, she knew who'd be first in the firing line.

*   *   *

Mary unlocked the passenger door. Margaret slid into the Cavalier beside her. She was still shaking. Mary put her arm round Margaret's shoulders and gave a squeeze.

'Margaret, I'm sorry. I had to let her have her say. She's rather over-wrought, you know, she's taken those two deaths much too much to heart – she has to take it out on some person. I'm sorry it had to be you.'

So much compassion, Margaret recognised, so much love. They moved into traffic. This, too, was the Zelaszny effect, that a woman could steel herself to assault the world's whole establishment structure and yet remain caring, feeling, conscious of others. Margaret hated herself, despised herself. Because it wasn't just Mary Abbott who was good as a person, it was the good in Fight's ideals that appealed to her.

'Lorraine's perfectly sound at heart,' Mary said. 'She's just apt to take a sometimes too serious view of Fight's philosophy. Lorraine is a perfectly normally oriented young woman and she's taken a sort of private vow to avoid male entanglements. She acts sometimes as if she feels threatened by someone she sees as sexually more attractive.'

Absurd, absurd. Lorraine's gold curls and snub nose and sheer personal confidence, and Margaret, so tall and skinny with her glasses. Mary couldn't be right, Lorraine couldn't possibly even think in those terms in the context of a guerrilla cell. Irrelevant.

'And don't worry about the operation,' Mary added. 'You and Lorraine won't even be working in the same area.'

CHAPTER 10

Briefing took place in a private room over a meeting hall in Bayswater and when Margaret followed Renata up the steps she found their coats and dresses blended them nicely with the other women going in, a Townswomen's Guild or some such. It was two weeks later, Thursday, March 29, drizzle on the pavements, gusts at the windows. Lorraine's jeans didn't blend. Lorraine earned a critical comment from Mary when she walked in with a woman Margaret hadn't seen before. Thirtyish, tanned, fawn hair cropped to an efficient-looking bob, her clothes conventional, navy skirt and jacket with a brown print blouse.

Mary ran through the introductions. 'This is Coral Bargellini. Coral's a senior Fight executive, based in America. She's here to lead Operation Tulip.'

It was the first time anyone had named it.

Coral Bargellini's grip was powerful. 'Hi, Margaret, good to meet you.' The grin displayed flawless teeth. Coral's eyes were hard, with the same aggression as Lorraine's showed. Strikingly, they were different colours: one brown; one grey above the pupil but green below.

Mary sat them down. Coral and Renata lit cigarettes, Renata with a defensive flick of lank hair. Margaret picked nervously at a snagged thread on her sleeve.

'This operation is for Sunday coming.' Coral's voice was quiet, authoritative. Glancing at her, Margaret realised suddenly that Coral was another one who'd worshipped at Zelaszny's feet. The confidence, the messianic light in her eyes. 'We named it for the Dutch connexion. Our target is a cargo on board a regular commercial airline flight into Heathrow airport.' She waited.

Lorraine said it, nose wrinkling in the cigarette smoke. 'What's the cargo?'

'Tulip bulbs from Amsterdam.' She grinned knowingly. Lorraine shrugged, annoyed at walking into it. Coral said: 'Regular run, this time of year. Top-quality bulbs for UK growers, they go into quarantine for a routine period, customs check them coming off the plane and they send someone down from the importers to count 'em. Routine, boring. That's why a certain cutting house in Amsterdam picks the tulip flight at random intervals to send diamonds into the UK. That flight will carry two million dollars' worth – just under a million sterling at present rates – in the charge of a single security guard, named Poelmans.' Again she waited.

'You mean it's only one man on the plane,' Renata said.

'Right. The whole key to this diamond run is its low profile. Take diamond merchants themselves: walk out in the street with a steel case locked on your wrist and they'll all know you have jewels on you; so they don't, they put 'em loose in a pocket and no one knows. Same with this one. When that guy gets off the plane, the only people expecting his diamond parcel will be one customs officer, airside, and one further security guy, non-customed, who'll be there in plain clothes in a plain car and looking just like the growers' importer – who will also be there but who won't know anything about the diamonds.'

Margaret's heart rate had quickened. She remembered that night in Fenchurch Street.

'How do we get in there?' Lorraine said. But Renata was saying, 'Y've a lot of assumptions going there.'

Coral grinned at Mary, motionless, taking it all in, then at Margaret. She was enjoying herself. The ones with the sense of humour, Margaret thought: they were the truly dangerous ones.

'Right, Renata. But the basic assumption is accuracy of our intelligence. You don't figure we just called them up and asked them?'

Renata grunted. So they had someone inside the cutting house, or with access to it.

Coral smiled at Lorraine. 'I'll tell you how we get in there. One: commonly, the airline has groundcrew meet the plane, liaise with customs, talk to the importer, that kind of stuff. Sunday, there will be two uniformed groundcrew, and they'll be Fight guerrillas. The importer will be there in a Range Rover. Only, once again, it won't *be* the importer, it'll be one of us. We

59

heist the diamonds airside – that way we have only one security man to tackle, not two. We take the diamonds outside, and there's our Range Rover, ready waiting. We ditch the Range Rover, we have a further car waiting for a stretch across country, rough-surface work. It ends at an uncompleted motorway section where a light plane of our own will be waiting, having flown in from France the night before.'

Renata glanced at Margaret, and again Margaret felt her heart rate rise.

Mary tilted her head. 'And may we know what happens to the diamonds once they're safely out of Britain?'

'Re-cut,' Coral said. 'We have women with the skills. When the diamonds are no longer identifiable, we market them. To the same recipient that's supposed to have them now – even though they'll then be illicit. That market system is symptomatic of a sick, male-run economy: they're so shit-scared of illicit diamonds upsetting their price structure, they'll even buy back what's stolen off them.'

'Do we kill the guards?' Renata said. Her pale eyes glittered, Margaret noted, with the tension of a theorist who preferred others to put her ideas into practice. Others would, though, sure enough.

'Not unless we have to. Two guerrillas with good unarmed combat can take Poelmans good and fast before he joins his escort. An outside squad can then very easily isolate the escort while our couriers get in the Range Rover – which won't arouse suspicion, as it'll be the real importer's vehicle.'

Lorraine said drily, 'Where do the jammers come from for the escort's VHF?'

'Jammers?' Coral frowned, then widened her multicoloured eyes. 'Hey, that's good, Lorraine, we never thought of that. I guess we should try that some time. Nope. For this operation, we were figuring on the escort using all the VHF he wants – 'cos the outside squad, when it's isolated him, will then create a big, big diversion aimed at attracting every cop in miles.'

Lorraine nodded, sceptically, watching Coral. More rain spattered the window.

Mary said, 'May we know the names of any of our cell who are to be involved?'

'Sure. You personally are ground co-ordinator – I'll go over the skeds with you afterwards. Renata, you're driving the rough-surface leg from ditching the Range Rover to the airstrip. Lorraine, you lead the outside unit isolating the escort and creating the diversion. Margaret . . .'

Margaret blinked grey eyes shakily behind her glasses. Coral gave her a direct look.

'You're the person who knows southeast English airspace. You'll co-pilot the plane in – you'll go to France first thing Saturday and pick it up. You and I then intercept Poelmans, wearing airline stewardesses' uniforms, we run the diamonds to the Range Rover and then separate. You go with Renata to the plane, and fly out.'

Night was claustrophobic at the dusty panes. Margaret sensed Mary eyeing her, still and compassionate, and sensed clearly the growing rage and disbelief inside Lorraine. For a moment Margaret disbelieved it herself. Then, slowly, she began to see what lay behind it.

Coral smiled tightly. 'Do we have any questions?'

Tense, scared, thinking rapidly, Margaret said, 'Yes: why all the complication?'

Coral frowned. 'Complication?'

'Certainly. All this relay-race business could be dispensed with and the whole operation made vastly more secure if, once the diamonds have been seized, we land the light aircraft straight on at Heathrow, transfer the diamonds – and ourselves – to the aircraft, and fly out again.'

'That's *more* complicated, I'm afraid, Mags.' Coral smiled apologetically. 'You just have to have the least delay in the freight plane arriving and you have ours making a spectacle of landing at Heathrow with nothing to pick up.'

'Radio. The pilot could orbit, listening-out on Heathrow's frequency, and she'd know immediately when the airliner landed.'

'You'd be in and out of all that heavy traffic, with the turbulence the jets cause.'

'On the contrary, you'd avoid it quite easily. Heathrow has huge grass areas a light aircraft can use and the jets can't.' She was getting desperate. Not just because she didn't want this mission.

Coral straightened her shoulders, formally, and the movement, unintentionally, emphasised her figure. 'Mags, you're fairly new as a cell member. But one thing I can tell you right now: Fight is the most effective thing that ever happened to the women's movement, but it'd be as much use as a secondhand condom if cell members ever forgot that Fight has a seniority structure that is adhered to unswervingly and unquestioningly. Okay.' She nodded. 'When you get a tactical plan from your leadership, you carry it out, no mods, no messing. Fight is not a democratic assembly, it's a guerrilla army fighting for half the world's population.'

Margaret knew. And what she knew scared her. She shifted her glasses on her nose and stared down, terrified of looking at Lorraine.

Coral wasn't terrified. She said: 'Right, Lorraine?'

'Oh, for Christ's sake, Coral, not when you've got bloody *lunatics* writing the tacplan!' Lorraine was white with fury. 'What the hell d'you want *her* at the sharp end for, she isn't this cell's unarmed-combat whiz! Stick her in her little plane and let her play all the Red Baron games she wants, but if you want a fighter, what's wrong with Renata? What's wrong with me?'

But they all knew that answer. So, obviously, did Fight command.

'Okay, hear me good, sister.' Coral's eyes had narrowed and her voice was dangerous. 'Just give me one more whisper about insubordination in this cell and you're for it. Sunday, you fix that diversion and you fix it with no snafu. I want it slick, I want it fast, and I want absolutely no rumble. And no one in your squad draws firearms.' She watched Lorraine harshly. 'Any time we need you for tacplan writing, we'll come ask you.'

A snub over the Oxford disaster, and at top level. Lorraine's face boiled. Margaret avoided the steel-blue eyes, but in the edge of her vision she couldn't help seeing Lorraine's hand, grasping the big knife with the notch in its hilt.

*   *   *

The aircraft was a Cessna U206, single 300-horsepower engine, high wing, cambered leading edge for better slow flying. Margaret had flown its type-ancestors in Peru. Fight kept it at a farm strip in Normandy. Its pilot was Thérèse Boucher, forty or so, divorced, a tallish, dark Frenchwoman with a tennis-and-skiing robustness and no doubts about where men were in society and where they ought to be. And the way she strapped herself into the instructor's seat and fixed critical eyes on Margaret left Margaret under no illusions about what was going on.

She was taking her test.

In London, Mary had tried her out, purely operationally. Word had gone back to Fight command, Mary had said as much. Now they wanted a look for themselves.

Crossing the Channel, low down at last light, Boucher flew the Cessna, Margaret navigated, the harder chore. Their landfall was below radar. West of London, Boucher gave Margaret back the controls, and she handled the landing on the bumpy hardcore surface of the unfinished motorway.

Guerrillas were waiting, from a cell Margaret didn't know. They set guard on the aircraft and took the two pilots to join Mary and Coral at operational headquarters, in a group of old buildings beside a derelict gravel pit just outside Slough.

* * *

Dawn on Sunday was foggy. All Fool's Day, Margaret thought, pushing away the blanket and swinging stiff legs off the camp bed. Massive preparations, a great military-style plan, and now the diamonds would get diverted to Glasgow. She splashed water in her face from a plastic bowl.

'This shit's gonna lift,' Coral said. 'We heard it on the aviation weather.' She was in her stewardess's uniform, the demure skirt incongruous among the other guerrillas' jeans and anoraks and Renata's Nomex racing overall.

They were eating. Fat crackled in a pan. Among the nervously confident faces Margaret felt bitter with loneliness and self-contempt. She admired these women, their fervour, their energy, the dedication that made them risk their lives. Yet all their meticulous organising was for destroying life, not saving it, and Margaret wished more than ever that she could make them believe that warfare wasn't the way to win women the equality she herself so passionately believed in.

Sometimes in her isolation she would pray, just in her mind. Here among the fog-shrouded, derelict buildings, she was afraid to, in case the others read her thoughts.

*   *   *

On the buttons of the sky blue jacket Margaret's fingers shook. She caught Coral's eye. From withdrawn solemnity the American's face flashed to a broad, tanned smile, and her multicoloured eyes were knowing.

'Quit worrying, Mags, we'll hack it.'

In the mirror, Margaret's cheeks were pale, her grey eyes big, dark. Tension drew down the corners of her small mouth, sharpening her chin, hollowing her cheeks. She pinned up the chestnut hair under the uniform cap and went with Coral to the inoffensive, four-year-old Mini.

*   *   *

It was seven-thirty, the grime-grey roads deserted. South past the airport perimeter and a TriStar took off, whining over them. Margaret wasn't worrying about the diamond flight now, visibility was three quarters of a mile, improving.

The airside passes were superbly done, they got them through. Margaret nosed the Mini myopically in beside the freight shed. Security would get this car afterwards and there wasn't a lot they could do about that.

Eight. The airfield lay brooding, grey grass reflecting grey mist, a low-ceilinged backdrop with the passenger terminals merging into it and the jetliners half-seen, huddled round the piers. Either Squad C would by now have immobilised the real groundcrew stewardesses or they wouldn't, in which case very shortly Coral and Margaret would have some explaining to do. Or some sprinting. Margaret hated every instant of this.

A Concorde joined four 747s, two Tridents and an A300 in the queue to the holding point. It hadn't moved for almost a minute and Margaret felt her heart jump as she realised why.

A tractor was there with airstairs, very oldfashioned unless you were used to the Andes; in an office with the light switched on to cope with what passed for daylight the customs man settled his cap on his head and reached for his coat; a Range Rover appeared, two people of indeterminate sex in it, and Margaret didn't look. White-faced in the cold, she edged closer to Coral, standing there relaxed with her hidden, dangerous grin as if this was simply some prank that beat scrumping apples.

Then it was over the threshold, flaring out smoothly and sinking on, a Merchantman, the freighter derivative of the old four-turboprop Vanguard airliner. Brakes, taxiway.

It came up to them slowly and with growing menace as its unexpected hugeness filled their view and the scream of its propellors filled their brains. For a moment Margaret thought the dread rising from her stomach to fill her whole body would prevent her from moving.

Then the propellors spun down and the man with the tractor towed the airstairs into place and Poelmans was there immediately, clattering down the aluminium steps.

He was in airline uniform, in keeping with his cover as crew supernumerary. His jacket flapped and he clutched his cap in case it blew off. The customs man was at the foot of the airstairs. He obviously knew Poelmans but was asking for his passport nevertheless. Coral nodded at Margaret. The rap of their heels started clacking back off the freight shed wall.

Poelmans got a leather pouch out of his inside pocket. The customs man opened it. It looked very small for two million dollars' worth, Margaret thought, but that was it all right because now Poelmans was handing over the papers.

In the edge of vision, the Range Rover, edging forwards. The customs man glanced up, looked at them, smiled, two pretty stewardesses. Margaret tried to smile back but couldn't. He was a chubby, homely fellow, the customs man; and Poelmans was balding, older than she'd imagined.

'Did you have a good flight?' Coral said. Meaning *go*.

Clockwork. The easy hard finger-stab under the rib cage, the customs man muffled in pullover and cotton vest but still keeling over as predicted, *chop* to the head as he went down, not behind the ear in case you killed him, *spin* to support Coral but Coral had laid Poelmans flat and seized the pouch. Beside the freight shed, men were shouting, but the Range Rover was there now. Margaret hadn't even looked at it to see the big crash bar across its grille. She piled in. She hadn't thought she'd be panting like this, sweating, after so little exertion.

The Range Rover was crossing the wet grass at 90, right out in

65

the middle of Heathrow airport. It was heading south, Margaret realised. Her uniform cap had gone, so had a hairpin, and her hair was falling around her eyes. Driving in, she'd used the sliproad to the cargo section off the B379 Staines-Slough road and now they were going parallel to that. And neck-and-neck with them, on the sliproad, a police patrol.

Then she saw Lorraine's diversion.

A battered old Transit towing a battered old caravan was starting a turn in the road that happened to jack-knife the rig. It left no way through. Margaret saw the police driver put his car sideways to use his rims for braking but she shut her eyes just at the bang and, when she opened them, saw the impact had shifted the rig yards down the road. Big flashes made her jump, and in horror she thought Lorraine's squad must have drawn guns after all and be shooting the policemen; then she realised it was thunderflashes and smoke grenades.

The Range Rover slammed through the wooden fence at 50mph with the crash bar shattering the pine and any spectators staring firmly at the crashed cars and pyrotechnics along the sliproad.

CHAPTER 11

Raised voices in the next room came from chapel officers and national-level union negotiators engaged in meaningful dialogue with the management. A lot of unusual people were coming and going by the street door, which made another winner for Robin Barrington Yorke.

'That name Thérèse Boucher and the registration number of the plane,' Richard Caine said. 'It seems to have been all Brouzet needed to blow a cell based in Paris. Once again, he's waiting, natch, but he says if they attempt any ructions in France, he'll have 'em. It's all entirely new, of course. We're improving our credit in Parisian circles.'

A bit primly, Barrington Yorke folded his hands over the tip of his stick. Caine was an ambitious director, possibly ruthless, certainly efficient; but in Barrington Yorke's view, in a transnational inquiry you exported information for its own sake, not as a means of amassing favours to be collected later.

'Did Brouzet comment at all on the numbers involved?'

'Well, he certainly agreed there were a hell of a lot.'

Fight had a lot of women to call on. Zelaszny's writing had spread so far, so quickly, that a whole cult had grown up believing in the ancient matriarchies. The ones who'd joined the cells were a tiny fraction of the overall numbers of the feminists who believed the time had come to restore the matriarchy. And many of those had been prompted to join by seeing how efficiently Zelaszny's original cadre of guerrillas had carried out terrorist operations. Barrington Yorke was candidly impressed with the way Fight had conducted the operation. It had been big and complex, nearly twenty women had taken part, the scope for mistakes and mishaps had been correspondingly great. Yet the whole thing seemed to have run largely to plan.

'The name of Coral Bargellini was also new to New York,' Caine said. 'Again, discreet surveillance, no action, until they're sure they can get the lot. And, again, they're impressed with Rahab. Bargellini's a big fish, she'll lead them to Fight command.'

'Assuming Fight command is where Pasarell thinks it is.'

'It *must* be: deep United States somewhere, it's the only thing.'

'Desatnick has her doubts.' He watched Caine: Caine shrugged. 'Did you speak to Pasarell or Desatnick?'

The voices rose again but were more unanimous this time, and a door slammed. Some paper's labour correspondent was going to have to wait for his no-comment.

'Pasarell,' Caine answered in faint surprise. 'I've been going through to him ever since he took over the inquiry.'

Barrington Yorke wasn't sure whether he liked that. DI had just started to develop a certain rapport with Assistant Special Agent-in-Charge Carla Desatnick when Frank Pasarell had been moved in. Desatnick was bright, career-conscious, mid thirties, she was destined for higher things and knew it. But she'd been in charge of the disastrous operation in which women FBI agents had attempted to infiltrate Fight's agitprop; the failure had been embarrassing politically and hadn't improved her standing; and the FBI had brought in Pasarell over her head, nominally on the ground that the inquiry was going international (true at the time) and that the US Government wanted a senior officer to liaise with foreign agencies.

Desatnick wasn't stupid, she was working perfectly well with Pasarell, as she'd done from the outset. But still Barrington Yorke wasn't convinced that the Americans had made the wisest available move.

'Did Pasarell mention anything else?' he said.

'Yeah. Like Lieutenant-General Andreyev's still quote training Cuban spies, unquote, and the CIA says the 9mm slugs all those Thais on the trawler were full of definitely came from M3s, but they can't prove the KGB sent the M3s to the people who butchered them – let alone *were* the people who butchered them – and our suntanned friend Gregorio Tabio is now licensed on at least two sorts of light planes and is now learning how to fly them without looking out the windows.'

Instrument flying, Barrington Yorke understood. He still

didn't care for Caine's manner.

*   *   *

Outside, the church with its blue-black stone columns had all the voluptuous curves of a Spain that had been mistress of the world, or most of it; but sooted now from the hot, honking traffic of the Puerta del Sol in Madrid. Inside, groups of candles lit the gloom and the nave, with no service in progress, was a grey haze where even the few tourists moved silently. No one was worshipping except in a side chapel, where two veiled women knelt, a little apart, at a saint's feet. The tourists took care not to disturb them.

The taxi that pulled up the opposite side of the Puerta del Sol had come straight from Madrid airport. The woman in the back had got straight off an Iberia 747 from Mexico City, but the taxi driver didn't know that. She paid him, and he glimpsed her going into a hotel as he pulled away. He didn't see her crossing the square to the church.

In the cool shadows of the nave, Wanda Zelaszny, who wasn't travelling with that name on her passport, pulled the veil over her hunting eagle's face and walked measuredly to the side chapel. She knelt in the space the original two women had left between them. They scarcely glanced at one another. But the one on the left with the tennis-and-skiing robustness was Thérèse Boucher, who was on Fight's Command Cell Europe, and the one on the right with the curvy hips and the aggressively squared shoulders was Coral Bargellini, who ranked level with Boucher in the States.

Zelaszny judged her interval before speaking, her voice soft, level, as if in prayer. 'One of the best so far. On everyone's part.' She nodded to her left. 'Now, technically?'

Thérèse Boucher hadn't met Zelaszny before. The reputation conditioned her reaction, but what she felt was much more than that, she could feel the sheer, cool power and command and conviction of Zelaszny's presence. She had to swallow, briefly.

'I couldn't fault Stubbs's flying. She lacks absolute experi- ence . . . but she has the gift.'

'Thank you.' Still Zelaszny spoke quietly. In the acoustics of the chapel, they probably couldn't have been heard six feet away. 'And has Stubbs'–she'd turned to Coral–'the

69

gift for operations?'

'Again, inexperience,' Coral murmured. 'That's all. Nerves before the start, cool as all hell when the rumble's on, a real pro. She could lead, too.'

'So what's the drawback?'

Coral hadn't even mentioned a drawback, hadn't even realised she'd implied that one might exist. Yet it was there in her mind, and Zelaszny had read it, and again Coral was unnerved by her leader's uncanny ability to hear the unsaid.

'Well, I guess she argues. She's got to put her own ideas across, she comes on like she really believes them. She tried to modify the tacplan.'

Boucher said nothing.

Behind the veil, Zelaszny smiled. 'Well, initiative is no bad thing.'

CHAPTER 12

Darjeeling, Margaret Stubbs thought, that was it; it was the same sort of tea that timid little Surekha had brought them last time the cell had met in the cosy room over the sari warehouse. Tuesday, April 3. Lorraine and Renata had all Monday's dailies spread over the floor. The raid had been pushed out of the lead position only in the *FT*, which preferred the latest increase in sterling M3, and the *Guardian*, which sometimes couldn't make its mind up, anyway.

'Bloody fantastic,' Lorraine muttered again.

Mary sat straight-backed, white hair immaculate, eyes clear and probably sharper than Margaret's, which were blinking as she realised she had dust all over her glasses, and took them off to polish them.

'I've had two messages of congratulation for you, one from Fight's Command Cell Europe, one even from Supreme Command. Tulip was a total success. The diamonds are with our own cutting expert now, and we expect to raise three quarters of a million sterling from them – not as much as the original market value, obviously, but a substantial sum that will make a measurable difference to Fight's major international project.'

Lorries on the main road set up a barely perceptible, low-frequency resonance in the building. Margaret toyed with the belt buckle on her jeans, watching Mary. This was the big planned coup she'd mentioned before. And time, Margaret started to sense, uneasily, was running out.

'Bloody fantastic,' Lorraine repeated, still gazing at Monday's papers.

'Who's read this morning's *Times*?' Mary asked. Margaret had; she knew what Mary meant.

'*Morning Star*,' Renata said. She didn't read the capitalist

71

press, only read a male-run newspaper for want of choice.

'Last night, Anthony Grieves asked a question in the Commons.' Grieves was the MP whose constituency included Heathrow. 'In reply, the Home Secretary said, without specifying, that measures in the inquiry into Fight were being stepped up. He also, for the first time, named the Scotland Yard officer leading the inquiry: Detective Chief Inspector Eve McKnight.'

Lorraine sat back with her legs apart and dug her thumbs into her jeans pockets. 'Right, then, there's number one on the hit list.'

Renata said with quiet venom: 'Not so much a pig, more a sow.'

Another passing lorry shook the window and, more distantly, an emergency siren brayed. Margaret held down her anger.

'Kill her,' Lorraine said. 'Get her, quick. She's no threat to us but she's a traitor to all women. It'll throw 'em – loose ends in the file, trouble finding someone else to stand up and get shot. Think of the psychological gain. That's what Wanda Zelaszny said – women'll win on 5 per cent action, 95 per cent psychology.'

'How far', Mary said with an edge of Zelaszny's own steel in her voice, 'do you think we're conforming to that ratio?'

'Shit,' Lorraine sneered. They all thought of Oxford.

Renata shifted her legs, fiddling with the hem of the granny dress. 'This *is* a psychological thing, much more than it's action. Kill the bitch.'

Mary looked at Margaret, the tall guerrilla solemn, troubled.

'Kill her if you must,' Margaret said. 'But don't expect to get a propaganda gain out of it.'

'Screw the propaganda,' Lorraine said fast, 'she's after *us*, she's . . .'

'You've just said she's no threat,' Margaret answered. 'You're right. So the only reason for killing her is propaganda, and it'll simply work against us. Don't you *realise* the difference between a killing and an operation like Tulip?' She had them all listening, suddenly. Her voice was urgent. 'Tulip has made tremendous propaganda for us, and here's why. One: the victim was male sexist business and no one but its shareholders cares a jot if it loses diamonds. Two: we've surprised everyone, because women aren't supposed to be capable of running a big, military-style operation with split-second timing and complex equipment. But we did it, and we made the company and the security forces look stupid, and men as well as women in the street are laughing at them. We've given the public some fun, for heaven's sake! Three: no one got killed, no one was even seriously hurt.' Margaret paused, breathing quickly, grey eyes bright. She'd combed every newspaper to assure herself about that. Poelmans, a bit of concussion; a headache and no internal injuries to the customs man; one collar-bone, three ribs and a wrist broken between them for the policemen who'd crashed. 'We'll get support at street level as long as the injuries after an operation read like the outcome of a rugby match. But look what happens when we kill people!'

'We made yon bastards in Glasgow sit up and think,' Renata sneered. 'There's less males coming home pissed and bashing their wives now!'

'Glasgow's a classic example. One Saturday-night squad squirting off with a submachinegun, and the next thing isn't just armed police, solid on the streets for six months – it's a sudden big shift in people's thinking, wondering if the women's movement really is a good thing after all.' She let them think for a moment. 'Just imagine the reaction if we killed this McKnight person. A woman makes much bigger headlines than a man as a victim of assassination. Is she married, has she got a family? All the support we've gained over Tulip would switch immediately to McKnight's children and widower. We'd never fully get it back.'

Lorraine said what Margaret had known she'd say. 'Crap. You don't seem to realise we're a fighting organisation. That's what the name means. If you can't face a fight, cop out now and leave it to the people who can.'

Lorraine scared Margaret. But the plea had to be put. 'Even when the revolution comes, we need ordinary people's trust and support. We can only get that by using peaceful means wherever possible.'

'If you can't stand *action*, lie on your back – and whore, for *intelligence*! That way we might get some use out of you!'

Margaret felt her cheeks burn. The thought of sex scared her. Even more frightening was Lorraine's attitude of using her body as a weapon.

Detached, Olympian, Mary murmured, 'That will do. I will

not have personalities brought into discussion of operational priorities. As far as McKnight is concerned, this cell will make no recommendations to Fight command and there'll certainly be no action.'

*   *   *

In Cannon Street the lonely pavements were as well brushed down as a stockbroker's suit. Not a fast-food carton, not an old newspaper blew in the wind. Oddly, they weren't far from the building Margaret had bombed, that night with Lorraine. It still scared her, Lorraine's readiness to use sex as a weapon.

'Don't let her provoke you,' Mary said, halting the Cavalier at a traffic light. 'I don't think she quite realises your feelings.'

Margaret wasn't sure she realised her feelings about sex herself. It was hard to think objectively about a set of attitudes you'd had burned into your subconscious since before you could remember. Sexual morality always had been inextricable from religious morality in the mission home in the Andes. Restraint was the key. Not just physically but emotionally, economically, intellectually, sometimes, she thought, even spiritually. You were angry but you didn't show it; you needed new clothes but couldn't afford them; you avoided certain areas of thought because of the threat they might pose to your faith. And yet there *was* aggression, there *was* anger, perceptible in her parents' personalities. What happened was that it all went channelled into the mission. That was the one place they felt free to act unrestrainedly. Maybe that was the reason why the one place Margaret felt free to act unrestrainedly was in her own, special, secret mission.

Mary went through the gears again as the lights changed. 'And I do agree with you about McKnight.'

It was so good that she'd carried her argument. That was the important thing. You could find danger in Fight, you could find evil; but you could find so much good, also, not least in the real love and compassion that united these women who were risking life and freedom for something they believed in. It was vital to coax them into bringing out the good and suppressing the evil, if only she could influence them enough.

'It's almost your end of term,' Mary observed.

'Yes.' A bit more flying, a lot more studying, catching up on lost time. She wouldn't get that when she started her third year, all ward studies and tutorials and only four weeks' holiday in the twelvemonth.

'We may want you to go abroad for part of the time, perhaps to meet some people.'

Oh, no. Oh, please. Didn't they want her to qualify? 'I'll watch out for the signal.' But she hoped they'd change their minds and it wouldn't come.

It did, though it wasn't what she'd expected. A day before the end of term, Margaret checked her pigeonhole and found an envelope in it containing US immigration documents and a ticket to Kennedy airport, New York.

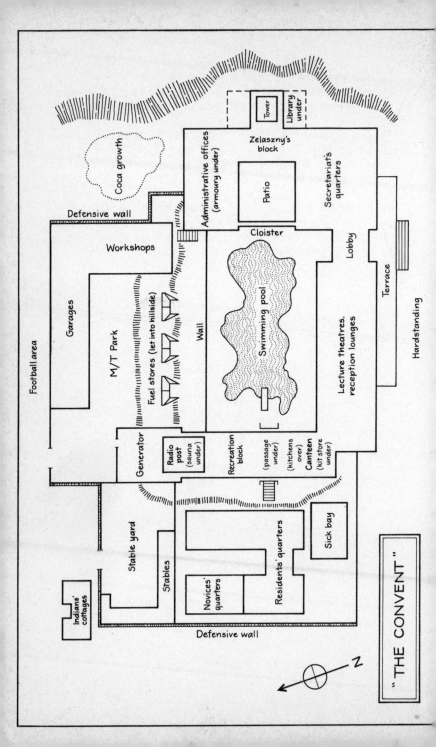

"THE CONVENT"

NOVITIATE

Through the exhaustion of a seven-hour flight, the antiseptic corridors of JFK were claustrophobic. Tension pervaded Margaret's movements. She'd half-expected contact from one of the 747's stewardesses but there'd been nothing and now here she was in New York with no idea where to go, whom to see, what to do.

In the rack in arrivals a yellow envelope said *Ms M. Stubbs.* She opened it. Phone number, cash, hotel confirmation. *Why* couldn't they, just once, give her some *human* contact?

She boarded the airport coach, guiltily reflecting on the ease with which her parents had believed her when she said she'd got a late cancellation on a special clinical course, readily noted the New York phone number Fight would answer if they rang; and then, schizophrenically, wondering how much they *did* believe of the lies she told them. It was six, local time, she'd taken off at half past two; her body clock made it eleven. Easter Monday and the airports full of couples with confetti still in their hair. She'd watched them holding hands and had to fight her own longing.

The hotel was Manhattan, one of the biggest. *Yes, ma'am, you're in one of our Style Suites, please take the elevator to the fifty-second.* Seventy-odd storeys, this place had. The bellhop placed her suitcase in the lift but stood back deferentially as another woman entered, wearing what looked like the hotel's livery. Older than Margaret, less tall, black hair severely swept and the predatory eye of a store detective. As the lift rose she looked straight at Margaret.

'We've met – weren't you at Mrs Lowell's?'

Was it or wasn't it? *Your contact will use an L keyword, follow it with an M.* 'Maine or Mayfair?' She was exhausted, this stretched the imagination.

And an M with an N. 'North Audley Street.' The woman smiled, hawk-eyed, and the lift stopped. 'There's my floor. Why not let's meet up for a chat, if you're staying a day or two?' The bellhop held the doors. 'Call me on the internal, here's my number.'

The lift went on up and Margaret fumbled the card hurriedly into her shoulder bag.

'Thank you, ma'am.' He straightened from the suitcase and took her dollar and she shut and double-locked the door. She looked round. She should have remembered this one, there'd been a bit of ballyhoo about it in the papers, special treatment for the visiting woman executive, feminine appeal. Ordinary Americans had a pithier term for it. But the flowers were nice. Margaret flopped into the armchair and dug out the card.

Wilma Sternberg, she was called. The phone number wasn't internal and was marked *emergency only*. On the back it said, *put messages in soil of floral display, frequent pickup*. Margaret memorised the number and destroyed the card. She could still see Wilma Sternberg's face, severe, honest.

She dialled the number she'd found in the envelope from Fight.

The polite American girl's voice said: 'Saratoga-Global Corporation, good evening to you. This is a recording for your convenience. If you'd care to record your wishes on this tape, we'll make sure you get our soonest possible attention.' Margaret sighed.

She gave her name and said, 'I'm at the hotel'; couldn't think of anything else and so hung up.

Trust them. Keep it sterile, keep you at arm's length. Not like the FBI. A really human touch, that, giving her a face, if just for a glimpse. Contact, linking Rahab with Richard Caine. And courage, too, because if Fight once discovered that Margaret Stubbs was a DI operator with a smartypants codename, then all her contacts would be blown as well and Wilma Sternberg could expect rapid revenge.

In the room's perfection she thought for a moment she was going to suffocate, and she went out on to the balcony. It was nightmarish. Her head started to go, and she clung to the rail to stay upright.

Fifty-two floors down, East 50th Street was a slow snake of

cars' lights in the last of the evening. Margaret loathed any height not viewed from behind an aircraft engine, her taste based on the aerodynamics of an average chunk of masonry. Even the cool moisture of the air reached her full of the sound and stink of traffic.

She trudged back in and flopped forlornly on the bed, pulling off her glasses to rub eyes itching with fatigue and depression. City loneliness was a truism she'd never before recognised quite so inescapably. More than at any time since she'd moved to England, she longed to be back, to stay, among the empty, echoing, windblown, enfoldingly familiar and friendly trails and cols and pastures of the Andean valleys where she'd ceased to be a child.

* * *

She was down for breakfast late enough actually to want to eat, her appetite perking up after weeks in which she'd done no more than pick at her food and make her mother think she'd got anorexia nervosa. No letters, though, no messages, nothing.

She lingered over coffee; killing time; comparing the flavour with the coffee Thérèse Boucher had made her in Normandy; and once when Richard Caine had treated her at a snob Mayfair hotel; and thinking still the best she'd had was the coffee Mario Roca's wife used to make in Peru. But that had been before cancer claimed her and these days Mario Roca made his own coffee.

At half past eleven Margaret sat down in one of the lounges to wait. She skimmed the *New York Times* and then started on the bit she needed to revise in Muir's *Pathology*. Still nothing. She finished the section in Muir and turned to the next book, medical microbiology.

Then at well after twelve a uniformed lackey from the hotel's vaunted staff of two thousand stooped politely. 'Ms Stubbs? Your cab's here, ma'am.'

'Oh?' She almost fell for it. Almost. Then she recalled that however well this might fit in with Fight's devious ways there were still unexplored dangers outside the airconditioned cosseting of the hotel. She put on her best county accent. 'I'm afraid there must be some mistake. I sent for no taxi.'

* * *

Over lunch, still in the hotel, a coffee-coloured, business-suited world expert on travel, New York and women tried to pick her up, which was nice in small doses but not what she was there for. She pleaded preparations for an appointment and hid in her room, but she'd only just got there when Coral Bargellini came through on the phone. At least, it sounded enough like Coral.

'Hi, Mags. How'd you get on yesterday?'

She was straining her ears for any nuance of trickery. She felt so badly exposed. 'Better than today.'

'Hey? What happened today?'

'Something strange about a taxi. I don't want to talk over the phone. Where are you? Why don't you come over here for a coffee or something?'

'Not right now,' Coral replied smoothly. 'I have a message for you: be in the foyer at two-thirty, you'll be picked up by a black chauffeuse called Poppy with a Rolls. It's safe. So long, Mags.'

That sounded better.

* * *

On the dot of half past the young woman walked in, black, short, in an olive uniform that might have been hotel staff or US forces or just something out of Sears Roebuck.

'Ms Stubbs? I'm Poppy. I have the Rolls right here.'

It was taking up most of the hotel pull-in bay. It was glossy brown, a Silver Spur. It hadn't got satellite-tracking radar, but it seemed to have everything else, Margaret noted as Poppy closed the rear door after her and slid the Spur's long snout soundlessly into East 50th.

She picked up the Henry Hudson Parkway, driving north. The speed limit showed as 50mph and she stuck to it. Over her shoulder she said agreeably, 'There are cigarettes or cigars in the cocktail cabinet if you wish.'

'Thanks, I don't smoke.'

Over the toll bridge, into the Bronx. Sweep right, into a tunnel. A truck baulked Poppy, she blew the horn. Out of the tunnel now, out of the city and into the state, suburbia, fake colonial villas among the trees.

'Where are we making for, Poppy?'

This time there was surprise when the black woman turned her head. 'Where? I figured you'd know. I have to pick up directions at this address in Dobbs Ferry, that's all I know.' They were at the turning, and she started the indicator.

* * *

The edge of the town was sprawling, tree-shaded houses in development-lot-sized grounds and Poppy's address led them to a green-shadowed driveway running through a shrubbery towards something pretty massive. Poppy had the message wrong, Margaret thought, this was journey's end, not a stop for directions. She was right, but not for the reason she'd expected.

The hedges of the driveway took a bend. Margaret glimpsed a big house, beyond, in the instant that Poppy braked sharply.

Blocking their path stood a wheelbarrow loaded with compost. Impatiently Poppy blew the horn to summon the idiot gardener who'd left it there and immediately an ancient Dodge came from behind and slammed into their bumper in a shower of gravel as a Chevvy pickup bucked to a crash stop barring the way ahead. Two men, one with a moustache, the other lean, in a yellow T-shirt, jumped from the Dodge for each of Margaret's doors as a limp-haired Puerto Rican pitched out of the Chevvy and dived for the driver's side.

Poppy screamed.

Margaret's panic vanished and as the seconds lengthened into cool clarity of reflex she remembered this was the precise situation for which Mario Roca had trained her, back in Peru. She launched herself across the long, hide-covered seat and out through the rear door, Poppy's side, an instant before the man with the moustache reached it.

He'd expected her to run. He was accelerating into the impact as she turned, bunched tautly and balanced, and dealt him a chop in the groin that folded him like a pair of socks. As she turned, even before he'd fallen, the man in the T-shirt was up on the Spur's boot and jumping at her, arms out, a gaunt, gangling figure with his teeth bared.

She took one pace back for a come-on, then as the man sprang full-tilt at her leaned her left arm at him, fingers aimed at his eyes. He jerked away with a gargling cry but his feet kept on coming and Margaret hooked hard with her right into the

83

proferred stomach and saw him crash his head into the Spur and bounce face down on the gravel.

Gunfire blasted shatteringly right next to her.

That did frighten her. She hit the gravel and rolled half under the Spur and was aware as she shielded her head of movement close by, scrambling, scared; a vicious yank at her hair and a kick at her head, too angry to hurt; then nothing. Just the echoes in her skull now, the shooting had stopped. Margaret rolled over, rose on a knee and shook back her hair.

Poppy was kneeling, supporting herself against the Spur's open door. She had a short-barrel Colt Cobra in her hand and she was trying to snap the cylinder open, one-handed, to reload. The two men Margaret had thumped had disappeared. Margaret saw the blood darkening Poppy's olive uniform in the same moment that she registered the Puerto Rican, lying in a huddle with one side of his head missing. Why, why did they have to do it?

'Where does it hurt?'

'I'm okay, I guess.' Then the pain got her and she had to drop the Colt; she was gasping.

Eyes wary for the two who'd run, Margaret got Poppy propped against the Spur's sill and opened her jacket and shirt. A single .32 or 9mm bullet had caught her glancingly under the ribs.

'Breathe in. I know it hurts, but you must. And out.'

No leaks, no pink blood. Just the sinew damage, then, superficial almost. Margaret was trembling slightly. She realised what had happened. The Puerto Rican hadn't reached Poppy's door in time to stop the chauffeuse pulling her gun; he'd taken fright, drawn, and shot her; and she'd fired back, killed him, and scared off the others.

'I'll get help at the house.' And there was a thought: why hadn't someone come out at the sound of shooting? Margaret looked properly.

The house was derelict.

'No go. All right, back to New York.'

She found the first-aid kit. Antiseptic and bandages weren't much for a bullet wound but they'd keep some of the blood off the seats. She got Poppy inside, the black woman shivering now. 'Brandy.' She'd got it from the Spur's cocktail cabinet. 'Careful, not too much. Good. Wait a sec, I'll be back.'

84

The Dodge started more readily than she'd feared. She backed it out of the way. She had to keep flicking hair out of her eyes and she thought her glasses must be dirty because of her vision blurring periodically. She was starting to see some of it now and it still made no sense.

She got into the Spur and clipped up Poppy's seatbelt, the black woman fighting her pain; at the last moment remembered the Colt, and climbed down from the wheel to retrieve it; then started working out how to make the car go. She got it. She was on the expressway, driving the big Rolls-Royce south for New York City, when the shaking started.

CHAPTER 14

If anywhere was going to be watched, it was FBI headquarters at 26 Federal Plaza, so instead they'd set up operations in a couple of grubby rooms where Richard Caine could watch the tarts and junkies below in Times Square. He stared down into the neon-lit darkness. Behind him Carla Desatnick was saying, 'Right . . . right', into a phone and Frank Pasarell was leaning forward looking simultaneously alert and half-asleep with his elbows on the desk.

Desatnick set down the phone and, as Caine turned, placed her elbows on the blotter, forearms together and hands clasped, and gave Caine a toothy, hard grin. 'Your angel of mercy Rahab has delivered Ms Poppy O'Quinn to a Fight-approved female doctor and is now back safe and sound in her ridiculously expensive Style Suite.'

Caine sat on the edge of her desk. Desatnick was very careerist, she had no kids and a husband who sold stocks on Wall Street and let her do her own thing. She was five nine, with permed hair and heavy thighs, and wore designer jeans and a lacy blouse that showed Caine she had a better bust than Rahab's. Pasarell was the same height but looked shorter with his thickset, powerful body, crewcut and deep tan, and he wore a slate woollen suit with a tie: a quiet, conservative, family man. Desatnick was a New Yorker born, but Pasarell came from Arkansas; they both had the FBI's mandatory law-school training.

'And?' Caine said.

The toothy grin stayed on. 'She passed the exams again. *Wasn't* she a clever little girl?'

'She was damn lucky, then.'

'Oh-ho, you surely do underestimate we ladies.' She battered

86

Caine's knuckles with a ballpoint. 'Those calculating bitches had a support squad all ready to break it up (ref, getcha glasses on!) if it got out of hand. But with that amount of atmospheric lead pollution, I hate to think what the cutoff point mighta been.'

'You didn't have a bad day, though, altogether.'

'Hell, no. I was staggered to see O'Quinn *casually* tooling around in her official employer's car! They are so goddam cocksure, those bitches. Of Rahab, too.' She chucked Caine an approving glance. Pasarell was still looking sceptical and sphinx-like. 'Marlena Kuhr, president of Saratoga-Global, bit of a recluse, home on Long Island, pots of money. One very shrewd lady, apart from this. It's not yet a proven connexion, but we'll sure watch her closely from now on. We have checked her out in the past, I have to admit, and although we've had our suspicions we never had anything substantive to go on.'

She waited. Caine waited. Pasarell waited.

'Yeah, well, thank you, Ms Desatnick, Mr Pasarell,' she said, 'allow me to buy you dinner on my HM Government expense account.'

'I was just going to say that,' Caine said, 'but Queen's Regulations prohibit me from entertaining anyone who takes the piss out of Britain's economic state.'

Pasarell chuckled. He said, 'Richard, we've had a look at Rahab now. She's a very impressive young lady. Can you, as of now, give us any background on her? All we know so far is that she's a rank amateur who's doing some incredible work for your outfit.'

Caine considered. 'Hm. Okay. Born in Britain, parents went to Peru as Protestant missionaries in a remote area when she was four and she lived there till she was seventeen. She took unarmed-combat and survival training in Peru from a guy named Mario Roca. In Lima, that was, initially. She went to local schools out there until she was twelve, then they sent her to an English-language school in Lima and Roca more-or-less took her under his wing. All very proper, mind you – he wanted the girl to know how to look after herself; he did okay. She was up in the Cuzco area at a time when a series of earthquakes killed some people she knew. She formed a decision to pioneer an Andean flying-doctor service and accordingly took the relevant sixth-form exams and entered medical school in London. She also began flying training in Peru, although she took a British test for the licence. And here comes the snag: to get a commercial licence, which she needs, she has to have a lot more money than she would normally have; also she needs marginally better eyesight.'

Desatnick whistled softly. 'And HM Government figures it's cheaper to buy Rahab's flying hours than have Fight create havoc all over Britain. What about the eyesight?'

'We know doctors who'll stretch a point.'

'Oh, naughty, naughty, the blind flying the blind-terrified. Why doesn't Fight wonder where the flying fund comes from?'

'Rahab's dad runs a church which has acquired an anonymous benefactor who is as loony as Rahab is about Andean flying-doctor services. What the hell do Fight know about how much money a church usually has, anyway?'

'How did you inveigle her into this? I can't see a loony-intellectual missionaries' daughter volunteering as a penetration agent, even for the flying money.' Desatnick was annoying Caine. She was a nitpicker; this time she'd picked the top off the weak spot in his operation.

'No one inveigled the girl into anything. She was a friend of a student called Julie O'Dell, who was trying to join a Fight cell. You know how meticulous Fight is. It checked her out, decided she was dangerous, and sent a guerrilla to kill her.'

'*And* Rahab *just* happened to trip over the body on her way to church.' Desatnick shook her heavy hair. 'You are not a fool, Richard Caine. You are a goddam fool.'

He eyed her sidelong. She shook her head again. If Fight was cocksure, Caine thought, Carla Desatnick was even more so and he had no option but to lay her at his earliest opportunity.

CHAPTER 15

One of the big Sikorskys on the regular run to Kennedy was lifting off the rooftop heliport when Coral Bargellini walked out with Margaret into the gusty sunshine. The exec helicopter pilot was thirty-odd, wind plucking light-brown hair, not quite Margaret's height, fray-ended denim shorts on her smooth, tanned legs. 'Mags, this is Sharon Levenson.' They strapped into the Hughes 500 six-seater and Sharon Levenson spun up the rotor and then they were out in the middle, not on the ceiling and not on the floor, of the box that is New York. They threaded their way amid the skyscrapers.

Wednesday, scarcely twelve hours since the Puerto Rican had died. She'd been cat-wary in the morning, but Coral had smiled with her multicoloured eyes and said, 'C'm'on, I'll take you this time,' and she'd had to trust her. Even in the knowledge that this time her destination might be a trap with no escaping. The Hughes with its traceable registration reassured her, although so had the Spur done yesterday.

Islets and blue water, sprinklers on lawns held apart by Dobermann-guarded driveways, eastern Long Island. The cedars that gave Cedar Point its name were Lebanons, beautiful and spreading as Sharon Levenson set down the helicopter. Cropped grass, white-porticoed mansion, very Scott Fitzgerald. They didn't get a look at the house, though; Coral took them down to the jetty. Several people were there, black as well as white faces, but Caine would want to know about the boat and Margaret gave it a good look. She was big, a seagoing cruiser built in Italy around an extended Riva Superamerica hull, her twin diesels growling already. Margaret went aboard and found that the black woman smiling at her was Poppy O'Quinn.

She was relaxed, looking informal in jeans, T-shirt, denim

jacket, but the loose clothes didn't hide the bulk of the wound dressings. Margaret had forgotten how short Poppy was. Her flatmate, who'd helped Margaret get her to the Fight doctor and who was behind Poppy now, was taller. Jodie Sadler, she was called. Margaret wasn't sure she liked Jodie, she hadn't Poppy's humility or her ready smile; and Margaret thought she detected the Zelaszny effect in this woman's air of suppressed bitterness.

'How are you, Poppy?'

'Whole lot better now. I got a week off, to recover.'

Jodie Sadler had cast off. In the control cabin, a tawny-blonde head was talking to a chubby, greyish head and they were doing things with the throttles because now the cruiser was moving quickly. Coral placed a strong hand on Margaret's arm and escorted her down the companionway into the walnut-and-solid-gold lounge.

*   *   *

They were well into the Atlantic, coastline just visible but blurred in spume, when the cruiser hove to. Poppy O'Quinn and Jodie Sadler went up to the foredeck, Sharon Levenson with them, and the tawny-blonde woman who'd been at the controls. Coral took Margaret aft. A woman sitting opening a wicker box of fishing tackle turned and smiled at them. She was the grey-headed one Margaret had seen from the jetty. Her face seemed assembled from little fragments of hard material and her eyes held kindliness but authority, too. Her body was chubby as well as her face, shortish, and she wore dark slacks in a soft synthetic fibre, and a heavy woollen sweater with a floppy rollneck. Coral, too, wore a thick sweater under an orange sailcloth trouser suit that looked vivid in the sun. She hadn't told Margaret they were going sailing, Margaret just had a light vee-neck over her blouse. She had a bright woollen shawl, though, that they'd given her years ago in Peru.

'Marlena, this is Margaret Stubbs. Marlena Kuhr.'

'Good to meet you, Margaret.' The hands, battered like the wise, watchful face, the grip decisive. Margaret hadn't known the name. Marlena Kuhr smiled as she clung to Margaret's hand, her old eyes less than clear at close range, brown, narrowed now in the glare off the sea. Margaret liked the smile but she wouldn't want to cross this person.

'Sit down, you're at home on my boat. Cigarette, cigar, drink?' She was smoking a black Sobranie. In a built-in cocktail locker there was whisky, bourbon, French champagne, Löwenbräu.

Coral lit a Camel with her eyes on Margaret and Margaret, not for the first time, felt the oppression of Coral's air of command, and critical competence, and devotion to Fight. None of them drank. Kuhr sat square and stocky on the folding chair and baited and cast two lines, then clamped the rods to the rail. She crushed out her Sobranie in an ashtray, a thoughtful touch: she might simply have tossed it overboard. She turned to Margaret again.

'It's good to have women like you in the Fight cells.'

'I'm . . . glad you think so.' They were a bit far from land for detailed discussion of her allegiance to Fight. Margaret pulled the shawl closer round her.

'Not a talker, huh?' Kuhr clapped a friendly hand on Margaret's knee. 'What d'you think of New York?'

'Dangerous.'

The cruiser rolled gently on the grey Atlantic swell. Gulls called. Margaret stared defensively at the narrowed brown eyes as they summed her up, relentlessly.

'Not to you, kid,' Kuhr said. 'That was what we needed to know.'

As she'd thought.

'How *can* you just sit there and tell me you put Poppy and me through a deliberate test yesterday?' She was furious. 'It's not only rank insolence to refuse to believe the reports you must obviously have had from London! It's stupid and immoral to hazard two guerrillas' lives in . . .'

'Listen, kid.' The hand on the knee calmed her slightly, but Kuhr was ruthless. 'Fight command is not justified in accepting other people's opinions on anything, even, allowing the best of intentions, other executives and cell commanders. For starters, if you were the kind of dum-dum to get in a cab you never called, you'd'a been out of New York so fast your feet never touched the ground. If you . . .'

'A man got killed yesterday!'

Chillingly, Kuhr said: 'It's one less.'

'Poppy and I nearly got killed!'

'Not killed.' Kuhr was sitting straight-backed on the chair,

91

knees apart, eyes harsh. 'We had a squad standing by to intervene if necessary. But if you'd been damn fool enough to get trapped, we'd'a let those guys rape you.'

The world closed in to a little globe, Coral indifferent at the edge, Kuhr's cruel eyes at the centre. For a long while Margaret was too incensed to answer. When she got her voice back, it was shaking. 'That does it! Let's get this boat back to shore! I'm taking the next flight back to London and having nothing more to do with Fight!'

Kuhr put her hand back on Margaret's thigh, heavy this time, detaining as well as calming. 'You're staying right where you are, kid. Fight needs you.'

Maybe it was the cold and the motion of the boat. Margaret was shivering, she felt slightly sick. 'You're insane! How do you know you could have stopped them at rape? If we'd been killed, there'd have been an international investigation that would have blown Fight wide open.'

Kuhr said: 'Didn't happen with Julie O'Dell.' Margaret froze. Kuhr paused, squinting out at her fishing lines. 'O'Dell got you interested in Fight, right?'

Margaret swallowed. 'We were close friends. Julie was very dedicated to the women's movement, she believed in force to fight male force, she'd have made an ideal guerrilla. I think Julie's aggression provoked the aggression of the man who killed her. That was what made me realise that Julie was right. Men who fight and kill are going to have to be fought and overcome themselves.'

Kuhr turned and fixed her glare-wrinkled eyes on Margaret's face. 'Suppose I said you have it all wrong?'

'How d'you mean?' The boat was rocking, maybe in the jolts from Margaret's heart. She pulled the shawl tighter on her slim shoulders but went on shivering. They were a long way from land for a person to go accidentally overboard.

'No man killed Julie O'Dell.' Kuhr's voice was cold, quiet. 'A woman did. O'Dell was in contact with a known agent of British Defence Intelligence. She was a spy and Fight had to execute her . . .'

Just like you. Margaret heard it, ringing round her brain, and she braced herself, calculating how to react. It scarcely seemed possible when she realised the words hadn't come.

92

*　　*　　*

She used the pay phone in Macys. Thursday morning, time off, and Fight surely couldn't have bugged this one, although if they had the risk was covered. They got Caine for her.

'What's the flap?'

'Look, I . . . I just needed to speak to you.' You in your cosy office full of armed guards and me out here never knowing when the next step behind me isn't going to mean a knife in my ribs.

'Oh. Okay.' This was the emergency number, and anyway he didn't like Desatnick and Pasarell watching him listen to his agent cracking up.

'Richard, I'm scared.' She was having to blink. She'd once loved this man, or thought she had. 'I want to see you. Is . . .'

'For Christ's sake, Rahab, we've been over this.'

Oh you contemptuous fake professional. Haven't you ever known what it's like? She whispered, 'Goodbye, then,' and hung up.

*　　*　　*

In the afternoon Sharon Levenson flew Margaret back to Cedar Point and a spindly-legged, doe-eyed Puerto Rican girl in a uniform like Poppy had worn led her to Marlena Kuhr. The library was pure, startling white, and modern as next year at Cape Canaveral. Electronic indexing, concealed rheostat lighting, push-buttons on the consoles beside the low, contoured armchairs, spacious in the sunken central bay. Kuhr was wearing dark red silk.

'I see you speak Spanish.' Margaret had been talking to the Puerto Rican in her own language.

'I've spent most of my life in Peru.' She declined a cigarette.

Kuhr lit her own. 'Any other languages?'

'Only Quechua, the language the Indians speak in parts of Peru, Bolivia and Ecuador. Peru's official second language.'

'You been in Bolivia?' Kuhr saw the nod, thought a moment, then shook her grey head. 'But I guess you would've been too late anyway to run across Guevara. Interesting person. Ever read his books?'

93

'A little. Then I went on to Wanda Zelaszny.' Keep those answers right.

They'd sat down, Margaret in her jeans, Kuhr gathering the silk of her skirt.

'I dragged Julie O'Dell into it yesterday for a reason.' The hardness was back in Kuhr's beaten-copper face, the ruthlessness. 'Now you slept on it, how d'you feel about Fight, knowing we killed that woman for spying?'

'Angry.' She waited; Kuhr listened, head tilted. She said, 'I'm angry with Julie for making a fool of me, I'm angry with British security for using her as a stooge. I'm angry that that's the kind of trick they have to stoop to to get back at us.'

Kuhr nodded, watchful, benign now, the Sobranie resting between her fingers. 'And you still want to quit Fight?'

'Your ambush test was thoroughly irresponsible.' She said it straight, small chin high, her anger apparent. 'But we've got a lot of fighting to do and I can't opt out of that.'

And the tension went as Kuhr smiled. She'd scared Margaret yesterday. But now the warmth came through and she was loving, and genuine, and magnetic.

*   *   *

Sunlight filtering into the library well and Margaret unconscious of time, gesturing her emphasis, leaning forward to make her point to Marlena Kuhr. If only. All that love and courage locked up in the movement, like energy in an atom bomb, if only Margaret Stubbs could be the one to turn it to constructive use. Caine and the others only wanted to break up Fight, they just wouldn't realise what a force it could be for good.

'Why', Kuhr was saying, 'did you put the brake on Easson's plan to hit McKnight?'

'Because of the propaganda result.'

' "Women guerrillas hit ace investigator." That sounds like good propaganda to me, kid.'

'On the contrary, it's negative propaganda. I agree there are times when we must fight, but if we acquire an image as wanton butchers, we'll alienate the very people from whom our most important support *must* come: ordinary women.'

Kuhr blew smoke thoughtfully through her nose. 'I'll buy it.'

94

It was working, it was working already.

*　　*　　*

They'd got on to history, Castro and Guevara, when the doe-eyed Puerto Rican girl brought them English tea. Kuhr stood up as the girl left, and poured it. She sat down closer to Margaret on the divan. The library was silent, you couldn't even hear the airconditioning. The silk of Kuhr's dress rustled richly and the clink of bone china was unreal.

'Know what really got you out yesterday? Kuhr murmured. 'Rape. Just thinking about it.'

A shiver ran up Margaret's spine. The anger was back instantly, and the dread.

'Listen, kid. We're not in the nineteenth century now, no one still figures it's a fate worse than death.'

'Maybe not.'

'Forget it!' Kuhr's voice had turned harsh again. 'I could introduce you to a kid, just turned thirteen now, came out of Vietnam on a refugee boat that got caught by Thai pirates. They killed nearly all of them, she was one of a handful of women and girls they took on their boat. They kept her for a month and raped her seven or eight times every day. Eleven years old. She hung on because she's got guts, and because she knew living – even *that* way – was better.'

Kuhr turned. It shocked her to see the tears flooding silently down Margaret's cheeks, shocked her to realise that, mentally, Margaret was there, on that boat. With compassion, Kuhr watched her a moment, then she put her arm round Margaret's shoulders. Margaret felt the contact, and the spasm of crying went faster, out of control. Kuhr pulled her gently close, Margaret conscious of her perfumed body, touching, and she stroked Margaret's hair. The chestnut colour, the heavy texture, she adored sense impression. And her gift for hardness had never stopped her recognising and loving sensitivity in another. But Margaret was whispering, 'No,' and she had too much compassion to convince a person against their will.

From a little distance, she watched Margaret mop her eyes, defenceless without her glasses.

'You're an ascetic, Margaret,' Kuhr said. 'You know, so was Guevara.'

Daringly Margaret looked at her. She smiled, and Margaret smiled back. Lesbianism, in the abstract, sounded something horrible; she didn't want it; yet the warmth, the contact, had appeal when you so much needed warmth and contact.

'I'm glad you're with Fight,' Kuhr said. 'There'll come a time when our movement, Fight, will be sparking off revolution wherever women are victims of phallic tyranny. When that time comes, women will be rallying to Coral Bargellini as their leader, the action personality, the spearhead of the whole movement. But it'll be words that get the movement moving. Words, ideas. And they're going to come from you, kid. Coral's the toughie, you're the intellectual, you know that?'

Margaret's lips were parted. She could scarcely believe the naïvety.

But the roles had been cast; the talk of Castro and Guevara hadn't been accidental. Castro, the tough, fiery commando leader. Guevara, the doctor, the quiet, fervent academic. Argentinian, a foreigner amid a principally Cuban revolution. Just like Margaret, a foreigner amid a principally American revolution.

*   *   *

Clear of the windstorm under the Hughes 500's rotors Kuhr shook Margaret's hand, her left clutching her hair as the leaves blew across the lawn.

'Goodbye, kid. Good luck – I mean it.' Kuhr smiled up at Margaret. 'You'll leave New York first thing tomorrow. Report to executive departures at La Guardia and ask for the Kuhr flight.'

'Where am I going?'

'You'll find out when you get there.'

96

CHAPTER 16

Black was winning in the pavement chess match down in Times Square. Caine didn't think much of the players, one Latin, one mostly negro. He was looking at white and thinking, mate in three moves.

'Those binoculars are FBI property,' Carla Desatnick said. 'FBI property is not to be used for the purpose of ranking women in order of desirability.'

'Nothing of the sort,' Caine said. 'I'm reading the subversive messages that that fast-food merchant is passing to his customers written on his hamburger wrappings.'

'Ah, now, he's one of ours, under secure cover. Yesterday he blew a conspiracy by Mauritanian intelligence to subvert the Tibetan navy.'

'Just 'cos Rahab's got another breakthrough, it's no excuse for you to bring what passes for the wit down to that level.' He groaned as white made the wrong move.

It was true, though, that Desatnick was mildly niggled about Rahab's making a discovery the FBI had been working on for months: Fight's underground structure. She'd got it from Marlena Kuhr that day on the boat. A national or continental network would consist of cells comprising four guerrillas, one appointed as leader. The cells would be responsible to an overall command cell, numbering perhaps half a dozen senior executives: there was a Command Cell Europe; a Command Cell North America, embracing also Canada; a Command Cell Latin America; possibly others. The command cells were responsible in turn to a supreme command, which obviously included Zelaszny. They still didn't know where that was.

'Okay,' Desatnick said, 'well, now zoom in on some real work.' Something went *slap* on her desk. Caine turned and

97

saw a file of papers.

He set down the binoculars and picked up the file. Desatnick leaned back, raised her arms and adjusted a hairgrip somewhere behind her head. The motion reminded Caine what a sound choice she'd made in putting on the blue denim shirt.

He looked at the sourceline. 'Finance Office? Whose expenses are they investigating?'

'Okay, dodo, since that thing has big words in, like "balance-sheet", let me explain it to you in kiddie talk. Rahab turns up a line to Marlena Kuhr, right? Kuhr is big business – but big. So we go talk with the Finance guys (how come they only have guys in that office, anyway?). And after a discreet but somewhat intensive second run through Kuhr's corporations' accounts, what do they deduce? You guessed it: when the Commerzbank in Main Street, Düsseldorf, gets ripped off by thugs with high voices, or when a certain diamond house gets mugged by lady flight attendants at Heathrow, all that cash disappears down the labyrinthine sewers of Kuhr's profit-and-loss.'

'She's laundering Fight money.'

'Hold it, baby, we Americans are supposed to have the crude-simplification lines. Let me tell you what is *odd*. Down Mexico way . . . uh, like Mexico *City* way . . . there is a mad millionairess with a Midas touch, by name doña Alma Múñoz. She's big business in Lat-Am, although not so big as Kuhr; but the two have done deals and joint ventures together lots of times in the past. One concerns an outfit called Cadal. Mean anything?'

Caine's eyes narrowed. 'Aircraft, isn't it?'

'Go to the top of the class. Construcciones Aeronáuticas de la América Latina. A small but constant thorn in the side of US-Mexican diplomatic relations. It's at a remote place on the Gulf of California called Alameda and it specialises in overhauling military aircraft, chiefly first-generation jet fighters of the Mirage III era. Cadal's board includes at least one Mexican government top kick; Mexican policy is traditionally independent and they will not stand for Uncle Sam meddling, even if it might safeguard their oil; consequently we – I don't mean we, I mean CIA – can't get closer than satellite altitude to find where their clapped-out junk comes from or, more to the point, where their shiny, refurbished jets go to.'

Caine nodded. 'An important question in the light of US policy of restricting arms for Latin America except for countries with petrodollars to spend at McDonnell Douglas.'

'You are a cynical jerk.'

He sat on the edge of her desk, leaned over her, and looked down. Desatnick hit him accurately on the nerve in the knee with a volume of police law. 'No, no,' Caine said, rubbing the injury. 'Men use physical violence, women use verbal torture. Let me sum up what you're saying. Kuhr is subversive, Kuhr owns half Cadal, therefore Cadal is at least half subversive.'

'Broadly.'

'Where does friend Fidel fit in?'

Desatnick narrowed her eyes suddenly and shifted her gaze past Caine, out through the dusty window. Clouds were playing tag with each other somewhere above, but you couldn't see much of them from this level. 'I'd sure like to know,' she said softly. 'That guy General Andreyev isn't sitting on his butt in Havana just because he likes the climate better than Sochi.'

CHAPTER 17

A Gulfstream III will carry up to nineteen passengers for more than four thousand miles at 500mph. On Marlena Kuhr's aircraft the seating had been cut down to twelve but only eight other women were on board when Margaret Stubbs ducked through the door on Friday, April 19. She wasn't surprised to see Coral Bargellini but she was to see Lorraine Easson.

'Wotcher, Maggie.'

Lorraine grinned to see the shock on Margaret's face. She was dressed as usual except for a shapeless T-shirt instead of the rollneck. The greeting was exaggeratedly English, theatricals for her American hostesses, and the attitude seemed matey, in contrast with her old antagonism. But her eyes were still steely.

They took off, Margaret near Coral, along the cabin from Lorraine. Through the gaps in the cloud, the patched brown and green below might have been anywhere; with no compass in front of her Margaret couldn't tell which direction the Gulfstream was flying. The seatbelts sign had gone off and now a petite American with big, slanted eyes and a pointed chin, whom they'd introduced as Tina Zeiss, brought coffee for Coral and Margaret.

'Presumably we're going outside the States,' Margaret said, 'since they told me to bring my passport.'

'Right,' Coral said. 'Ever heard of Tequísquepec?'

Margaret frowned. 'No.'

'Okay. Ever heard of "the convent"?'

'I . . . believe I have.' That theory session they'd had with Mary Abbott. *Even in the convent there are men.*

'Good.' Coral set her coffee in the holder and leaned a little towards Margaret. It wasn't always easy to hear in the noise of the pressurisation. She caught Margaret's eye, the grey, green and brown of hers oddly accentuated. 'Fight's secret structure breaks down broadly into three circles: the nucleus, consisting of a very few powerful guerrillas responsible for policy and strategy, at world level; the inner circle, a rather larger number of reliable, highly valuable cadres; and the outer circle, the ordinary guerrillas in the cells.' She glanced at Margaret. 'You're one of the inner circle now. It's only the cadres who get to go for training at Tequísquepec. It's Fight's world operations centre, Wanda Zelaszny's base.'

Coral sipped coffee. Through the thick noise came laughter. Tina Zeiss and Lorraine were joking with Jodie Sadler, the black New Yorker who was Poppy O'Quinn's flatmate. Poppy, it seemed, should have been on this flight, but she'd swapped with Jodie because of her wound. Jodie had been to Tequísquepec before. She held higher status in the cell structure, she was tougher than Poppy.

On this aircraft Margaret was beyond reach of Caine's contacts, but now curiosity overcame her fear. 'What is Tequísquepec?'

'We call it the convent. Kind of an in-joke. We call Zelaszny "Mother Superior" and the trainees "novices". It's near a place called Alameda, on the Gulf of California in Mexico. Little, broken-down town, the only industry's the port and an aircraft repair shop. Just outside town in the furthest western reaches of the Sierra Madre there's a pre-Aztec site. Nothing spectacular, a few broken steps and what might have been an altar, not even much to attract the archaeologists – they go down to the big pre-Columbian sites in central Mexico and Yucatán. The hill's called Tequísquepec. Back before the revolution, the Spanish dug up a few ounces of silver at a mine on the hilltop they called the Oraboca, but that was derelict for almost a couple of centuries until a few years ago, when a rich but eccentric rancher-businesswoman called doña Alma Múñoz figured on redeveloping and landscaping the old mine workings into an *hacienda*, in the grand style. Then she got tired of it – and decided to turn it into a mental home for women suffering from stress.' Coral eyed Margaret. 'Or so the official line runs.'

'Doña Alma is one of us.'

'Right. Okay: a ranch full of women is going to get noticed in a lonely neighbourhood, specially with planeloads of us coming in

101

and out periodically. You gotta keep the rubberneckers out, okay. Small towns are superstitious, so you create a bad-luck legend around the old mine and the pre-Aztec site. That just leaves you the young rowdies – except that one thing that'll put the fear of God up them is mental illness. Human monsters who look just like normal.'

Funny, Margaret thought, that they should choose that for a cover image.

'And for those who *do* get through – well, you give 'em a guided tour. Treatment centre, wards – locked, of course – lecture-size halls for group therapy. It's all there. We even have a brochure in Spanish and English that we give to visitors – emphasising, of course, the astronomical fees and the strict screening applied before we accept potential patients.'

Margaret watched the grin in the multicoloured eyes. 'You're very thorough.'

Coral jerked her chin, and the bob of fawn hair swung. 'C'm'on, Mags, let's go look in the cockpit.'

*   *   *

Loneliness. Coral was at the other end of the cabin now, Margaret back in the deep, rich seat by the window, watching the other guerrillas nodding as they listened to Coral. Rapt, all of them, even Lorraine, methodically, automatically honing the big knife as she listened. Only once before had Margaret been lonely like this, lost overnight in the Andes, when she'd found a coca bush and chewed the leaves the way Mario Roca had told her, to ease her hunger, thinking she might be days more before she picked up familiar country. Now she was lonely because she'd had her contact with Caine broken and she didn't know how to pick it up again; yet the paradox was the same as that time in the Andes, that she felt so calm about it.

Pressurisation noise wrapped itself round her and insulated her from the others. *For Christ's sake, Rahab, we've been over this.* She'd been more scared then than now, yet, objectively, here she was in deeper danger. Odd, that it should no longer be an issue that, once, she'd thought she loved that man. There was nothing personal to her dilemma of whether to betray him.

He'd never seen how much good there was in the women who

made up Fight. He'd seen the dead drunkards in Glasgow, and the kneecapped brutes who'd beaten up their wives. He had no concept of these women's energy, and talent, generosity and dedication and sheer force for sanity in a world turned mad by men.

Vengeance wasn't his prerogative, either.

For a moment, behind her glasses, Margaret had to blink. She stared hard out through the pressure window, forty thousand feet down to the Sonoran Desert. If only she could do it. If only she could wield the influence to direct Fight's methods away from violence and towards peaceful ways of taking power.

If only she could be sure of doing that, she would happily go to Wanda Zelaszny as a convert to Fight's cause.

*   *   *

The tower when they taxied in was an architectural mongrel of World War Two USAF and Spanish baroque. The whitewash was flaking, dulled with sand, but a banner in harsh, clashing, cheerful colours proclaimed BIENVENIDA A ALAMEDA. Three aircraft stood parked: a Cessna Stationair single-prop; a Beech 18 twin; and a Super Constellation that took Margaret back mentally to tatty airstrips in Peru. It was almost a museum piece, but a beautiful one, a classic of elegant design. Immigration was a Portakabin, reception a single-storey building in international motorway style, and drab offices huddled among the stunted fan palms.

But it was the hangars that caught Margaret's eye. Five of them, massive structures big enough to house a fleet of aircraft the size she trained on. *That* wasn't normal for the back of the Mexican beyond.

They went through the Portakabin with a speed that told Margaret someone very high up was pulling strings. Coral was the one who knew the place. She led them into reception.

At the bar, a shock-headed waiter in a white coat polished glasses and a figure on a high stool sipped mineral water. Five eight, short blonde hair, a powerfully built woman with an angry strength of will in her round, alert face as she turned.

Coral said, 'Hi, Sabina.' And Margaret knew who she was.

She was German. She'd been on a long wanted list Caine had

103

given Margaret, and she remembered this woman particularly because her daughter was wanted, too. Sabina Stamm, ex-Baader-Meinhof urban guerrilla, dedicated feminist fighter who'd kidnapped her young Giselle from the girl's defector father to save her from becoming another cog in the male machine. And who was here, at the nerve-centre of Fight.

She looked as pugnacious as her reputation suggested. The ferocity in her eyes, the savagely cropped hair; the fair skin, peeling with sunburn, that she plainly didn't give a hoot about; her energy, her air of dedicated ruthlessness.

Caine had told Margaret that the daughter would lead her to the mother. Now Margaret wasn't even sure that she wanted the mother to lead her to the daughter.

Coral said, 'Okay, I guess we can't all get in the plane. I'll ride shotgun with García and the luggage.'

In the edge of her eye Margaret was aware that someone had joined them. But it still gave her a start to see the man so close.

He was Sabina's height but his shoulders were twice as wide. He wore gymshoes, jeans, blue denim shirt, limp black hair to his collar, and less expression than a sun-bleached boulder. He had the copper complexion, the flattish cheekbones and the slit eyes of the Amerindian. And the way he'd simply appeared like a ghost made Margaret cold, despite the day's heat.

'Okay, García,' Coral said, and nodded at the luggage.

He went wordlessly, like a well trained dog. Outside stood a Toyota Land Cruiser. Margaret glimpsed him with two big suitcases on one massive shoulder, held by an arm, and an even bigger one held in a hand like a steel grab. Then she was following Sabina Stamm to the Stationair.

They were taxiing in five minutes and in another four they were landing at Tequísquepec.

Margaret hadn't seen a landing strip like Tequísquepec's since she'd left the mountains of Peru. It was half the length of a strip you'd call short anywhere else and it sloped at thirty degrees and you didn't turn upwind and approach conventionally, you touched down uphill, whatever the wind, and let the steep slope brake you. Tina Zeiss cried out in fright when she saw what was happening. Sabina Stamm was a first-class pilot but she didn't give a damn about nervous passengers, she'd carried too many. She slammed the wheels on the threshold like a handful of change in front of an awkward customer and swung up on the flat parking ramp as the Stationair ran out of speed. Under an awning Margaret glimpsed a propellor, but she didn't see any more because a young woman was there in another Land Cruiser, and the party walked across and got in.

CHAPTER 18

Wind off the Gulf of California lifted Margaret's hair as she climbed the steps stiffly to the terrace that ran the length of the frontage of the *hacienda* that was Fight's HQ. The convent. Even that near the sea, the air was hot, dry. Local time was half past one, but they'd been five hours in the air from New York, where the time was three-thirty, and part of Margaret was still on London time anyway. She felt exhausted. But not too exhausted to take note.

Tequísquepec was the sharp, steep tip of a razor-backed spur stretching westwards from the Sierra Madre, hard, high and blue in the haze towards the interior. The girl, no more than a teenager, who'd driven the Land Cruiser had climbed it in low gear up a steep cinder track with the woods stretching down to it from the crest on the right, very green in the sunlight, oak and cypress, and eucalyptus peeling like Sabina Stamm's tan, and, to the left, the crags falling away to a slope of acacia, prickly-pear, and yellow flowers amid the tumbled boulders. Here and there, yuccas stood spikily where the scrub had been cleared to widen the trail for cars. Then above them they'd seen the convent, orange tiles and white walls that suggested ancient Spain, and, directly overheard, at once startling and threatening, a tower, tall as a belfry, on the cliff that reared now beside the track.

The hardstanding, cinders again, sloped, but less steeply than the track. The tubs of lupin and juniper on and below the terrace weren't new. A group of women waited as Coral led her novices to the top of the steps. One wore a dress fastened with a belt but the others, Margaret saw, wore the same pale khaki shirt and trousers and brown boots and belt that the teenage driver had on. And two of them carried American M3 submachineguns.

Through the glass doors of the entrance lobby a corridor to

the left led them into a room like a lecture theatre. At a table, another woman smiled at them and gave them *margaritas*, the sweet-and-sour mixture of tequila and curaçao and lemonade, with salt crystals on the rim. Then the woman in the dress sat them down and got into her speech of welcome.

She was called Catalina Sánchez. She spoke English but Margaret guessed she was Mexican. She was in her forties, a thin, dark figure with a fire of fanaticism not quite hidden. She was efficient, intelligent, a good manager; but Margaret didn't like her eyes, too blank, too empty.

Rules. Fight was a military-style establishment and the novices were privileged to see its headquarters but you had to have discipline. Training took place in the mornings and the late afternoons with a siesta break between two and five, and you turned up on time for your details. And you wore uniform. Uniform on your training details, civilian clothing at siesta and in the evenings.

Sánchez explained the uniforms. Tequísquepec was managed by a group called the Secretariat with Zelaszny at its head and Sánchez herself as executive officer. The resident staff all trained to fight; but among them was a specialist security corps called the Bodyguard. They were Bodyguard members Margaret had seen with the M3s. Secretariat members wore the belted dresses, the rest wore the khaki shirts, trousers and boots with which the novice party would shortly be issued. And the unit flashes, the small rectangle of coloured cloth they all wore on the left shoulder: red for the Secretariat; blue for the residents; black for the Bodyguard; white for the novices with a blue band to indicate any previous visit; and for visiting VIPs or command cell members – Coral was one – an orange flash.

'You will not carry handbags or shoulder bags,' Sánchez said. 'You will learn to move with your hands unencumbered except with firearms. Equipment to be brought with you will be carried in webbing pouches on your belts.'

Limits. Anywhere on Tequísquepec hill was on limits, anywhere down below you got special authorisation. Pilot training would be carried out at Alameda airfield but, again, only those novices selected for flying would be authorised to go down there. Alameda town was strictly off limits.

'And to outline the training and its purpose I'll hand over to

Sarah Kuhr.'

Sarah Kuhr. Margaret had noticed the thickset, thirtyish woman who'd joined them, in the belted dress of the Secretariat. She could see the resemblance now. And of course if Marlena Kuhr had a daughter who shared her mother's ideals, this was where she'd be: right at the nerve centre.

But Margaret's head was nodding, she was barely taking it in. She'd grasped that the principle consisted of all-round experience – unarmed combat for a guerrilla like Tina Zeiss, who lacked those skills; field training for a city-raised woman like Jodie Sadler – but not a lot else before, vastly to her relief, they broke for lunch.

* * *

In the refectory another party was just finishing. It looked maybe twice as large as the New York group and they were speaking mostly Spanish; they'd come in a few hours previously on the Super Constellation Margaret had seen at the airfield, flying Rio to Caracas to Havana, and on here. The refectory was in a building that formed a right angle with the reception block with its lounges and lecture theatres. The HQ complex stood on a hillock, but what surprised Margaret when she walked out of the lounge to go for lunch was to find that the hillock was hollow in the middle like an old volcanic crater.

The big swimming pool in the bottom must once have been natural. But doña Alma Múñoz's architects had cleaned it up and concreted it and landscaped the sides, and now there was a flagstone walk right round the rim of the slope to the pool, and even, at the refectory end, a diving board built out from the flagstone walk.

Exhausted, Margaret didn't even get all her lunch down. Coral sat next to her, chatting, but Margaret scarcely followed her words. She was barely aware of uniformed residents moving among the tables, clearing plates, talking in English and Spanish, before Coral put a hand on her arm.

'Let's go draw uniforms.'

The kit store was in the same block as the refectory and Margaret, as she followed Coral down the stairs, cold suddenly, remembered the story of the Oraboca mine. This chamber was cut into rock, limestone, she thought, and she wondered if it had formed part of the old workings.

'Uniforms,' Coral said.

The kit store was shadowy, shelves running back to an unseen area. The woman who glanced Coral and Margaret up and down, went away, and returned, to set the neatly folded uniforms on the worn oak counter, was Vietnamese.

* * *

At six, Margaret woke in her novice's cell. Light through the closed shutters barred the shadowy chamber but the air was still warm, and her eyes and body sticky from sleep. They'd showed her a shower room, and she thought about that. Then she remembered the pool. Swimming gear was the last thing she'd thought to bring from England, but in Macys, when she'd gone to place the call to Caine, she'd bought a bikini, partly for the excuse, partly because the New York hotel had a pool and she'd fancied using it.

From the whitewashed H-block that housed the residents as well as the novices, she followed the grass-strewn path to the steps up to the passage through the refectory block. The diving board was straight ahead. Margaret dropped her towel on the flags, placed her glasses with it, then just walked down the board and dived.

For a moment there was nothing, just the roar in her ears and the cool, smooth weightlessness washing the tension from her skin, spreading out her hair. It cushioned her from the hazards of being alive. She broke surface. Coral waved. Most of the women from both novice parties seemed to be there: Tina Zeiss; the hard-eyed black Jodie Sadler; a woman from the South American flight whom they'd called Paquita; and another small person, Margaret noticed, looking very young, although it might have been her eyesight. Then, surprisingly, a man.

He sauntered down from the flagstone walk to a ledge by the poolside, grinning down at Coral: she was swimming naked, Margaret realised. The man was a lean, youngish Mexican, his Spanish descent evident in the lines of his brown face, and he wore cream flares and a flame-coloured shirt, and long black hair like El Cordobés.

'*Hola, Coralita. ¿Has vuelto a jugar un poquito, ha?*'

Coral yelled in Spanish, 'Get back to your goats, peasant.' She wasn't there for games and she didn't like being called 'Coralita'. The Mexican grinned; he seemed to relish the insult.

'Why are you so angry, Coralita? Can you still not arrange a transplant of *cojones*?'

She splashed water. He hopped nimbly out of range, jeering as Coral clambered out. Margaret trod water, watching the show with the others, incredulous that the man should let Coral with her unarmed combat training get within reach of him. But he did. Coral got his arm and went for the throw and the Mexican shifted his hips and an ankle. Then stepped back from the splash as Coral hit the water.

He was hooting with laughter as Coral surfaced. Angrily she shook fawn hair out of her eyes. 'Okay, smart-ass, c'm'on down here and sort it out.'

'*En seguida, querida.*' And he pitched in on top of her, classy clothes and all. He held her head under. Water thrashed.

Sharon Levenson, the helicopter pilot, was beside Margaret; she'd been on the Gulfstream. She muttered, 'Meet our deputy chief flying instructor.'

Margaret turned her head.

'Don Martín de Navásquez y Molina,' Sharon said. 'Finito to anyone he tries to get his legs around. Arrogant Mexican bum.'

She struck away from Margaret. The small young person was climbing out, and Margaret turned again, half-expecting to spot Sabina Stamm's daughter, but it wasn't: even at that range, Margaret could see the youngster was another Vietnamese. Coral came up in a cloud of bubbles and Finito broke for the side, paralytic with laughter.

*   *   *

By eight, sun was down, afterglow turning the sky turquoise low over the Gulf, a line of violet cloud underscoring the cutoff where the stars were coming out in the indigo. They kept Mexican hours here, the siesta, the late supper, and in a normal Mexican town eight was the hour of the *paseo*. Tonight at Tequísquepec it was time for the reception where Mother Superior met her novices. Margaret couldn't guess what to wear. In the end she settled for the sole dress that she'd brought from

110

England, with the old bright shawl that they'd given her in Peru.

But jeans would have done. The first person who recognised Margaret, and delivered a curt smile, was Sabina Stamm, and she was in jeans. She wasn't the only one; although Margaret spotted Tina Zeiss wearing an amazing floor-length gown.

Sabina spoke English. So Margaret was a pilot; what types, what experience; she hadn't been to Tequísquepec before, did she know anyone here? Lorraine, Margaret answered, and relaxed a fraction. Sabina was older than she'd supposed, mid thirties, a big-boned woman with small but tough, restless hands that betrayed energy, anger. The teenager who'd driven the Land Cruiser walked by, fair hair in a bun, in a uniform with the residents' blue shoulder flash, and Sabina said, 'Hi, Cathy.' She told Margaret: 'Cathy Latta. She's on duty tonight. Patrol.' Margaret realised she'd seen a holster on the girl's hip.

They were at the opposite end of the pool from the refectory and the diving board. A cloister, all Spanish arches, separated the poolside walk from a flagstoned patio full of stone benches, and plots with yuccas and juniper, and opposite the cloister the tower rose, hard black against the night, the tower Margaret had seen driving up from the *altipuerto*, the sloping mountain airstrip. On the other two sides of the patio, buildings stood, linked to the wing with the tower: one side the Secretariat's living quarters, Sabina explained; the other side, administrative offices. Tonight, one of the offices had been turned into a bar, and Sabina took Margaret in and a woman gave them champagne.

Back in the open, they drank it; Margaret sparingly; Sabina knocking hers back and not noticing. Starlight in the pool quivered like the bubbles in their glasses and the yellow lights under the junipers drew mosquitoes and made the night darker. Margaret thought about Wanda Zelaszny, nervous that she, with the other novices, was to be presented to this awe-inspiring woman tonight. She thought also that she was a long way from Richard Caine. But she didn't know how much that mattered.

'There,' Sabina said. 'Nadezhda Sokolova.' A tall, bird-like woman, hair silvered in the lamplight, talking to a group Margaret recognised from the South American flight. She was wearing a very plain dress and a cardigan. 'She's Russian,' Sabina said. 'Brilliant, a former Soviet academician. And those

111

sexist pigs don't let many women in. She's our Comecon Command Cell leader.'

Margaret watched Sokolova a moment. The Russian woman's hand movements looked balletic; but then she moved and almost fell over a flower tub. A black woman in an orange dress walked up to her and Sabina said, 'Miranda Nwokoye, Nigerian, she leads our Command Cell Africa-Asia.' Margaret tried to get a look, but just behind her a voice said, 'Sabina,' and then a mutter of soft German that Margaret wouldn't have understood if she'd caught it. She turned.

The girl was slight, early teens, not quite Sabina's height, wearing jeans and thin pullover. Margaret saw wavy blonde hair falling to the girl's waist, a round head, an intelligent set to the face. But the light was wrong, and Giselle Stamm, the daughter Sabina had kidnapped to train her to fight beside her mother against phallic tyranny, had her eyes in shadow. Margaret couldn't guess what might be hidden there.

Sabina was answering brusquely, monosyllabically, Giselle leaning at her, her shoulders tense, as if wanting to be close to her mother, yet still as wary of her as of all the other people in the world.

She said one last thing to Sabina, chucked Margaret a suspicious glance, and vanished among the guerrillas. Now someone else was there.

'*Buenas tardes*, you're the very two ladies I'm looking for.'

Finito. He'd changed now into a dark suit with an ivory shirt, silk again, the trousers cut tight across the hip to draw the eye to his small buttocks and the frontal bulge he wanted noticed. His shirt was open almost to the waist to show dense, black hair and the flash of a crucifix, but it was his dark eyes and wide, white smile that Margaret liked. He was broadshouldered, tough, but not so tall as Margaret; he didn't like that.

Sabina gave him a look she'd just mixed up in a cauldron. 'Finito Navásquez, one of our instructors,' she told Margaret.

He obviously knew who Margaret was. He gripped her hand. 'What a great pleasure, I'm so glad to learn you're my pupil.'

Margaret felt herself starting to go.

Then she caught Sabina's eye and re-entered atmosphere with a jolt.

*   *   *

Half past nine, the evening colder, and still they hadn't called supper because Zelaszny still had novices to meet. Coral Bargellini had appeared wearing a jacket and skirt that suggested that if she gave up being a guerrilla she could always go in for beach contests. She was sitting with Margaret now on the edge of the pool, and in the light of the patio they saw Lorraine Easson come out of the door the novices were being led through to see Zelaszny. Lorraine was walking on air. Margaret wondered what Zelaszny could have said to her, she was in a dream; she scarcely seemed to know where she was until Jodie Sadler took her arm and steered her to the cluster of guerrillas round the bar. Margaret saw Catalina Sánchez go into Zelaszny's door with the South American guerrilla called Paquita.

At a corner of the pool Finito had become the centre of a little knot of guerrillas, Tina one of them in her long gown. He was playing guitar, confident Spanish cadences, a bit of thumping, impromptu jokes with the music. Coral was muttering seriously at Margaret. At the opposite corner from Finito another guitar had set up in competition but it was stuff out of the old protest songbooks, a bit mechanical. It was Giselle, Margaret noted; she was with a mixture of American and Vietnamese faces. Odd that she should take up position directly opposite Finito and then cause deliberate jamming.

'See that kid,' Coral said. A Vietnamese girl about Giselle's age, the one Margaret had seen swimming; she was wearing boots and combat gear and kneeling with the jamming party. 'Pham Anh. She was with a load of refugees on a boat out of Nha Trang that got caught by Thai pirates. The Thais killed the men, the oldest women and the youngest girls, and took the rest of them on and raped them repeatedly. We managed to rescue that party.'

Something had stuck in Margaret's throat. She remembered the Vietnamese storewoman; she'd spotted other Vietnamese here. They must all have been from the same party. Victims, alike. Vividly Margaret remembered that day, talking with Marlena Kuhr, and she had to bite her lip. Sex combined with violence, her greatest dread. Yet that kid had come out of it sane, which was more than Margaret Stubbs would have done.

'That's what we're up against,' Coral said. 'That, in symbolic form, is what all men are doing to all women, and we have to overthrow that tyranny.'

113

By the way she said it, Margaret knew, unmistakably, the essential Coral Bargellini. She was tough, she believed in herself, she was a person who could be gifted in any sphere; and she believed in Fight and its objectives. Not because Wanda Zelaszny had convinced her but because Coral knew an inevitable shift in history when she saw it.

Margaret thought she did, too. But, unlike Coral, she felt no need to be the force that led the change; Coral's ambition wasn't just different, it was greater; far greater.

Unexpectedly, and in friendly formality, Coral touched Margaret's hand. 'You have a leading role to play in that. Oh, yeah, Mags. It isn't for me to go into detail, but I can assure you that right now you are one of the key women in Fight.'

Trapped by Coral's multicoloured eyes, she didn't know what to say. Her heart was thumping and the guilt of her deception haunted her. She opened her mouth.

Then by the makeshift bar there was shouting, movement, and they both jumped to their feet.

Margaret saw guerrillas shifting quickly back, Lorraine among them, with Jodie. As the ring broke, she saw two women, one of them their teenage driver, one a short, wiry person with curly, red hair, wearing jeans. Heavier than Cathy Latta and fighting her savagely.

Cathy Latta went on her back, hard, on the flags, and the woman in jeans saw the next move coming and broke aside, evading the stomach throw. But Cathy Latta hadn't let her go and she was back on her feet fast, and Margaret realised this wasn't like any fighting she'd ever witnessed between women or girls. It was no more angry, no more vicious. But it was trained, skilful, co-ordinated and much more dangerous.

Then from the crowd a tall woman strode in, wearing uniform with the black flash of the Bodyguard, and broke it up. In the patio lighting her face was strikingly beautiful, but she didn't let that bother her.

Margaret and Coral swapped glances. Margaret breathed: 'What on earth . . .'

But she didn't get an answer, because Catalina Sánchez was there.

*   *   *

114

'Stubbs,' Catalina Sánchez said through the open door high up somewhere towards the tower that dominated the track to the *altipuerto*. Tired yet tense in the dull dress and bright shawl, Margaret went in.

The shutters were closed. The room was lit by a desk spot and a standard lamp set between two armchairs, and the woman waiting wasn't at the desk but in one of the armchairs. She stood up as Margaret hesitated on the threshold.

Sánchez murmured: 'This is Wanda Zelaszny.'

It unnerved Margaret to be shaking hands with the world leader of Fight.

In the shadows Wanda Zelaszny was slight, five foot six, greyish, in a plain blue dress cut below the knee. She'd been reading, but she put on a different pair of glasses, and in the moment that her eyes were unprotected her face with its gaunt cheekbones, its shadowed hollows, was that of a hunting eagle. An impression reached Margaret of religious asceticism, as befitted Mother Superior. Then Zelaszny smiled, and instantly Margaret was at her ease.

'Margaret, I'm really glad to meet you. It's a privilege to have talented women such as yourself fighting alongside us.'

Margaret mumbled something. Zelaszny gathered her skirt and sat, and, with a gesture, invited Margaret to do likewise.

'You had a tough few days and a long flight this morning, so I imagine you're tired. I won't keep you long. I just want you to know Fight is really pleased with what you've done for our movement. And not just your performance in action. You're a thinker. That's important.'

Marlena Kuhr, Margaret thought: that was where she'd got that from. She replied: 'Possibly. But any thought of mine has been strongly influenced by other people's ideology – yours in particular.'

The smile conveyed kindness. Margaret realised that she wasn't just awed by Zelaszny's radiation of command, her lawyer's precision; she was attracted, too, and strongly. Caine was hardly in her mind. So this was the Zelaszny effect: to make another person want, immediately, instinctively, to do whatever she said; to believe that she was right.

But Margaret could feel Zelaszny's will urging her and yet could feel, in some secret depth of her own, that she knew better

115

than to believe unconditionally.

'Ideology is impotent,' Zelaszny said, 'until you support your ideas with action.'

The desk spot kept reflecting in Zelaszny's glasses. Margaret wished she could see her eyes. Yet she was picking up their impression even without the sight. 'On the other hand, action is futile outside a framework of ideas.'

'Which would you rather do? Have the ideas or command the action?'

Margaret smiled. 'Choices are never that simple.'

'Meaning?' But Zelaszny knew her meaning.

'That the idea itself obliges one to act and, often, to take a hand in leading.'

'You are a paradox.'

Margaret straightened her shoulders, surprised. 'You don't agree?'

'I agree wholeheartedly. I'm talking about you, personally. When you talk, you're cool, you're clinical. You're a single-minded professional. But what makes you talk at all? Sensitivity, Margaret. You're a highly sensitive, highly caring person. Yet you have this tremendous capacity for restraining that and hiding it behind your ideas.'

Margaret could see Zelaszny's eyes now. But she was scared, because Zelaszny could see more than just Margaret's eyes, she could see right through to her mind.

CHAPTER 19

At 1402 mountain time, 1602 in New York, a USAF Boeing E3A airborne warning system roughly over Yuma, Arizona, tracked the Gulf Stream landing at Alameda and radioed base. Richard Caine was sitting in the back of a JetStar with Frank Pasarell and Carla Desatnick at Floyd Bennett Naval Air Station and the moment they got word, Pasarell selected San Diego, California, off his prepared list of possible destinations. The JetStar climbed steeply out over New York.

'I still say she should have had radio,' Carla Desatnick said.

Nitpicking bitch. 'They'd kill her as soon as she used it,' Caine repeated. 'They're paranoids, you should know if anyone does.'

Desatnick threw him a weary look, bored with cheap cracks. 'An agent's no good if you don't have linkage, for Christ's sake.'

'Hold it,' Pasarell growled. Off the satcom link they'd now switched to, a new message was coming from the E3A: the shuttle, Alameda to Tequísquepec. 'Hell kinduva place is that?' Pasarell grunted, and punched the question into the computer terminal. If anything was on file about Tequísquepec they'd be getting it shortly off the ground link.

The JetStar was still climbing. There was solid cloud below and not much sensation of movement. Desatnick said: 'Let's ask the computer if it's nice weather in San Diego. I guess I'll call my old man and say dinner isn't in the oven.'

Caine lit a cigarette, resisting the bait.

Pasarell muttered: 'Carla's right about link . . .' then his answer started flashing on the VDT and he pushed *print*. He looked it over critically as the keys made quacking noises like an electronic duck. 'Right on, doña Alma Múñoz, old friend Marlena Kuhr's playmate.'

'*Is* she?' Desatnick threw in.

'Also,' Pasarell reminded them, 'the owner of that Super Constellation reported by CIA this morning as having been watched flying out of Havana by Gregorio Tabio and General Andreyev.' He went on reading. 'Rahab landed at Tequísquepec. Kind of a ranch run as a private loony hatch by Múñoz, who is also in partnership with Kuhr at Cadal in that same area.'

He tore off the sheet and gave it to Caine. Caine read it, gave it to Desatnick.

'Gusher at Borehole 47,' she said.

Pasarell nodded, sighing softly as if both his colleagues bored him, and looked at Caine.

'Short of confirmation from Rahab,' Caine said, 'I'd agree. Obviously we must *get* confirmation, but, from the circumstantial . . .'

'Yeah, right, we got the Fight Incorporated global head office telex number.' Pasarell was still sour; he wasn't looking forward to the next few moves. 'So we have two problems: the immediate practical issue; and the political issue.'

The political issue being that if they really had found Fight's nerve centre, a lot of nations were going to feel entitled to demand instant action.

'We have to get a radio to her,' Desatnick told Pasarell. 'Just let Capitol Hill get a whiff of FBI straying into Mexico and you, me and everyone we touched in ten years'll be on a supermarket shelf labelled cat food.'

'She is not having radio,' Caine said.

The seatbelts signs were on. They were in light, clear-air turbulence and the JetStar seemed to be riding on cobbles. Desatnick leaned towards Caine, against her belt, got as far as, 'Okay, wiseacre . . .' then realised where Caine was looking and tucked angrily at her blouse.

Pasarell, cool, said: 'Richard, what's up your sleeve?'

'I'd like to use that satcom link. We've got someone we can move in, but it won't be overnight, and besides, it's a man, so he won't have easy or regular access to Tequísquepec.'

'Go ahead.'

Risking the turbulence, Caine unclipped his belt and went aft to encipher the message.

When he got back, Pasarell and Desatnick were arguing about bringing Mexico in.

Pasarell spread a big, tanned hand. 'Okay, I'll tell you what our ideal move is. We contact Rahab, we have her get comprehensive detail on Fight's worldwide structure, then we get Mexican government approval to go in there and clear out the whole stable. But that will not work. We already have a somewhat sensitive diplomatic issue in the form of Cadal, and the Mexicans won't stand for interference. Strictly, they're right: anything that happens at Tequísquepec is primarily a Mexican domestic matter.'

'There's an international inquiry in progress,' Caine said. 'They've got Americans and Brits and God knows what there – it's international already.'

Pasarell eyed him uncomfortably. 'You're forgetting a little history. Europe has its pool of information-sharing in the Fight operation, based on Interpol in Paris, and in which your officer McKnight participates. The suggestion was raised, some months ago, that the US should join in that pool. As you'll recall, nothing came of it. We over here pointed out that, since, one, FBI had the most advanced national inquiry; two, Fight first crawled out the woodwork in the States; and, three, in the information-sharing process, FBI had up till then done most of the giving and precious little receiving, then for those reasons the international inquiry should be superimposed not on Paris Interpol but on the FBI operation. What we now have is a European operation, a US operation, and a tenuous link between the US and UK in the form of you and Rahab.'

'Leaving aside Mexico.'

Again Pasarell sighed. The seatbelts signs went off and the woman USAF sergeant from the crew asked if they'd like coffee. Pasarell said yes, three, and resumed.

'Mexico is one headache. Co-ordinating a strike against Fight in twenty or so countries is something else, and something that can't be worked out on the back of an envelope in ten minutes. Thing is, as soon as Mexico realises Washington really is keen on Tequísquepec, they'll go right in and bust the place open, just to show anything the Marines can do, the heirs of Pancho Villa can do better.'

He was oversimplifying, Caine thought, but the substance was correct. He said, 'Thanks,' to the sergeant and set the coffee cup in its holder.

'My vote,' Pasarell said, 'is for a rather casual approach from Washington, just so we can say we told Mexico about Tequísquepec, but not letting them realise how interested we are – thus giving them time to get ready for a sensitive look at the place while we set up the big hit, working from Paris. Which at this stage of the game is where it's got to be worked from, since the Europeans aren't going to come to Washington now.'

Desatnick eyed Pasarell sourly. 'You are a big shit,' she said. And gave him the wide, toothy smile.

'You New Yorkers always did have a way with words, specially when talking to a senior officer.'

She appealed to Caine with an outflung hand. 'We're just going to assume all Mexicans are stupid, right? We're just going to assume they won't see right through it when they get the word from Washington?' She turned back to Pasarell. 'Washington just better lay it right on the line when they talk to Mexico City.'

Something in the noise had altered. They were climbing again, they must have entered a new traffic control zone and been given a new height.

'And have Mexican forces go in there?' Pasarell said.

'We can't *know* . . .'

Caine said: 'Frank's right, Carla. If we don't stall off the Mexican authorities, Rahab will be endangered immediately, and none of us can risk that.'

'That is not the . . .'

Pasarell said: 'That's what we're doing. Okay. Carla, when we get to San Diego you're in sole charge of the operation, on the spot. Richard, you get your linkman in real fast, get the orders to Rahab and the world membership and structure out. I won't be with you. I'm going to Paris and set up the international strike against Fight in conjunction with Brouzet and his Interpol guys.'

CHAPTER 20

The rifle sight wouldn't keep still. Even with glasses, Margaret could scarcely see the square card of the target on Tequísquepec's 100-metre range, let alone the bull. Maybe she was still shaky from the gym workout that had started their day. When Tina Zeiss and Sharon Levenson started shooting, on the stands next to her, the noise scared her and she lost the target altogether.

She squeezed, because she had to, and the FAL 7.62mm selective-fire automatic rifle slammed its butt plate into her thin shoulder.

'You know where that went?' The marksmanship instructor was French-Canadian, Charlotte Rondeau, small, intense, on her uniform the blue residents' flash barred black to identify her as a qualified instructor. 'Okay, why not?'

Margaret said nothing.

'Clipped the card,' Rondeau said. She had 6 × 30 binoculars round her neck. 'Didn't even hit the target. C'm'on, now, you can do better than that.'

The gym instructor had been the strikingly beautiful American Bodyguard who'd broken up the fight last night. Annabel Hardy. She'd started fashion modelling when she was seventeen, she'd grown a political consciousness later. Sharon had found that out. Sharon always knew the gossip. It was Sharon who'd discovered that the fight between Cathy Latta and the red-haired woman in jeans, a Bodyguard called Kelly Thane, had been over a disputed girlfriend called Cornelia Piotti. And that was a name from Caine's wanted list, an Italian ex-Red Brigades guerrilla.

'Okay,' Rondeau said.

Aiming the rifle was like aiming two bags of potatoes. Margaret hated its polished wood and its smell of grease and burnt cordite; but she tried.

'No, no,' Rondeau said, 'put the rifle down. That's way too long aiming.'

The range was above the HQ complex, high amid the deep-green oak forest on Tequísquepec hill. Heat blurred the grass; Margaret felt sticky; insects kept diving at her.

'Deep breath.' Rondeau was very dedicated, a bit severe, a bit formal. 'Keep relaxed. Squee . . . eeze.'

Again the jolt of the butt plate, and Margaret realised in surprise that she'd fired.

Rondeau raised the binoculars. 'Much better, an inner. Now find where you're aiming off, and start correcting.'

*   *   *

Halfway down the hill as the novices carried their rifles back to the armoury, a patch of woodland had been cleared, to extend the vegetable garden, and four women, stripped to the waist, were breaking up the soil with mattocks. Margaret recognised Cathy Latta, her hair awry, body glistening, movements obviously weary in the high sun. It wasn't until she saw the uniformed Bodyguard standing over them that Margaret realised this was a punishment detail.

Kelly Thane got her punishment immediately before lunch and all the novices were marched into the patio to watch. There'd been a disciplinary tribunal before breakfast and Catalina Sánchez, presiding, had heard the evidence and decided that Thane had started it although not without provocation. Thane, wearing boots and uniform trousers, took ten strokes with a cane across the back from Jo Colwell, the head of the Bodyguard and a woman who, Margaret knew from Caine's wanted list, had killed several men in the States. Colwell drew blood with every stroke but Thane didn't make a sound. Tina Zeiss did. Afterwards at lunch Tina couldn't eat a bite and Margaret herself had a job to.

Cornelia Piotti didn't escape, although her part in the fracas had been indirect. When Margaret left the refectory, Piotti was in full uniform, in full sun, standing to attention, and that was how she was going to spend her siesta time.

Coral Bargellini, ignoring Piotti, took a few lazy strokes round the pool and then joined the others in the cool behind the closed shutters of the living quarters. Margaret went to investigate the library.

With your back to the pool and your face to the tower overlooking the *altipuerto* trail you were in the patio, on your left the offices where they'd had the bar last night, on your right the Secretariat's quarters. But the Secretariat lived on the first floor, you could tell from all the closed shutters. On the ground floor there were other offices, among them one that produced a news-sheet for the HQ complex and the disinformation brochures Coral had talked about. There was also a way into the library.

The ground floor when Margaret went in was galleried. Above it stood another gallery; below, a basement, which, she realised, had been sunk into the edge of the cliff where the tower stood. No one was there. Thin light through Moorish windows slanted on to a writing desk, on a corner of concrete cantilevered over the basement; a slender catwalk linked it with a spiral staircase rising to somewhere unseen.

She couldn't find the lights. Afraid of the silence, she stole round to the writing desk, searching for switches. And for no reason glanced back.

García, the Indian, was inside the door, motionless, silent, a squat silhouette. Something primitive inside Margaret tried to scream.

She swallowed hard. She said in Spanish: 'What do you want?'
García said nothing.
Margaret said: 'Where are the light switches?'
García turned, indicating a panel Margaret had missed. Edgily Margaret said, 'The basement,' and García reached, and the fluorescent light flickered. Still expressionless, García vanished through the door, silent as the afternoon heat.

Margaret stood, shuddering. She had the sensation that García, like Zelaszny, could read thought. Nerving herself, she went down the steps and began exploring the shelves and cabinets.

*   *   *

This time when the spiral stair creaked Margaret whipped round, looking for García before she realised García wouldn't even have

123

made that slight sound. Wanda Zelaszny peered over a rail above.

'Don't you take a siesta, Margaret?'

She mistook the tone. 'I'm awfully sorry if I've disturbed you.' It was like getting caught out of bounds by the housemistress.

'Not a bit.' Zelaszny smiled hawkishly. 'Come up, Margaret, let's have a chat.'

Margaret climbed the cedar steps. The cantilevered platform had a strongroom door at one side, she noticed. Zelaszny's office was immediately over the strongroom. It was the one Margaret had been in before, the shutters open this time, the rough-look plaster, the desk, armchairs. Last night Margaret hadn't noticed the steel filing cabinets or the weapons rack with the HK53 submachinegun and the Mondragón semi-automatic sniping rifle. And, of course, the comprehensive electronic alarm systems panel.

'We came in the back way,' Zelaszny said. Her cool voice was nasal. She was in a different dress today but cut similarly plainly, in bleached-blue cotton. 'I have access to the main administration block and to the library. What'll you have?'

'A soft drink, thanks.'

'Fine. I only drink sometimes with supper.' She opened one of the filing cabinets to reveal a fridge and television, and poured two orange juices. 'Come look at my roof garden.'

It was through the tall shutters, a platform with a low parapet, blankets spread, big flower beds with juniper, dwarf mesquite. They flopped on the blanket. Zelaszny's formality, her asceticism, seemed to criticise Margaret, and she knew she was afraid. She didn't dare let Zelaszny read in her mind what she'd come here for.

The mental breakaway was deliberate. 'What's that place on the hill?'

'The Sacromonte. Pre-Aztec holy place.' Zelaszny smiled. Margaret remembered now, Coral had mentioned the place. 'We get archaeologists over once in a while to study it. Finito Navásquez looks after them, keeps them away from here. You can see the steps where they say the priests stood.' She glanced at Margaret. 'Funniest part about it is underneath. There's a big pool from an underground source – I run the swim pool off it. Down at Alameda airport the Mexicans have permanent offices for their Water Commission, to study the terrain and try to discover any more water.' Her fingers, toying with a twig on a tub plant, betrayed energy, restlessness, the way Sabina Stamm did. But Sabina hadn't Zelaszny's intellect. 'Underneath the Sacromonte it's honeycombed, a real labyrinth, and all natural passages in the limestone. And that's before you get to the old Oraboca workings, down under where we are.'

From up here, you could see from the blue haze of the Sierra Madre right round to the silver shimmer off the Gulf of California, and the yellow brown fields and olive groves round the dust-blurred, unstirring airfield. Margaret snapped a leaf off the shrub, broke it, and sniffed.

'Not quite ready.'

Genuine perplexity crossed Zelaszny's eagle face. 'Margaret, what is that?'

'This?' She stared, it sounded like a catch question. 'Coca.'

'*That's* coca? Why, nobody tells me! We have a stack of it in back, growing right up here.' Zelaszny indicated about five feet.

'I wonder if that's all that healthy. Although this is a bit far north for coca. The best Peruvian grows to seven or eight feet.'

'Okay. Coca is the plant cocaine comes from, right?'

'Yes.' Margaret snapped another leaf, remembering Mario Roca. This was like delivering a lecture. 'The juice in this is virtually pure cocaine. Indians chew it like we drink coffee.'

'Right. You can trip out.'

'Not the way they take it, say for a hunt or a long foot journey. It's a powerful local anaesthetic. You can feel your mouth go numb when you chew it – quite a pleasant feeling, actually – and then when it lands in your stomach it anaesthetises that as well, so you can go for long periods without food or sleep.' She passed the leaves to Zelaszny, and their fingers touched. 'You can tell by sniffing when they're ready.'

Zelaszny sniffed dubiously and chucked them back in the tub. 'So this stuff toughens you physically in the short term.'

'You could put it that way,' Margaret replied cautiously.

Through the two pairs of glasses, the two pairs of eyes met, Margaret's soft grey, Zelaszny's violet like deep sky.

Zelaszny said: 'What *you* need, Margaret, is psychological toughness – but in the long term.' She paused. Uncannily, Margaret knew what was coming. She said: 'I want you to kill a

125

man. Ideally three or four, but certainly one. When you've killed, you'll be tough enough for us.'

Something had stuck again in Margaret's throat. Violence, that was what scared her, almost as much as the thought of sex did. 'But . . . I . . . you must realise killing should be avoided wherever possible. I . . .'

'I don't question your arguments over McKnight.' Zelaszny's voice had gone hard, like her eyes. 'But there are men around who well deserve killing. We'll find one for you, one you'll *want* to kill. If those guys in New York had raped you, you'd have wanted to kill them.'

Maybe she would have, too. Maybe she'd have lost that much grip on sanity. Maybe for that very reason these terrible women had wanted Margaret to suffer.

Zelaszny's eyes and voice softened. In the afternoon sunlight she leaned towards Margaret, sister to sister. 'You owe it to Fight, Margaret, but most of all you owe it to yourself. You *know* what these men are capable of. You know what they've already done. And it isn't just the odd one, it's all of them.' The violet eyes strove to convince her, they were winning. 'Unless *you're* tough enough, the whole world's women don't have a chance. That's how important you are to Fight. You *have* to kill a man.'

Except that Margaret didn't want them to win. And she wasn't going to let Zelaszny's mind-probing eyes read that. Last night, dimly, she'd been aware of a potential clash of wills. Now it was open battle. Her will against Zelaszny's.

*   *   *

When she went out, Cornelia Piotti was still at attention in the relentless sun. At the novices' quarters, Lorraine Easson and Jodie Sadler, in uniform ready for the afternoon's detail, turned away from Margaret. At first she thought it was for keeping them waiting, but then little Tina Zeiss went all huffy, and Margaret realised. She was in the convent. She'd been getting the exclusive ear of Mother Superior and the other novices didn't like it.

126

CHAPTER 21

Flies whined in the heavy heat and Margaret knew she'd made a mistake in not sleeping her siesta. The deep, irregular thump from the rifle range, another squad training, made her tense and her hot eyes kept her from concentrating.

'The double-action semi-automatic pistol is more complicated than the single-action I've just explained. Movement of the finger on the trigger cocks the firing mechanism separately from the stroke of the bolt. Thereafter, the backward stroke of the bolt cocks the firing mechanism, as in the single-action type.'

Giselle Stamm couldn't be more than fourteen, Margaret was thinking. She was demonstrating the Walther PP with the cool professionalism of some armourer sergeant-major. Singleminded, thorough, like her mother. Straight out of school, they'd taken her, and into weapons and survival and combat training; ponies to pistols in one jump. But what chilled Margaret was the depth to which this kid believed in what she was doing.

'Now I want to see you reload, blindfold.'

Tina Zeiss tied the scarf round Paquita Villegas's head. Paquita was Cuban, a short, dark, broadshouldered woman with bushy hair. Her sensitive hands broke the empty magazine out of the automatic pistol's crosshatched plastic grip, selected the full magazine, fumbled a moment at the feed, then slotted the mag home. Paquita checked for safety.

'Four point two,' Giselle said, glancing up from her stopwatch. 'You should need only two seconds to do that. What are you going to do when it's night, or you're in smoke, and your pistol jams and you have only a few seconds before the soldiers come?'

Tina said: 'Use a revolver.' A couple of voices laughed.

Giselle, perfectly serious, said: 'Revolvers jam also.'

Somewhere behind the kid's seriousness there was anger,

127

Margaret recognised, bitterness. She was talking revolution, talking warfare, and she had a visible enemy. Yet this youngster hadn't had Pham Anh's experience, nor had her mother; Giselle had no personal reason to hate men. Something had happened to her, though, and Margaret found herself wanting to know what.

*　　*　　*

Pistols were far harder to aim than rifles. They practised, not on the 100-metre range but on a 20-metre miniature range, using man-sized, card targets. When they checked the weapons into the armoury, afterwards, the armourer turned out to be Cathy Latta's mother. Valerie Latta had been a Detroit factory worker; moved into extremist feminism when her marriage collapsed; served a spell as a Fight cell member, then been forced to run; she'd brought her daughter with her, a willing companion. For a person who combined weapons expertise with extra skills as a plumber, she acted with exaggerated femininity; Margaret had noticed that about other women here. Cathy wasn't one, though.

The armoury was a cellar under the admin block. Free for a while, Margaret wandered outside and through the gate into the transport park. Fight had horses, too, in a stable; some of Tequísquepec's trails were impossible for a tank; but the transport park was well stocked and Caine would want to know about it. If Margaret chose to find a way to reach him.

Sarah Kuhr, Marlena's daughter, and a guerrilla Margaret didn't know were under the back axle of a Ford pickup. Margaret counted four Toyota Land Cruisers and a Jeep Cherokee; a couple of Fiat cars; a tipper lorry.

She was about to wander away when a caterer's van drove in and a couple of women from the refectory, in dresses and overalls, met it. The convent, it seemed, wasn't self-sufficient in everything. Margaret had seen guerrillas drinking beer in the bar, and that had to come from somewhere.

Back on the flagstoned walk by the pool, Margaret tried to assess how many guerrillas were here. A couple of dozen novices; maybe sixty or seventy residents, among them an unknown number in the Bodyguard, the real killers. She couldn't even guess how they broke down into nationalities.

But it was time now for indoctrination.

* * *

All the novices were there, in uniform, in one of the big lecture theatres; with them, some of the residents, Giselle Stamm, Cathy Latta, a couple of Vietnamese, Kelly Thane. At the front, a couple of women with the Secretariat red flash and, with them Charlotte Rondeau.

Charlotte's whole small body was tense, her eyes alight, and for a moment, in the silence before they started, her tension electrified the waiting guerrillas.

Charlotte shouted. Her anger echoed all among the novices. *Who has the power*? Men have. *How do they use their power*? Tyranny over women. *Why do they tyrannise women*? Because their power has corrupted them and they're evil. *What do we do about it*? Take the power from them. *How do we take it*? We fight. We fight. We fight.

Margaret was shaking when she went out. Indoctrination, they called that. Margaret knew other terms for it.

She'd been in primitive religious gatherings before, and the emotional ferment, lacking as it did any mental component, had been frightening, frightening for its lack of restraint. This hadn't been far different.

* * *

Stars floated, silver, in the midnight blue of the swimming pool and Margaret hugged the bright shawl to herself defensively, waiting for supper, watching from the flagstoned walk. Finito Navásquez was chatting up Sharon Levenson and a black-haired novice from Rio. He'd spoken to Margaret earlier but she'd been too scared of the others' reactions to take the bait. Sabina Stamm was in the patio, talking in loud, harshly accented Spanish, but Giselle with her guitar was beside the pool again with some others. Giselle didn't seem to spend much time with her mother. It seemed paradoxical to Margaret that Sabina should go to the lengths she had to kidnap her daughter, and then hardly talk to her.

On an impulse, she got up. She went to where Giselle was kneeling, one hand resting on her guitar.

129

'Hi, Mags,' Coral Bargellini smiled.

Three of the residents were there, two Vietnamese, one American, with Pham Anh, tiny and vulnerable in her boots, belt and the uniform shirt that looked so inadequate for the chilly night. They were drinking Mexican beer, in the bottles with the special indentation in the base that would open the cap of the next bottle. Coral was the focal point, Margaret saw. She was getting respect from the residents and treating them with the cool superiority of a commander; she was getting adoration from Pham Anh, and Margaret guessed that Coral had been involved in, perhaps had led, the operation that had rescued the Vietnamese party. She realised that Coral was being compassionate, protective towards Anh, in the light of the kid's experience; the other residents behaved the same way.

But it wasn't suiting Giselle. The two were the youngest girls Margaret had spotted at Tequísquepec; yet they plainly didn't get on, they had too little in common. And Giselle's sulky indifference towards Coral told Margaret how she felt about Anh getting all the sympathy.

'You're very good with those guns,' Margaret said. 'Have you ever been in action?'

'No.' Giselle flicked her long hair as if irritated by Margaret, but then turned big eyes on her face. She couldn't match exploits with her mother. But she was glad to have someone talking to her.

'Were you good technically at school?'

'How would I know? Schools are a sexist brainwashing process: girls learn needlework, only boys learn technical skills.' Her anger was visible in the set of her head, and she was busy avoiding looking at Coral and Anh and the others.

'Do you ever miss your school?'

'No!' Still blunt, monosyllabic, an intense little figure with her knees tight together in the old jeans. Kids her age always had deep feelings, and they were entitled to them; but Giselle ought not to have been this angry.

'Why not?' Margaret murmured daringly.

'Schools are part of a system that brainwashes girls into becoming subservient, second-class citizens and shoring up the structure of phallic tyranny. Laws made by men trap children into a system made by and for men. When the female children grow up, laws based on ancient and immoral notions of property inheritance force them into the power of men, in the home.'

If only they could stop at the half they'd got right, Margaret thought. Giselle's English was good, but not that good; the slogan phrases had come from her indoctrination into Fight theory.

'So you aren't sorry to have left your home.'

'No!' She ducked forward, emphatically, then flicked back her hair with a hand.

'But what about your . . . your stepmother? Did you never get on with her?' Margaret had had the background gossip from Sharon Levenson; no one could prove she'd heard it first from Caine. The father who'd dropped out of the Baader-Meinhof group; who, released from jail, had married to give his daughter a home while her mother served her own sentence.

'I was taken in by her, I was deceived.' Giselle's urgent face was mostly a silhouette in the cool night, but Margaret caught the tremor in her voice. 'She's a traitor to us all, she's simply a cog in the machine of male authority. She talked about love, about loving me, and loving my father. And he might have done less evil if he hadn't been such a filthy coward that he sold out his own cause. This talk of love is just another excuse for enslaving half the human race. But our movement will free them.'

'Yes . . .' It sounded good. Like her guitar playing. Until you compared it with the real thing, Finito's music or Coral's ideas. Yet Giselle herself recognised the contradictions, maybe unconsciously. That long hair. It suited her, but it was an act of defiance. And she probably didn't even realise, so deep had they buried the real Giselle under the catch phrases and the uniforms.

Then Margaret saw Giselle start, alarmed, and she turned quickly.

Catalina Sánchez was there, and Jo Colwell, the Bodyguard chief, and another Bodyguard, a Japanese woman called Michiko Ishida. Horror grabbed Margaret by the gut when she saw their guns and her first thought was: *how*? But they hadn't come for her.

'Stamm,' Sánchez said, 'on your feet.'

Wordlessly, lips parted, Giselle scrambled up, her guitar forgotten. Margaret saw the colour drain from the girl's face. Colwell jerked her head and the three of them took Giselle away without a glance at Margaret. Baffled, Margaret watched them go.

In the shadows close by, a voice murmured in soft Spanish, 'She took water to Cornelia Piotti this afternoon.'

Margaret turned. It was Paquita Villegas, the Cuban. Devoted communist, devoted lover of people. They'd spoken before; that was how Paquita knew Margaret spoke Spanish; and Margaret liked Paquita.

'She thought nobody saw her,' Paquita said, 'but d'you know who did?'

'Who?'

'Sabina.'

The supper gong sounded. Margaret simply stared, incredulous. Paquita, sombre, crossed the flags to where Giselle's guitar lay, and picked it up.

'I'd better look after this.'

Margaret followed her, moving in a daze.

This was the real evil about Fight, she knew now. Not the killing alone, not the combat, not the wholly justifiable campaign against man's injustices to woman, and for a society based on real equality and on the sanity to will the world to survive. Margaret thought about Giselle's anger and intensity; her genuine toughness, side by side with the pony books she'd left on the shelf at home; her awareness of the abyss between what she said and what she felt, side by side with her terror that at any moment she might plummet into it. That was the evil. That, and the scheme of thought that could steal a child from its home, put a gun in its hands, and convince it that all the love people had ever given to it was a trick devised to enslave it.

She might have had doubts, once. But there was no supporting that philosophy. It couldn't even be turned to good.

CHAPTER 22

FBI headquarters in San Diego were off limits for the same reason 26 Federal Plaza had been. Instead they used an ordinary-looking house surrounded with palm and pine, between Mission Valley Road and the river, and within cheering distance of San Diego stadium. Carla Desatnick, in a housecoat, came yawning into the living-room, late after Friday's late night with the flight from New York, to find Richard Caine up, dressed, baggy-eyed, and deciphering a signal from London; and Frank Pasarell missing altogether.

It was Saturday, April 20, 1055 Pacific time, 1855 in London. Caine was looking relieved and apprehensive at the same time.

Desatnick covered another yawn. 'Harya ah?'

'Top of the morning to you, too,' Caine said. 'Frank's going to love this bit.'

'What bit?'

'Well, first the good news. The bloke I wanted has accepted the job linking Rahab to us and is being moved in now. And now for the bad news: Barrington Yorke's put virtually the entire thing to the Mexican government because he wants official local clearance.'

Desatnick slumped on the sofa. 'Oh, God. I knew I shouldn't ever have got up today.'

'Will it be one egg or two for madam?'

Ignored, as he'd expected, Caine locked the signal in the cabinet. He wondered fleetingly what Pasarell would do. Pasarell was in the air, he'd taken off twenty minutes earlier on a USAF transport for Washington and an FBI, CIA and State Department conference. Travelling against the sun, Pasarell wouldn't be in Washington with enough time to fly on to Paris the same evening. He would stay overnight. He would be in Paris late on Sunday at the earliest.

*　　*　　*

It was almost mid-day, Desatnick in her lacy blouse and designer jeans and the crickets shrilling in the bushes outside where the two plainclothes guards dozed watchfully in their Dodge coupé, when FBI Washington came through. This time the enciphered telex was for Desatnick.

CIA sources in Cuba had reported Gregorio Tabio taking off aboard a routine airline flight from Havana to Kingston, Jamaica. In Kingston they'd had a man waiting and the name on Tabio's passport wasn't Tabio, and the passport was Dominican anyway. Tabio was at that moment sitting on the end of the runway at Kingston while his jet captain spun up the turbines to take off. For Miami.

'We got him,' Desatnick said with satisfaction. 'We'll tag him from Miami on in and see what he does.'

Caine said: 'What about Andreyev?'

She consulted the signal. 'He didn't move.'

Caine thought about that. Then thought about Pasarell again and once more came back to the conclusion that Pasarell's plans wouldn't be materially altered.

*　　*　　*

Caine was right. The diplomatic contact in Washington was made at lowish level and was made rather before Pasarell's USAF transport touched down there. A State Department errand man handed the Mexican embassy a routine sheaf of reports and despatches, among them a signal from the FBI saying that it was investigating the activities in the US of doña Alma Múñoz and her business empire and that investigations by the police in Mexico might also prove interesting. If they felt like it.

The message would probably wait until Monday. On Sunday, all that happened was that Gregorio Tabio, using his fake Dominican passport, checked out of the Miami hotel where he'd spent the night, and boarded another airliner, this time flying to Dallas. But Tabio was booked through now, right the way to Los Angeles.

CHAPTER 23

Eighty in the hangar doorway at Alameda at just gone eight and the weather limbering up for a warm day. Margaret Stubbs and Sharon Levenson hadn't limbered up in the gym like everyone else because they had special passes for flying training. Stepping inside the shade of the hangar was like stepping back in time because the six aircraft, nose-high, big, four-blade props waiting, were P51 Mustangs. They might have been forty years old, Margaret thought, twice her own age.

The mechanics rolled out the two two-seaters and left the single-seaters in the hangar.

'Who's done these?' Margaret asked. 'Piper or Cavalier?' The natural-metal finish flashed sun. Forty years old these aircraft might have been, but they'd been refurbished, they might have just rolled off the production line.

'Neither, *muchacha*,' Finito Navásquez said, and the wide, wicked grin creased his brown face. 'Every one has been rebuilt here – expertly, or you wouldn't catch me flying them.' He gestured towards the hangars and the plant behind them. 'This is the main engineering base of Cadal.'

Margaret recognised the name.

She lowered herself into the front cockpit. A few yards away, Sharon was climbing into the other two-seater with Charlotte Rondeau. Sabina Stamm, the chief flying instructor, had given the pre-flight briefing. Margaret remembered Sabina's story. Her father, the Nazi fighter ace; her early training, her plans to become an airline pilot; that spectacular hijack after she'd joined the Baader-Meinhof group, when the captain had been shot and Sabina had landed the jetliner herself.

To Margaret it was a relief to be taking her training from Finito, not Rondeau. Not just because Finito was male and sexy but because Rondeau was highly intelligent and deeply fanatical, and that worried Margaret.

'*¿Está bien?*'

The cockpit well was hot, Margaret covertly unbuttoning her shirt under the flying overall before reaching to tighten the aerobatic harness. '*Claro*,' she said, turning, and Finito collapsed with laughter. She snapped: 'What's wrong with you?'

'Look at you! I guess I never flew with a pilot in glasses before. But I never saw sticking plaster used that way!'

Margaret grinned, realising. Once in a light aircraft she'd lost her glasses clean off her face in the *g* of a turn, and since then she'd taken the precaution of fixing them on with a strip of plaster down the bridge of her nose.

Firing up off the trolley-acc, Finito singing out the drills; the twelve-cylinder Packard Merlin booming across the parched, sandy earth. They'd begun taxiing before Sharon's propellor had started turning. It scared Margaret; forward visibility was a joke over that long cowling with the petrol smoke gusting in; yet on the intercom Finito might have been chatting over a beer in a bar. The canopy slid shut, bonking Margaret's bone dome. Brakes, boost, throttle. And the takeoff, blaring noise, dust, and a shove in the back like flat out in that Porsche.

Fifteen thousand feet, general handling, desert white below and the sparkle off the Gulf of California. 'Spin it,' Finito said. Half throttle, nose up. Margaret let the speed come right back and gave it the left boot, up to the stop. And the familiar empty-stomach feeling as the horizon whirled round and you started falling out of the sky, the white desert rotating fast beyond the nose. 'Shut the throttle. You'll never get a Mustang out of a power-on spin.' And so: power off, full opposite rudder, let it come out. It took a while. This aircraft was the heaviest she'd flown and by far the most powerful. Margaret pulled back the stick and then banked, to recapture height and position.

'*Muy bonito*, very pretty. Normally I have to take over when my pupils first spin a Mustang.'

She thought, I bet you say that to all of them. But then wondered, because Finito was a very *macho* man, didn't like a woman to upstage him.

Touch-and-go landings, twice for Finito to show how it was done. 'You have control.' And the old routines, brakes off, undercarriage down and locked, mixture, pitch, flaps. 'Don't three-point, you'll swing off the runway.' A trace of nerves, wary of a woman with something to prove. Margaret didn't try it, she just tucked down the long nose the way Finito had done, approaching in a wide curve, instead of the conventional straight line, to keep the runway in view as long as possible. Blind over the threshold she flared out, and the mainwheels touched almost together, then the tail came down. Margaret shoved on the power and the Mustang tried to go sideways left, and she ruddered it straight and by then they were climbing again.

'*Estupendo, inglesa.* I bet you flew Spitfires in the war.'

'You must have flown Sopwith Camels in yours.'

Finito laughed into the intercom, happy to be insulted back, and Margaret ran mentally through the checks again and set up the Mustang for another landing.

She was climbing away, for her umpteenth circuit of the morning, when an odd smell reached her and she scanned the dials in anguish, heart stopping. Nothing was amiss. Then she recognised the smell. Of all things, Finito had chosen to light a cigar, in the cockpit.

*   *   *

In Cadal's operations room as the mechanics refuelled the Mustangs the four pilots sipped iced drinks, Margaret and Sharon clammy with sweat. Finito unzipped his overall down to his pants elastic, the crucifix nestling in the curly black hair. Rondeau opened hers to halfway down the rib cage. She was wearing no more under hers than Finito was. Margaret and Sharon swapped glances. They'd had to take their overalls off.

'Where can we do something about this overdressed situation?' Sharon said.

Sabina Stamm jerked her cropped head, face still aggressive with its peeling tan; she'd debriefed them on the flying. 'The *señoras* is that way.'

It was a joke, a lean-to with *señoras* on one door and *caballeros* on another and a passage that met in the middle. But there was privacy to strip to underwear beneath the flying overall.

They went back to the Mustangs. 'Chopper girl,' Finito said chauvinistically, watching Sharon climb into hers with Rondeau.

'She's no good with a plank.'

Margaret settled her bone dome and glanced at Finito. She was strapped in but he was still on the wing root. 'Is something . . .'

'I'm not coming on this circuit,' Finito said, 'you can do this one solo.'

* * *

In the siesta-time heat Margaret swam and then sprawled on a blanket in what little shade she could find on the poolside flags. She'd found the convent's radio antennae, on a tower less tall than Zelaszny's eyrie and at the opposite end of the pool. She'd looked for radar but concluded there was none to find. She'd spotted the defences, though, or some of them: machinegun nests, possibly up to .5 calibre, hidden amid the roof gardens at key points and apparently on swivels to fire down at men on foot or up at aircraft.

She'd also spotted Giselle Stamm. Giselle was standing to attention in the sun. Catalina Sánchez's disciplinary tribunal had obviously chosen that as an appropriate punishment for a girl who tried to help a comrade in the same circumstances.

But there was nothing Margaret Stubbs could do, so she fought down her anger and ran over what she'd seen. The numbers, a hundred-odd all told. A good half of them American; say a fifth Mexicans or other Latin Americans; about a tenth Vietnamese, the group Fight had rescued from the Thais; another tenth European; and the rest a mixed bunch of nationalities including Sokolova, the Russian academician; Nwokoye, the Nigerian from the Secretariat; Ishida, the Japanese Bodyguard.

'*Hola, mi guapa.*'

She gave a start. Finito flopped beside her with a grin and nodded approvingly at her bikini. 'That's nice. Overdressed, though, this weather.'

Margaret ignored the bait. Finito, one knee bent, propped his shoulders against the wall and lit a cigar.

'I wish you wouldn't do that in the air,' Margaret said. 'I don't want to be in your aircraft when it blows up.'

'Blows up? It wouldn't dare.'

She rolled her head towards him. Beyond, in the sun, she

138

could see Giselle. 'What's a male chauvinist like you doing in a convent like this?'

'Keeping the novices at their prayers.'

So that was why they'd put Sharon with Rondeau. Sharon had been falling under the Finito influence last night, while Margaret had resisted. Now she thought of it, Sharon herself, with her ear for gossip, had answered the question of how Finito had come to be there in the first place. Sabina had the title of chief flying instructor, but the real CFI was Finito. Finito had been brought to Tequísquepec after leaving the Mexican air force to train pilots for Fight, and he'd sold his loyalty to Zelaszny for cash from Múñoz – vastly more cash than he could ever have got by signing on for another term as an air force instructor or by any civilian flying.

But that wasn't his only purpose here. His function as tame male served to stave off frustration in some of Fight's guerrillas and at the same time – whether he realised or not – to foster the same contempt for him in the convent as men felt for a female whore. Yet it was interesting that the stud role had its part in Zelaszny's scheme.

'Is that all you get out of it?'

Finito shouted with laughter. It echoed off the wall across the pool. Yet to Margaret the question hadn't seemed naïve. 'As a matter of fact' – Finito calmed down – 'that *gringa*' – he nodded towards Zelaszny's eyrie – 'pays me double what I'd get as an air force flying instructor. And I even get time to keep my old age provided for. I breed horses. Beautiful creatures, very valuable. I have a ranch in Veracruz, a couple of stable hands run the place for me, and a small stable here at the *cortijo*. Do you ride?'

'I'm more used to mules than horses.'

Then she started violently.

It was García again, squat, motionless amid the scant shadow, and Margaret knew instinctively that he'd been there ages, watching her.

Finito shouted angrily: '*¡Fuera, fuera, hijo de puta!*'

García vanished.

Margaret had gone goosefleshed. 'That man gives me the creeps.'

'Man?' Finito sneered. 'He's a halfwit. He's chauffeur, porter, labourer, handyman, patrolman, anything that doesn't require a

139

mind. He's a full-blooded Totonaco from the Sierra de Puebla – the hottest, wildest, foulest, bug-infestedest, godforsakenest bit of Mexico that I hope never to set eyes on.'

*   *   *

First thing after siesta was another half-hour's gym. Ishida instructed. Giselle Stamm was one of the forty or so guerrillas exercising. She was utterly exhausted after her spell in the sun, and Ishida knew it, yet spared her not a scrap of mercy.

CHAPTER 24

The big operation against Fight would be run from Paris when it came and they flew Robin Barrington Yorke in there in time for Sunday lunch with Brouzet at his office in the Invalides. Pasarell was expected on the evening's Concorde from Washington; the German and Italian investigators were arriving first thing next morning.

'And this man Pedragoza from Mexico City,' Brouzet said, handing Barrington Yorke the telex. 'Do you know him?'

'I'm sorry, I don't.'

Nor did Brouzet. The one thing obvious to both men was that Señor Pedragoza had been selected very rapidly for the Paris talks. That might mean that Mexico had its security forces so well organised that it knew the right man for the job automatically. Or it might mean something else.

Brouzet poured Barrington Yorke half a glass of Pouilly Fuissé. 'I must confess you've impressed me. To have placed an agent inside Fight's world headquarters! How did you find this girl?'

Barrington Yorke picked thoughtfully at his chicken salad. 'She was talent-spotted while much younger, actually, by a Peruvian who was operating in Lima as a routine although quite high-grade source for us. His name's Mario Roca. He's getting on now, he no longer regularly works for us, or, as far as one can gather, for anybody else. She turned up in Lima at an English-language school where Roca had connexions. She was twelve, then. Roca was, candidly, afraid for the girl's safety and wellbeing, and he trained her in self-defence and survival. He'd known her for perhaps two years before he formed the opinion that she had the character to operate for us – given only the motivation.'

Brouzet sipped wine; he'd finished his chicken. 'You are telling me that your source recommended a fourteen-year-old girl?'

'By no means. But when, shortly before her eighteenth birthday, she returned with her parents to Britain, Roca sent us a note with the suggestion.'

'And as for her motivation?'

'She detests violence. A friend of hers died violently at Fight's hands.'

Brouzet answered quickly: 'Ah, surely there's more than that!'

There was, but Barrington Yorke wasn't prepared to go into the mechanics of it. He sipped his wine, frowning, and set his knife and fork on his plate. He wasn't a big eater.

'You must understand . . . Picture a four-year-old girl taken from her home and friends in England to the opposite side of the world to live with her parents, who are missionaries. Picture the memory that is created in her conscious or unconscious mind of that home and those friends whom she never sees again.'

'A paradise lost,' Brouzet murmured. He could see it exactly.

'Then picture that girl growing up and listening to all her parents' promises of Heaven and warnings against Hell. She believes it. I think she believes it still; it need be no bad thing. Yet, whether accidentally or not, she connects, sooner or later, her paradise lost with those warnings of sin and damnation.'

'And does she see no fault in her parents' lives?'

Barrington Yorke hadn't finished with history. 'Next, picture that girl, a teenager and a part of her remote, Andean community, when that community is torn asunder by earthquakes. Friends whom she loves are injured and maimed. Some of them are killed.'

Soul-searching, particularly someone else's, came readily to a Frenchman. 'The new sense of loss reinforced the old,' Brouzet said.

'Indeed. And, as to her parents, she saw very little in them to blame. Many vocally religious people have the decency to be hypocritical in their lives. These practised what they preached. Rahab grew up finding that, however hard she tried, *she* could not practise what *they* preached.'

'Until', Brouzet concluded, 'she found a mission of her own. How ingenious.'

142

'The whole of Rahab's experience,' Barrington Yorke said, 'has driven her to over-achieve in whatever she does, and to find a mission to justify a life that any other way she would consider wasted. She is a brilliant agent and I feel most dreadfully sorry for her.'

Mario Roca had felt sorry for her from the start. But Roca was one of those professionals who can't leave any potential tool untouched. He felt, Barrington Yorke knew, a proprietorial, even paternal, responsibility towards her, enhanced by his guilt at having got her into this predicament in the first place.

But guilt was paramount with Rahab, too.

Half uncertainly, Brouzet asked: 'Rahab was talent-spotted by Roca but recruited by your man Caine. How did he go about recruiting her?'

'He went to her parents' church and very rapidly formed her acquaintance, since he was probably the only person there within roughly her age-group who was on the same intellectual plane as her.' Roughly, Barrington Yorke added mentally. Caine's brain didn't measure up to Rahab's.

'Did they have an affair?'

'I believe it was strictly, ah, platonic.'

But he couldn't be certain. Any more than he could be certain that Caine wasn't trying quite cynically to exploit Rahab's deep blaming of herself for the loss of that childhood paradise, the loss of her friends in the earthquakes.

CHAPTER 25

Amid the gypsum dunes as the guerrilla squad broke for lunch from its all-day field exercise a six-inch spider had run out and they'd killed it. Jodie Sadler insisted that it was a tarantula, but Margaret, who knew tarantulas well, identified it as a harmless wolf spider. It had given most of them a fright, except for Paquita Villegas, the Cuban, who was leading the exercise, and who never bothered telling one large spider from another but killed them all on principle.

Paquita and Jodie had crossed swords the night before, sitting round the pool, but they'd tacitly agreed a truce now. Paquita had maintained that communism was the best vehicle for establishing women's worldwide supremacy; but that had caused immediate friction with Coral Bargellini. Jodie, like Lorraine Easson, had sided with Coral in insisting that the first condition was a matriarchal benevolent dictatorship. They already had its elements at Tequísquepec.

The morning had been tough and the afternoon was no less so. The eight guerrillas were carrying packs, rifles and ammunition; much of their course lay on the fringe of the desert that, Margaret knew, stretched from here to well north of the US border. Periodically one of the Alameda Mustangs would come low over the dunes, hunting for them, a fictitious 'hostile', and they would fan out and hide. Margaret knew how to pace herself, she'd learnt, years earlier in Peru, from Mario Roca, but when Paquita stepped up the speed to march the last ten kilometres back to Tequísquepec it was as much as Margaret could do to keep up. Giselle was with them and from lunchtime on was at the limits of her endurance. Tina Zeiss, Margaret noted, was the one who marched next to Giselle, helped and encouraged her, and gave the kid the last of her water when Giselle's ran out.

144

*　　*　　*

The worst leg was the last, struggling up the steep slope through the hot oak and eucalyptus with the big insects zooming round them. Tina was physically supporting Giselle when they came out on the summit, holding the kid's arm. García was hanging round the Indians' cottages – there were three or four Indian men who handled the heaviest labouring – and Margaret saw him eyeing up Giselle as the squad crossed to the HQ complex. She thought: filthy brute. Finito was randy and conceited and probably cynical, but he had a better sense of honour or fair play than to have designs on a child.

She showered, Jodie and Paquita and Tina sharing the same washroom block. She couldn't tell now what it had meant yesterday when García had spied on her and Finito. She couldn't even tell what it had meant that Finito should seek her out. He presumably hadn't taken her for an easy conquest; yet she wasn't very used to men being attracted to her.

As a teenager in Peru she'd known only two sorts of response. On the one hand, the 'nice' boys were always warned by their mothers to avoid the dangerous foreign girl; on the other, the worst of the young bloods, who didn't mind what they got up to, considered her fair game any time and subjected her to the crudest of passes. In a sense, the 'nice' boys' mothers had been right, since Margaret would never have made the sort of docile wife their tradition demanded. But then, anyway, she'd soon shot up too tall for any of the boys to look at her any more. Except the young bloods.

Defensive, she'd retreated into her books. She read equally easily in Spanish and English, and she'd built up big stores of knowledge that had proved crucial to her getting the qualifications she needed to study medicine, and to fly.

It wasn't until she went to England, where she wasn't too tall for the boys, that she discovered that all that head knowledge, and the rarity value of her flying, had made her, in a different sense, 'too tall' for almost any of them.

'I'm going to try the sauna,' Paquita Villegas said.

They'd been told about a sauna, adjoining the recreation block with its games room, television lounge, bar. Margaret had only once had a sauna before; maybe, she thought, it was the thing to revive her after the exercise.

Paquita had already gone when Margaret walked wearily along the grass-grown path to the steps up. She couldn't rid her mind of García and his nasty eyeing of Giselle; nor of her own inadequacy.

In the changing room she hung up her clothes and went into the sauna. She didn't stay long. In the heat and shadows Sharon Levenson was cuddling and caressing one of the Brazilian novices, and Margaret simply didn't want to be around.

* * *

Very late, Catalina Sánchez caught Margaret coming out from supper. Margaret didn't want to go, she was physically and mentally exhausted, but you didn't ignore a summons from Wanda Zelaszny. She trudged up the stairs.

The office was as she'd seen it that first evening, shutters closed, globes of light round the spotlamps holding back the dark. Zelaszny gave a sympathetic smile, recognising the fatigue in Margaret's movements as she flopped into the armchair.

'Heavy day?' She saw Margaret nod. 'Okay. Got any comments so far?'

'Yes. You've got a terribly harsh system of discipline.'

'You reckon?' Zelaszny, thin and taut as coiled wire, arched her eyebrows, eyes hard on Margaret's through the gleam on her glasses. 'Have you any idea of what might happen around here if we relaxed that discipline and let people start beating up fellow guerrillas and getting away with it?'

'There are plenty of other forms of discipline. You should concentrate on reforming people's thought, not beating them, or putting them on heavy labour. And as for standing Giselle Stamm out in the sun all siesta yesterday just for taking pity on someone . . .'

Zelaszny's voice was gentle, convincing; yet the battle of wills was still on. 'Margaret, we have a responsibility not just to our élite guerrillas here, all of them, but to all women, worldwide. We have to free them from male tyranny. We cannot do that unless we all here can act in a team, under discipline, and without any risk of dissension. That's why guerrillas who fight one another must be punished. Not only that: any unauthorised attempt to lighten the punishment risks subverting our main purpose. That is why Giselle had to be disciplined.' She paused. 'Our punishments are not gentle. For too many centuries, women have been too gentle. We aim to be tough, because only by being tough can we hope to overthrow the tyranny of male government. Tough punishments are necessary in order to toughen up our guerrillas' bodies and minds and attitudes.'

There was another way of putting that: Fight was carrying out a deliberate programme of brutalising the women here, making them accustomed to violence so that they could deal violently with others. Margaret didn't say that. She watched Zelaszny, sitting there hawkishly in her plain, darned, cotton dress.

'Okay, now do you have any comments on the course?'

'I can see where we're going, but it's still terribly general.' Margaret was weary. 'It should be specific.'

'It *is* specific. It's filling in the gaps in our guerrillas' know-how. In your case, shooting. In Lorraine Easson's case, fieldcraft and desert survival; in Sharon Levenson's case, unarmed combat.' She placed a palm over something on the desk, and saw Margaret crane her head in the poor light. 'Oh, yes, we know all the strengths and weaknesses of all the women in our cells. I could tell you, from this, Renata Vernon's finishing positions in the last five rallies she drove, or Mary Abbott's latest pistol scores.'

'You keep dossiers on all of us?'

'Of course.' Zelaszny pointed at the floor. 'We keep them right here.' Her head moved, in the spotlighting, and Margaret saw her face more clearly than before: hollow-cheeked, thought-haunted, a hunting eagle. The fringe of grey hair didn't conceal the height of the forehead; this woman had once held a chair in anthropology. But the lines of the mouth showed a capacity for compassion as well as severity. The eyes, as Zelaszny changed from her distance to her reading glasses, were big and violet, probing Margaret's mind. This was a woman who had always been beautiful while never being pretty.

But she wasn't as clever as she thought she was if she kept written dossiers on her cell members, however securely she thought they were held.

She gave Margaret a direct look, imperative. 'You're another one who needs to toughen up your attitudes. And you will.

147

You'll shape up. Command Cell Europe is right now shortlisting men with backgrounds of crime and violence against women. You'll kill one of them. I told you that before. Now, do you have any preference how you wish to carry out the killing? Gun; knife; a car, say; or maybe you'd rather do it hand-to-hand?'

Margaret closed her eyes. She had to swallow. 'I . . . I haven't thought . . . really, there's been so much . . .'

Zelaszny placed a hand on Margaret's knee, cool, compassionate; but strong. 'Think about it, Margaret. You must. You have to be strong, for Fight's good, for the good of the whole world's women. A killing is the only way.'

Margaret didn't reply. Zelaszny sat back, settled her glasses on her nose, and studied the file on her knee.

'Let me explain what's in your own dossier. You have an unusual past, you're gifted intellectually as well as technically skilled, you're in Fight essentially for intellectual reasons.' Quite wrong, Margaret reflected: the reasons were almost exclusively emotional. The response to finding Julie O'Dell, the response to what they'd done to Giselle Stamm. She realised she knew where Fight kept its archives: immediately below this office, behind that strongroom door she'd seen from the library. Zelaszny said: 'Your weak points are your distaste for violence – which we'll overcome – and that you're too ready to compromise. Against that' – she glanced over the glasses – 'you're British.'

Margaret tilted her head. 'Has that a bearing?'

'We need a British national. We have a project planned that will make the entire world take notice of us.'

The very words Mary Abbott had used two months earlier. Despite the fatigue drumming in her brain, Margaret was wide awake and listening.

'There is a limit to the time we can continue to operate as an underground force,' Zelaszny said. 'When we come into the open we need a base for the movement, we need territory we can defend. We have our eye on an island called Guerrillera in the British Virgins group. Right now, it's uninhabited, but it has scope for development, and we have assessed it okay for coastal defence by boats and light fighter planes.' The Mustangs. It wasn't a stupid idea, either, even in an age of F15s and Foxbats. Zelaszny looked over her glasses again. 'Acquiring Guerrillera from the British Crown shouldn't be too problematical, once we've demonstrated the seriousness of our intentions. We have a plan that will pose a major threat to as many world cities as we want.'

Margaret fought to think clearly. 'What sort of plan?'

'You'll be briefed. Once the world sees what we're capable of, there'll be a lot of pressure for threat cities to be saved, and very little sympathy for an ancient imperialist nation hanging on to a piece of land it never bothered with before, anyway.' Rigid will, Margaret thought, that was the main thing in Wanda Zelaszny's make-up. Also the rigid refusal to let trivialities like broken bodies and human misery stand in the way of a tempting theory. Zelaszny said: 'We need a quick-thinking, technically skilful, intellectually strong and politically conscious guerrilla to handle negotiations with the British government. She will spell out our demands, impress on the British that we mean business, and if necessary conduct face-to-face negotiations with the relevant cabinet ministers. So you see it helps if she also is British.' The eagle face smiled.

Margaret was there. She felt cold inside. 'You're saying . . .'

'That's the task I want you to carry out. Margaret, that is your chief role in Fight.'

*　　*　　*

At gone one, the moonlit patio was empty but for two of the residents, talking softly in Vietnamese. Margaret halted, weary to indecision.

Maybe it was the best thing that could have happened. Maybe this key position could be exploited to counter Zelaszny's master plan. Yet the sheer size of the task appalled her.

Sound came close by and she jerked round, scared it might be García again. Instead, Finito leered at her out of the shadowy arches. '*Hola, guapa*. How does it feel to be among the élite?'

He came closer. Margaret got the tequila fumes. 'I hope you aren't flying in the morning.'

'Nothing like flying,' he slurred, 'for clearing the head. Two thousand metres, open the cockpit. *Estupendo*. You're the likely lass here, you realise, everybody loves you.'

Hates me, she thought. Some because Zelaszny keeps talking to me, some because Finito does. Poor Finito. He loved his

149

pure-bred horses more than he loved the women he satisfied, and probably got more love from the horses in return. It upset her to see him that drunk.

'Go home, Finito.' She started walking away.

He leaned on a pillar and called out, 'Teacher's pet!' Then shouted with laughter, echoing across the lonely pool, as Margaret ignored him.

CHAPTER 26

Half past two on Monday afternoon was the middle of siesta time and Alameda airport sat and sweltered in the heat haze while anyone who wasn't lying in the shade lay on the edge of the surf of the Gulf of California. The grey, three-year-old, Mexican-built Volkswagen Beetle was unobtrusive. It raised dust although it was driving sedately, coming in from the Sierra Madre. Its driver found no shade outside the government Water Commission offices, tucked away behind the Cadal plant, so he parked in the sun, and watched a big lizard flick away among the grass that traced the lines of the flagstones as he got out. He was broadshouldered, not tall, but barrel-bodied, with strong hands, and he wore a conservative suit several years old. His receding hair was silver, his deeply tanned features more Spanish than Indian, and sunglasses hid his eyes. He crossed the flags and went into the Water Commission without knocking.

His passport identified him as Mexican and his papers identified him as a civil servant working with the commission.

All the same, the average, ordinary civil servant probably wouldn't have noticed the man in the airport manager's block who picked up the phone as soon as the Volkswagen parked. And wouldn't have known the significance if he had.

*   *   *

No one at the Paris talks that opened on Monday morning knew the Mexican delegate, Pedragoza, but he made his impression rapidly. In contrast with Pasarell and the investigators from Japan and Brazil, Pedragoza showed hardly a trace of jetlag. He was in his early thirties, he knew his subject, and although his seniority stopped short of certain key decision areas,

151

he knew what he wanted.

Mexico had just – only just – been invited to participate in an international action against a nasty international menace. Even before the invitation had arrived, Britain had had one agent operating on Mexican soil – admittedly, not against Mexico's interests – and now, by consent, it had two.

What Mexico therefore wanted was every word of every report either agent filed.

Barrington Yorke answered politely. He quite understood Pedragoza's point about how Britain would feel were the roles to be reversed. But his agent's security was paramount. Pedragoza could see the reports as they came through, and see them at the same time Barrington Yorke did; not before.

Pasarell listened to the haggling with a weary sense of having been passed over.

*   *   *

Nothing happened all day Sunday in San Diego except a noisy match at the stadium and a phone call to Carla Desatnick from FBI in Los Angeles to say Gregorio Tabio had arrived as planned and booked into a hotel. That, and Desatnick's running battle with the US Justice Department to get authorisation for the air force to send up the E3A radar platform they'd used to track Kuhr's Gulfstream on Friday. No, said the Justice Department: we can't find anybody to rule on who pays the fuel bill.

'Goddammit,' Desatnick fumed to Richard Caine as the evening turned quiet at last, 'who cares who pays? We have to have the information.'

'We don't need the info,' Caine said. 'Sit down and stop pacing.' He should have been doing any pacing to be done. It was his agent they'd lost touch with.

With a bad grace, Desatnick sat down. She glowered about the room. 'Isn't that just typical FBI? Brand new stereo and not a tape or a record to put on it. I am going downtown tomorrow and buy some records.'

'They did leave us some whisky.'

'Yeah, great, Grandad's Special Old Rattlesnake Killer.' Desatnick sighed, considered, then looked at Caine again.

'Okay, iron nerves, make me a drink so I can't taste the whisky in it, then I want to ask you one question.'

Caine came back with two whisky sours.

'Ee-yech,' Desatnick commented, 'I can't even taste the whisky. Listen. Rahab took this job on when she found this O'Dell girl stabbed to death by Fight, right?'

'Yes,' Caine said cautiously.

'Like, she went to you and *asked* you for the job, having suddenly had a born-again experience as regards what she thought about Fight? How come she went to you, anyway?'

'She knew I had connexions with a secret department.'

Alert, Desatnick sipped her whisky sour. She'd conducted too many interrogations not to recognise evasiveness when she heard it. 'Were you and she going steady?'

'Not at that time.'

'Ah, but you had been?' The bastard. 'You *were* going steady with her. *Then* you asked her to operate against Fight, only she said: "Get thee behind me, Satan". So you two break up. Then we get this amazing over-reaction when she finds O'Dell.'

'Rahab has such a colossal guilt complex she's got to over-achieve on everything. *I*'d call it negligence of the first order *not* to use a girl like that against Fight.'

The bastard. Desatnick tilted her head. Actually, bastards attracted her. 'Is Rahab lesbian?'

'Now, how would I tell a thing like that?'

*   *   *

On Monday the Justice Department still wasn't prepared to pay an air force fuel bill for an E3A sent up on a Justice Department task, but Richard Caine got a signal to say that his linkman was in position, standing by to contact Rahab. But it was Carla Desatnick who brought in the big news. Gregorio Tabio had flashed his Dominican I/D and an American Express Gold card at the aeroplane hire man at Hollywood Burbank, had been checked out on a Cessna Skylane, and had arranged to rent the aircraft, from tomorrow. For a flight into Mexico.

She went downtown, shopping, to celebrate. They spent the evening drinking Jim Beam bourbon on the rocks, listening to old Beach Boys surfing hits on the stereo, and feeling good.

'Take that satisfied smirk off your face,' Caine said. 'Just hand it to phallic power for once. *I*'m on the point of making contact with Rahab.'

'Who said *I* was satisfied?' Desatnick answered. 'Just because I have a top-line Commie agent tippy-toeing through my patch and not realising he is in a trap and gets reported every time he scratches his fat black ass. I'd call that a certain success for female power.' She stuck her tongue out.

'How many females have you got tagging him?'

'That is *not* the point, wiseacre. The point is that *I* am the female who is going to bust that guy as soon as his true intentions become obvious, probably tomorrow.'

'*You* aren't. You're going to send a gang of men to do it.'

'Ah, but *I* call the shots. The gender of the people who carry out my instructions is irrelevant, anyway.'

Not gender, Caine thought, that was what German nouns had. Sex was the word to apply to people. He was half-consciously tapping a foot, picking up occasional fragments of Beach Boys lyrics. It didn't help him to guess what Gregorio Tabio thought he was doing hiring an aeroplane in Los Angeles, although to some extent it accounted for the earlier flying lessons. Anyway, he wasn't concentrating very strongly on that.

'As far as Fight is concerned,' he said, 'the sex of the people who pull the triggers and hand out the karate chops is entirely relevant, not to say crucial.'

They were sitting on the sofa, Caine in white slacks and T-shirt, Desatnick in the blue jeans and denim shirt. The living-room was dimly lit. Security was two men with shotguns in the Dodge under the pines and Mr Desatnick was in New York, scrutinising the closing prices.

'Ah, well, big news,' Carla Desatnick said. 'No one ever thought Fight wanted equality, baby, they wanted one step better. But one thing that *has* surfaced in the course of this inquiry is that one gender is doing better than the other in hunting down these bitches, and it doesn't happen to be your one.' She'd slipped off her sandals, and she reached with a bare foot and poked Caine's thigh.

'Do that once more,' Caine said, 'and my urge to have gender with you will become uncontrollable.'

'Oh, really, will it?' She gave him the toothy smile, eyes big and round and not a bit innocent. She poked him on the thigh again.

* * *

Drowsy in the darkness, Carla Desatnick moved slowly against Richard Caine to give him the feeling of her bare breasts against his chest. 'Bet you can't do that again before morning.'

'I could and would if I wanted to.'

'Oh, ho, ho.'

Nothing was immoral, Caine thought, about a romp between two people who fancied a romp. If immorality existed, it was in her comparing him with her husband, if that was what she'd secretly done, and in his comparing her with Rahab. Or rather, with what he thought Rahab would be like in bed but had never been permitted to find out. She would be taller than Carla Desatnick, with those superb legs making up the difference, but her bust would be disappointing, nothing like Desatnick's firm, full and stimulating breasts. She would move more shyly, less aggressively, so that there would be no doubt over who was having and who was being had.

Desatnick pushed Caine's shoulders flat on the sheet, levered herself partly on top of him, forced an arm under his neck, and grasped his shoulder with the other hand. 'You are now in an FBI-approved lock and I am charging you with carrying Anglo-US collaboration in a joint investigation way too far.'

'Guilty as charged,' Caine said, 'but I'm darned if I'm coming quietly.' It was starting all over again.

CHAPTER 27

Two levels underneath the convent the airconditioning wasn't working properly and the crowded chamber hacked into the limestone was stuffy and warm. Nadezhda Sokolova was blinking a bit but it wasn't her eyesight, it was the lighting, one bulb flickering and one out altogether. Margaret Stubbs wasn't feeling entirely well and she didn't think she was the only one.

'It would be wrong to describe chlorine as a nerve gas.' Sokolova was delivering her lecture in English, the main language in use at HQ. 'Nerve gas might be described as an especially potent insecticide. It is a chemical that attaches itself to an essential enzyme in the body and prevents it from breaking down acetylcholine, the means by which messages pass from one nerve to another. Acetylcholine then accumulates, the nervous system is overwhelmed by a mass of messages, and it fails. The victim will suffer from heavy sweating, vomiting and diarrhoea, then the diaphragm will cease to function so that the victim dies of asphyxiation.'

Tina Zeiss was going slowly green. Down here Margaret guessed they were in the old Oraboca mine workings. The limestone was honeycombed, natural as well as artificial passages running through it, and the chamber where they were listening to Sokolova was crowded with fewer than a dozen guerrillas.

'Chlorine, although not a nerve gas, does attack the central nervous system. The victim will die when the lungs collapse. Chlorine is important in our plan because it is perhaps the most widely used dangerous chemical commonly transported by road in the countries we propose to threaten. It is a heavy gas, pale green in colour, and when released from its pressurised container it spreads quickly and will not disperse.' Heavy lorries, Margaret thought suddenly. Heavy lorries were what they used to carry chlorine. Heavy lorries were what Renata Vernon had been learning to drive in London. Had she known? 'Chlorine is used in several industrial processes. Perhaps its best known use is as a disinfectant for cleaning swimming pools.

'Another possibility is sulphuryl chloride, $SOCL_2$, a gas carried as a liquid under pressure, and used as a reagent in chemical processes; for making pesticides; for dyestuffs. Also sulphur trioxide, SO_3; a gas that, like chlorine, spreads rapidly and attacks the nervous system. SO_3 is used in making concentrated sulphuric acid, H_2SO_4, commonly transported, used to make fertilisers, very dangerous, in this case because the victim simply gets dissolved.

'Again, any fuel tanker is a possibility. Petrol tankers, aviation spirit tankers. Other tankers carry toluene, a chemical intermediate used to make dyestuffs, insecticides, in the rubber industry, and a serious danger to any built-up area once in our hands.' Sokolova turned. Beside her Sarah Kuhr sat, hard-eyed, menacing. 'My colleague will explain our plan.'

Kuhr stood up. Sokolova managed to sit down without overturning her chair. On the desk in front of her, Kuhr had a pile of 10×8 glossies.

'Very simple plan,' she said. 'We get routine intelligence on tanker movements – gasoline, toluene, acids, chlorine, sulphur trioxide. We select the cities we're going to hit. We lay out Fight's demands, the demands are refused, we give a warning, our warning gets ignored. So we hijack a few tankers, drive them into city centres, and bam. Ignite the toluene, release the acid or chlorine, and see how they like it.' She paused. 'You don't think we can do it?'

No one replied. Margaret glanced at Tina, the little guerrilla ashen as she started picturing what would happen.

'Okay,' Kuhr said, 'let me explain how we already have shown that Fight can organise and carry out a tough operation and at the same time strike practical blows against male tyranny. A party of guerrillas led by Bargellini and including myself set sail aboard an ocean-going tug owned by a multi-national organisation that supports Fight' – Kuhr's mother's outfit, Margaret realised – 'and hung around the Gulf of Thailand in the knowledge that the refugee boats coming out of Vietnam were commonly attacked by Thai pirates who would rape the women on board.'

In Margaret's mind's eye, suddenly, was Pham Anh's face, big-eyed, vulnerable. She started to guess what was coming.

'We traced the captives from one of the boats. We were slow, a lot of women and girls suffered real bad. But we took on the pirates and beat them. We then'–she was shuffling her photographs–'executed them. Take a look.'

Lorraine Easson was in the front row. She reached for the photographs. From further back, Margaret heard her soft gasp, and she knew how much it took to shock Lorraine. She tightened up her stomach.

Then in the middle of them, something thumped heavily. Tina Zeiss had passed out.

*   *   *

At lunchtime they were still making a fuss of Tina, asking how she felt, asking if she was up to eating, but Margaret, who'd given Tina first aid despite feeling sick herself, got sent to Coventry. That was what you got for seeing too much of Mother Superior.

So with nothing to lose she took a brief dip at siesta time, then lay by the pool in her bikini and waited for Finito Navásquez to appear.

He was prompt. They went through the routines, hint, evasion, chase, tease, and Margaret despised herself because she was doing what Lorraine had told her: whore for intelligence. She was using her body as a tool, even if she kept Finito from laying a finger on it. But he bit, he offered to show her round Alameda airport.

*   *   *

Finito's car was a collector's piece, a soft-top Healey 3000, beautifully maintained, tuned, and sump-shielded against Mexican roads. Margaret hadn't been in or out of Tequísquepec by road before, and to do this, now, she was gambling her special pass for the airfield. The potholed track dropped steeply between sheer canyon walls, swung round the foot of a steep slope of mesquite, cholla and prickly-pear, and struck towards the coast through scruffy olive groves.

On the shimmering ramp, a Beech 18 twin was roasting. Finito vaulted out of the Healey, cursing. 'I've told those *hijos de puta* a thousand times, if they leave the tarpaulins off, the radio doesn't work for a week.'

He swaggered into No 1 hangar, shouting. Margaret sauntered after him. She'd put on sandals and just a bush shirt over her bikini; there wouldn't be many people around at siesta, and if there were, Finito was protection enough.

They were all Mustangs in the hangar, more than she'd seen the first time: nine altogether, all apparently airworthy.

Finito reappeared with a tubby guard puffing ahead of him going, '*Sí, sí, don Finito, derecho, don Finito.*' Finito left him getting busy and turned to Margaret.

'Impressive, no? All this belongs to Cadal. There's one workshop behind No 3 hangar and another behind 4 and 5. *Vamos.*' And he took Margaret's hand to show her the plant.

He had no idea what the simple, friendly physical contact did to her. It wasn't that such ages had gone by since she'd last held a man's hand, and he'd only manipulated her; Richard Caine it had been. It was contact, it was bridging the abyss between personalities, and for its promise of relief from eternal loneliness she was suddenly desperately and willingly dependent.

Jigs, lathes, panel-beating, engine test benches; the smells of lubricant and aircraft dope and the tang of metal shavings. 'I'll show you where the real money comes from,' Finito said, and they got back in the Healey. Hangars 4 and 5 were a bit away from the others. They drove the short distance and stepped out of the sports car.

'*Hé aquí . . .*' Finito gestured.

A tractor came out of No 5 hangar, behind it a Mirage III two-seater. Old, although not so old as the Mustang; serviceable; and a formidable aircraft in Latin American terms.

'Cadal buys them in,' Finito was saying. 'There are thousands of used Mirage IIIs in world air force service. For many countries, a Mirage III is an old aeroplane; but, for others, it's more modern than anything they've got. And the profits from sales feed back into the work of that *gringa* up there at Tequísquepec.' For a moment he was bitter; then he turned to Margaret with the wide, wicked grin. 'I'm sure you'd love a flip.'

*   *   *

Back on the ground it was later than they'd intended; they'd gone supersonic, Margaret for the first time, in the Mirage and the flight had delayed them.

It hadn't been shockwaves breaking off the trailing edge that impressed her, though. It had been the big screen in the middle of the aft control panel. That Mirage wasn't just there to train pilots to fly jet fighters with a landing speed of 200mph. It was there to train them on radar.

Tie that to a couple of brace of air-to-air missiles and you'd got an even more potent system for defending Guerrillera Island.

She wanted to get away, scared of questions back at Tequísquepec, but Finito ignored her protests, took her into the bar to buy her a drink and show her off. A bunch of Water Commission men were on the tall stools, just awake after their siesta, wide awake after Margaret walked in. She sat on a stool close by Finito as he ordered, and cast an arrogant eye over the men.

She stopped dead.

The man was silver-haired, very tanned, broadshouldered and barrel-built, with dark glasses tucked into the top pocket of his old suit. He had a square wedge of jaw, humour at the corners of his mouth, and deep, dark, wise eyes that Margaret knew very well. He'd recognised her, too, though he wasn't giving it away. He was flanked by Water Commission men and dressed like them.

Mario Roca. The one who'd taught her all she knew about self-defence and survival.

*   *   *

In the Healey Finito raised dust, heading quickly for the olive groves at the foot of Tequísquepec. 'Sabina Stamm and Charlotte Rondeau are qualified on those Mirages. We all three test-fly them when they're rebuilt.' Radar, Margaret remembered; that was one of Rondeau's specialities. 'So far, that *gringa* hasn't asked us to convert any of her novices on to them, but that day will come, and then you'll have a very formidable secret weapon.'

He glanced at Margaret, her chestnut hair lifting in the

160

slipstream. She wasn't paying attention.

'They keep a Mirage and two Mustangs on readiness down there,' Finito said. 'Did you know that? Armed. Four 7.62mm machineguns, those Mustangs carry. Rapid fire. And they keep them loaded. Do you *know* how fast they can scramble?'

She wasn't immediately interested. From Cuzco, where she'd last heard of Roca, to here was a journey of three thousand six hundred miles. He hadn't finished up five bar stools away from Margaret Stubbs by accident.

Finito braked unexpectedly. In a gap in the low, drystone walls a track dropped away into a hollow, and he drove down into it. You couldn't be overlooked here under the olives. He stopped the engine.

'You've gone thoughtful all of a sudden. Won't you tell me what you're thinking?'

She looked at him. He put his arm round her shoulders in their thin shirt. She drew in a nervous breath through her nose. She'd enjoyed a simple, friendly contact, but there were limits. She should have known better than to think she could entice him without raising his expectations too far.

'Finito, please. Let's go back to Tequísquepec.'

'We shall, *mi guapa.* Later.' On her thigh his hand was strong, warm, dry. And exciting, despite her rising fear.

'No, Finito, I don't want . . . I don't want to . . .' It petrifies me, that was what she meant.

'*Chito, niña*, relax, don't be silly.' Spearmint on his breath.

'Finito, I'll hurt you if you make me.'

'No, you won't. I won't hurt you, either.'

His face was close, wanting the kiss, wanting much more than that now she'd dragged him out here, and she jerked her head away. His hand started easing into the bikini pants. The limit, reached and exceeded.

She swung the flat of a hand and was surprised how loud it sounded in the stillness under the olives. He recoiled, but the glimpse of the light in his eye told her he'd just reassessed her, the sort that likes taking by force. Well, he was wrong. Before he could grab she used the same hand to chop him first on the shoulder nerve, numbing the arm, then on the thigh the same side to numb the leg. He muttered, '*Mierda*,' and doubled over the wheel. Still her left arm wasn't free, but she reached past him

161

with the right and shoved his door open. It swung to the check strap. She gave him the fingertip treatment, flat-handed under his right ribs, then, as the breath went from him, reached down for his ankles. Tipping him out of the sports car was simple lever action.

She was a mile up the road in the Healey before conscience overtook her, and she turned round and went back for him. By his anger and indignation as he slid back behind the wheel she diagnosed major trauma of the pride, and he didn't say a word all the way to Tequísquepec.

CHAPTER 28

Port door hinge, wired, security. Port wing strut, security. Port flap, freedom of movement, damage to flap tracks . . .

'Okay, this is the FBI.'

Gregorio Tabio turned smartly. He had the checklist for the rented Skylane in his hand, but not for much longer because two of the four agents who'd come for him grabbed his hands and planted them against the fuselage. A third agent frisked Tabio quickly.

He didn't even try to resist. He protested, because they'd expect it, and they handcuffed him and walked him to the waiting helicopter. San Diego was a short hop. They took him into FBI headquarters by the back route.

'I'm Assistant Special Agent-in-Charge Desatnick.' She picked up the Dominican passport and dropped it on the desk, at once familiar and contemptuous. The office was brown and shadowy. A tape recorder was running and there were blue-chinned guards by the door, out of Tabio's sight as he sat on the hard chair. 'Really, you oughta have more sense than use this kind of cheap fake.'

'Madam, I do not understand what is happening. I insist that you let me call the nearest Dominican consular office.'

Desatnick leaned forward happily, elbows clasped. This was what you expected: they stuck to cover, you broke them down. 'You keep on that way, baby, and I'll bring in all the Dominican officials you like, and we'll find where that passport *really* done come from. Why not let's quit screwing around and admit a few things? One, you're not Dominican but Cuban. Two, your name is Gregorio Tabio. Three, you're deputy head of Cuban counter-intelligence. Four, you're in the United States on an operation fronting for the Soviet KGB, which in the person of

Lieutenant-General Vassily Andreyev sent you in here in the first place.'

She gave him the toothy smile and waited for the denials. Tabio sat back a little in the hard chair, battered hands clasped, balding black head glistening a little, shrewd eyes studying her with interest.

He leaned forward and surprised her.

'Very well, madam. What you say is largely correct. But understand that my mission is not in the US nor against US interests and that I happen to be in this country merely for the sake of finding a means of travelling to where I need to be. And the reason I'm telling you that is that I expect you not to hinder my mission. It's running on close parallel lines to your own.' The intelligent eyes in the black face held Desatnick's, candid. 'You and I can help each other best if instead of getting in each other's way we pool our resources.'

Desatnick sat straight in her chair, head tilted, arms clasped defensively. If he'd wanted a way of putting her off her stroke he could hardly have chosen anything better.

'Right, you're Gregorio Tabio, Cuban counter-intelligence. You have any way of proving that?' This was getting silly. They *knew* he was Tabio, they didn't want to start proving he wasn't.

'Of course I haven't, madam, I'm using the identity in that passport. And you'll have a hard time yourself if you try to find evidence that I'm Tabio. Don't you even want to know what my mission is?'

'Hm. Okay, shoot.'

She pushed the cigarettes over. They lit up. Desatnick sent for coffee, trying to focus her brain.

'You're investigating Feminist International Guerrillas to Hurl down Tyranny.' Tabio had an arm flung now casually over the back of the chair, the other hand grasping an ankle propped on a knee. 'So is Cuba. So is the Soviet KGB. Do you know why?'

'Now wait a minute . . .' She broke off. A man came in with coffee.

Desatnick was starting to realise why Tabio was so confident, much more confident than her. All this had been covered in his mission briefing; he'd been cleared to say every word. What she'd expected to have was an abject Cuban spy, shocked by his slick arrest, possibly even asking to defect. Instead she'd got a tiger by the tail.

The man left with the coffee tray.

Desatnick said; 'C'm'on, Tabio. We have evidence that Cuba and the Soviets are backing Fight.'

'Name your evidence.'

She hadn't expected him to call her bluff so promptly. 'We know a lot of women wanted over Fight activities are active or former CP members. We know Cuba's been running ex-Vietnam weapons to Fight.'

'Communist Party members in the US and Europe seldom have anything to do with the Soviet Union, far less Cuba. As for your suspicions about gun-running, let's admit it – they are no more than suspicions.'

'We have captured weapons. We even know the channels.'

'Your captured weapons are American-made, all of them. And you do not know the channels.' Tabio paused. 'I could tell you some that we used formerly.'

Desatnick sat up, thrown again. 'Then you *do* admit Cuba's backing Fight.'

Tabio tapped a big finger on her desk. 'Cuba has sold to Fight American M3 submachineguns, a few American M16 rifles, and various handguns, all ex-Vietnam. We don't want the stuff, our Kalashnikovs are better. We have a reason for doing this.'

Irritably Desatnick flicked ash. 'Okay, hit me with a reason.'

'Fight has been found operating in Cuba. It has been found also operating in the Soviet Union and certain other member nations of the Warsaw Pact. In the Warsaw Pact countries it has been severely dealt with, but an evident danger exists. When the KGB in Moscow acted to arrest the handful of agitators and criminals active over there, the guiding brain behind them escaped and vanished. This was a former Soviet academician called Nadezhda Sokolova. It was obvious to the KGB that as long as Sokolova remained free, she remained a danger, in that, with her knowledge of the country, she could set up a whole new network of secret Fight cells. It was also obvious that Sokolova had gone to some secret centre of Fight's activities.' He drew on the cigarette.

'Go on,' Desatnick said.

'Now, at that time, we had not the slightest idea where that centre might be. We thought it was somewhere in the continental US. We now had to find it, urgently.'

'Okay.'

'At the time when Fight's Soviet section was crushed and Sokolova disappeared, an operation was also planned against Fight in Cuba. At the express request of the Soviet Union, that operation was cancelled. Instead, Cuba started selling ex-Vietnam weapons to Fight in the US. Now do you see?'

'Okay, I'm getting it.' Ash feel on Desatnick's dress and she flicked at it. 'You had to have Fight command trust Cuba. You had to leave the Fight operation in Cuba untouched so you could watch it.'

Tabio nodded. 'Results were very slow. We had to have something else. We were lucky. Through KGB sources in South-east Asia, we found the guns smuggled from Cuba to Fight being put to use – ironically, back in the Vietnam area where they'd originally come from.'

Desatnick frowned suddenly.

'We don't know how, but Fight caught a boatload of Thai pirates who'd sunk a Vietnamese refugee vessel, saving only a few women and girls whom they wanted to rape. Fight rescued the Vietnamese women – and then coldbloodedly butchered the Thais and scuttled their ship.'

'Okay.' Desatnick was liking this less and less.

'What little other evidence we could find about this slaughter suggested that the operation had been run from somewhere in the US. Now, to penetrate a terrorist HQ in the US, killing Sokolova and destroying her attempts to replace Fight's network in the Warsaw Pact nations, would have presented the KGB with the need for a massive, complicated, illegal operation, danger-ous, and expensive in cash and personnel.' Tabio shrugged. 'So Andreyev thought it would be better to let the Americans do the work for him.'

'Oh God,' she sighed softly. 'And we did.' That KGB bungling in the Gulf of Thailand. The whole thing had been done just to attract CIA attention. After that, the American agencies *had* to home in on Fight.

'My task involved penetrating Fight's secret cell structure in Cuba. A woman volunteer worked her way into a position of trust within Fight and was rewarded – by being sent for special

166

training to the secret headquarters.'

An exact parallel. Desatnick kept nodding, wearily.

'She was flown out of Cuba last Friday, April 19, aboard a Super Constellation owned by a Mexican business combine controlled by a doña Alma Múñoz. Soviet satellites tracked the aircraft to a Mexican town called Alameda and we traced our agent further, to a private mental home at a place called Tequísquepec. It was our first inkling of where Fight's base was. I flew to Los Angeles, hired that aircraft, and prepared to go to Alameda to contact my agent. If you check my flight plan from this morning, you'll see I was headed for Chihuahua. What the flight plan doesn't say is that I was going to declare an instrument malfunction and make a precautionary landing at Alameda.'

'Right,' Desatnick said gloomily. She stubbed out her cigarette.

* * *

She appealed to Richard Caine with an outflung hand. 'So what the hell do I *do* with this guy? It's absolutely straight, he just gave me the truth. If I hang on to him, he doesn't make contact with his agent. If I let him go, maybe he makes contact, maybe he doesn't.'

'Who is his agent?'

'He isn't saying.'

'What have you got to hold him on?'

'Passport irregularities.'

Caine squinted into the sunshine. Clouds reflected in the windows of a tall office block and a naval transport lost height over the sea, approaching Coronado air station. If Gregorio Tabio went free he might do a number of things, but one thing he would certainly do would be to remove one suspiciously acting woman from Tequísquepec, leaving only one other suspiciously acting woman to be caught. And he might or might not tell Caine and Desatnick what his agent reported. On the other hand, if Fight caught one agent, they'd hardly expect to find another in position.

He said: 'Play it safe, Carla, hang on to him.'

167

Light was fading on Tequísquepec hill and Margaret's heart missed a beat when she saw Catalina Sánchez bearing down on her; she thought she was going to get questioned about her trip to the airport with Finito. She needn't have worried, it was just an errand. They had something down at the airport that Sánchez wanted and would Margaret please pop down in the Stationair and fetch it.

Cathy Latta drove Margaret in one of the Land Cruisers to the *altipuerto*. Cathy looked none the worse for recent heavy labour. She was cheerful, competent, she looked about sixteen or seventeen. At the *altipuerto* she said could she come for the ride, and Margaret sat her on the right, ran through the checks, and drove the Stationair fast down the slope. It wasn't as bad as she'd expected. The aircraft accelerated well downhill and she got off with runway to spare.

At Alameda she kept glancing out of the corners of her eyes but she didn't see Mario Roca. She collected the parcel and took off and then had to hunt all round the hillside before she found the *altipuerto* through the evening haze. She swung up on the flat parking ramp and started shutting things down.

She gave the parcel to Cathy. 'Don't wait. I've got to tie the aircraft down, and anyway I'd rather walk back.'

Cathy drove off. Margaret tied down the Stationair and then went to see what the four-blade prop in the awning was attached to.

It was a Mustang, a two-seater. Margaret looked it over admiringly; she liked the old fighter's power and its handling. In more than idle curiosity, she reached to the fuel filler cap and looked inside. Full. That was worth knowing.

She walked back to the convent along a narrow path under the oaks. Jays swooped among the shadowy branches and the first of the evening's moths blundered about. Her path brought her out opposite the transport park with its wall that enclosed also the garages and workshops, and she spotted, not for the first time, the coca growth Zelaszny had mentioned, a sprawl of dark vegetation between the admin block wall and the near-vertical slope down to the cinder track. Not for the first time, either, she contemplated trying the stuff out. She'd been feeling much too tired lately for her own good.

A dozen young women were playing football, a goal mouth drawn clumsily on the transport park wall. Margaret walked round the edge of the game. Giselle Stamm was there, but not playing. She was simply hanging round sadly as if hoping they'd ask her to join in and yet knowing they wouldn't.

García was hanging round, too, behind Giselle's back, and again Margaret thought: filthy brute.

*   *   *

It was almost two in the morning when Catalina Sánchez called Zelaszny to the radio room. Zelaszny hadn't quite got to bed. Sánchez was in a rush, fear, anger and impatience in her fanatic's eyes, and all she'd managed to get by way of escort was Sabina and Giselle Stamm; but they both had M3s.

The radio operator was a Mexican called Ana Ramírez. She wore the residents' blue flash on her uniform. She was good, she'd been trained by a Fight instructor who'd learnt the job during her spell with the US forces.

'We've traced the signals,' Ana Ramírez said. 'It's a cell in the novices' block.'

Zelaszny's cheeks were hollow, lips compressed a bit, she was blinking and unsure whether she'd brought the right glasses. At her knees the cotton dress hung limply. 'And these signals, they're . . .'

Ramírez said: 'It's an HF wave transmitting cipher groups on a directional antenna, beamed towards the north, the United States. On a night like this it might carry fifteen hundred kilometres, putting the receiver anywhere from San Francisco to Denver or New Orleans. We've picked up no incoming signals, although we might have missed the frequency. But the fact that

169

the cipher groups appear to be the same ones, repeated at intervals, suggests that no reply has in fact come in.'

Nobody moved.

Zelaszny said: 'Okay, let's go get her out. Who's guard supervisor tonight?'

'Hardy,' Catalina Sánchez replied.

'Okay, have her detach her three best Bodyguards, meet us here. Wake Colwell to stand by Hardy in the guardroom. And wake Bargellini. I want her in on this.'

It took six minutes.

Then Coral Bargellini was there, and Giovanna Piotti, Cornelia's sister, and Kelly Thane and another from the Bodyguard, and Sabina and Giselle to make up numbers. Ramírez led them, carrying a sensitive receiver that just flashed lights, didn't carry the sound.

It was two-fifteen. The whole complex was quiet and their rubber soles were soundless. In the novices' wing, only one door had a line of light under it. For a moment they waited. Then Coral nudged Giovanna Piotti's arm, signalling.

Giovanna Piotti kicked the door in.

Paquita Villegas, the Cuban guerrilla, was crouching over the HF transmitter. The set was built into a Spanish-English dictionary. From the hopelessness in her eyes she'd been waiting for a return signal and not had one. But she wasn't too hopeless to put up a fight.

Giovanna Piotti saw the Stechkin APS coming up and dived forward flat, firing immediately to throw Paquita's aim. Kelly Thane piled in behind her with the other Bodyguard and behind them were Catalina Sánchez and Giselle. Shatteringly in the confined space the Stechkin was blasting and it couldn't miss. Nor could Giovanna Piotti, from four feet with the Smith & Wesson .38 Military Airweight.

Giselle heard Sánchez scream, stumbling back, but she was looking at Paquita Villegas. Five .38 bullets hung the woman flat-shouldered against the wall, shock on her face, the APS falling loose. Then the energy dissipated. She collapsed face forward on the bed.

Sánchez was clutching her forearm, face white, blood trickling through her fingers. But she'd caught the bullet secondhand, it was one of those that had killed Kelly Thane.

Coral shouldered her way into the room. She breathed: 'Shit.' Aloud she said: 'Well, *she* won't be answering any questions.' Zelaszny was looking tottery, sick. Coral gave her a hard look, recognising the weakness. The sole flaw, possibly, but a dangerous one, for a theoretician to show such revulsion at the outcome of her theories. One day, that weakness was going to give Coral an opening for her ambition. 'Okay.' She hid her thoughts from Zelaszny's probing mind. 'Piotti, get a guard on the door, keep the rubberneckers out. Stamm, Ramírez, escort our Leader back to her quarters – not you, kid.' Giselle had started to move. 'You go fetch Dr Arias.'

*   *   *

Everyone knew about it, nobody spoke about it. The shadow of death was there. The group Margaret led in the morning for unarmed-combat training was subdued, taciturn, the feelings of betrayal and anger mostly hidden deep.

'I am not going to teach you judo or martial arts. If you want to, you can learn those openly at a club, and you'll probably find the discipline helpful. But they are not a substitute for unarmed combat.' In her mind, the face she saw was the one she'd seen yesterday: Mario Roca's. These were Roca's lessons to her that she was delivering to these guerrillas. 'Judo is a sport. Karate is more adaptable to combat, but its moves, even for an expert, tend to be formalised if not stylised, and intensive practice can lead to rigidity in thinking that will hinder, not help, in real combat. Always remember that in real combat your opponent can and will play dirty.'

They were gazing at her, Lorraine Easson nodding, hard-eyed; Tina Zeiss scared, like Giselle with her luminous eyes; Sharon Levenson, the helicopter pilot, simply bored.

Margaret smiled at Tina. 'But that isn't to say that you aren't in with a very strong chance, even assuming that.' Mario Roca again. 'The first requirement is to *believe* that you'll win.'

Tina didn't. But she went at it with a will when they practised, picking up the techniques, using the moves. Then, matched with Giselle, she dropped her opponent a bit heavily in a throw, and made the cardinal error: she broke off the combat to find out where Giselle had been hurt.

171

Sharon Levenson was Margaret's own build, leggy, well co-ordinated. She lacked practice, though, and she seemed unwilling to come to grips with an opponent. Lorraine was still the one who scared Margaret most. Since arriving at Tequís-quepec the two had hardly exchanged a word, although in the ambience of Zelaszny's comradeship Lorraine's old antagonism seemed to have vanished. But Lorraine was heavier than Margaret and at least as skilful, and in intent Lorraine was much more deadly.

In a similar way to Lorraine, Giselle put every fraction of her energy into her combat; yet something there wasn't right, Margaret sensed. The kid was scared. Not of fighting, not of potential adversaries, but of getting her lessons wrong. She couldn't make herself fight against Margaret, she was fighting *for* her, tacitly longing for a word of praise, for the hint that just someone was actually pleased with her.

CHAPTER 30

It was after lunch when Finito Navásquez took Margaret aside. He did it subtly, so the others wouldn't notice; she appreciated that. '*Oye*, Margarita.' The Spanish version of her name. 'I want you to know I made a mistake yesterday. About you. You aren't like the others . . . I didn't realise . . .' He couldn't quite voice the apology. But, for him, getting this far was difficult enough.

Margaret smiled. 'Forget it, Finito. I ought to appreciate you, really.'

He relaxed, surprisingly, with a vivid smile. 'Are you going to *dormir la siesta* now?'

'I might.'

'Or would you like to come to the *cortijo* and see my horses?'

*   *   *

The last hundred yards of the cinder track brought the Healey 3000 perilously close to the rim of the canyon by which Margaret and Finito had left and returned to Tequísquepec the day before. Finito parked. The *cortijo* was a sprawling bungalow wrapped round with old vines, its whitewash gone yellow here and there, russet tiles, around it a jumble of lupin and prickly-pear. Three sides round it a terrace ran, and Finito escorted Margaret along the terrace until she stopped, with a gasp.

The terrace had been built up to the very edge of the canyon at its sheerest point. It had nothing but a foot-high, tile-topped brick wall to break a fall and Margaret was suddenly back, mentally, on that balcony in New York.

Finito grasped her arm and chuckled. She felt safer with him holding her. 'I make sure never to get drunk up here,' he said. 'Don't you like the view?'

173

She had to admit she did. She could trace the road from Tequísquepec with hardly a break, right through the olive groves to the airport; she could see the distant, brown rooftops of Alameda town, and the silver shimmer of the Gulf.

Despite herself, even despite Finito's arm, Margaret found herself edging back from the long drop at the edge of the terrace. Close by her she noticed full-length shutters. They opened out from Finito's bedroom, she saw. She'd have taken a while getting used to sleeping there.

'Look down,' Finito dared her.

It was the one slope on the whole of Tequísquepec where hardly any living thing had found purchase to take root. One solitary, old mesquite balanced on the edge, not far off; a few traces of green amid the brown rock suggested chollas; and the next sign of life, a sprawl of brittlebush and prickly-pear, was on a ledge a hundred feet down, with still another sixty or so to go before you hit the road.

Then she spotted it, squarish, tan and matt to tone in with the rocks, and tucked among the less inaccessible roots of the old mesquite. A television camera.

Margaret glanced at Finito, his dark face close to hers. 'This place would make an ideal lookout point.'

'It does, *mi guapa*, it does. And if any of these professors who come to look at the Sacromonte spot that thing' – he indicated the TV camera – 'I take them inside and show them my photographic workshop and my darkroom.'

'But you haven't got infra-red on that?'

'Naturally not.'

'And Zelaszny trusts you to crew a lookout point in the dark?'

Again he pealed with laughter at her naïvety. 'What she does when I'm alone here I really don't know.'

Of course. Margaret kicked herself. Probably there'd be a different woman up here every night, and in better shape than Finito as the hours went by to keep an eye on that road through the olives. She'd hardly need to leave the bedroom.

Hand grasping her arm, Finito moved Margaret on. 'But photography's really no more than my hobby. The horses are my real passion.'

They were in a stable, a paddock attached, judiciously away from the canyon rim: two-year-olds, big and supple and glossy,

174

their manes brushed until not a hair lay out of place. The wooded hill behind the paddock blocked any view of the Sacromonte. Finito smiled, watching Margaret mount.

'You don't know horses like you know aircraft.'

She smiled. 'Sorry it's that obvious.'

'*Vaya*, you can ride.' Finito grinned. 'Have you been to the Sacromonte? *Bueno, anda.*'

Resin smell hung in the heat-laden air. Even the insects seemed too tired to fly. Leather creaked and the hoofbeats fell dully. Margaret had never ridden such a fine horse. A sound pension insurance for Finito, she thought as she followed the trail over the crest and then rode downhill through the trees.

The Sacromonte was parched grass, sun-bleached stone, broken into glimpses through the shadowy cypresses. When they came out into the clearing Margaret could see the structure, the broken steps, a dark gap at their foot like a missing tooth, much bigger than she'd imagined, more impressive. Her scalp tingled.

Her horse was stamping now, swinging its head, trying to mark time. Finito bounced down from the saddle and took his mount by the bridle. 'Tether them here. They won't go near the Sacromonte.'

They walked across the ragged clearing. Mostly the Sacromonte was just a weed-grown mound; it reminded Margaret of a disused air-raid shelter. But at its western end, where they were, you could still see where the steps had been, make out the platform at the top. Once there'd been carvings, but they'd weathered away now.

Margaret felt cold, despite the heat. 'It's spooky.'

Finito's laugh echoed in the trees. 'The day women stop reacting to imaginary atmosphere, that's the day they can start thinking about world domination.'

'And the day men stop pouring scorn on what they can't understand,' she replied evenly, 'that's the day we can worry that we might not get it.'

He clapped her on the arm. 'Make love, not war, *I* say.'

'Does anyone know what they did here?'

'It's a sun temple. On the great annual religious festivals they offered human sacrifices. The priest cut open the victim's breast with an obsidian knife and took out the heart, still beating. They would be the purest of the young men or women

175

from some conquered tribe.'

Margaret shuddered.

Again Finito laughed at her. 'Don't look like that, no one's been sacrificed here for five hundred years.' But in her mind Margaret could still see the blood. Finito grasped her hand. 'Come, I'll show you something.'

She followed him reluctantly, ducking into the utter darkness beyond the doorway at the foot of the steps.

Finito flashed a torch. The tunnel was narrow, low-ceilinged, and sloped down. Damp air touched the cooling sweat on their faces. Margaret hesitated, wanting to go back. But still Finito clasped her hand, and she made herself follow. A right turn, steps; a level stretch, a left turn, a steeper slope than before. Finito knew his way but Margaret still didn't like it. And an echo filled the tunnel walls, the sound of water.

They came out suddenly into a high, wide cavern. Margaret caught her breath. A dark lake stretched in front of them, the area and roughly the shape of the weed-grown mound above.

'Zelaszny's water supply.' Finito raised his voice over the echoes. 'It's tapped off underground for the convent.'

'So it's a *water* temple up there.'

'It's a temple of life. Sun and water, you need both. But to ensure life, they had to sacrifice life to the gods.' He pointed. 'There's where it rises.'

Spring water was running freely from the rocks at the end of the lake. Close by, another small pool on a pillar jutting from the cavern like a pulpit dripped very slowly into a slender runnel to the lake. Finito shone the torch. Its light caught two metal stakes, beaten into the limestone either side of the dripfall.

Margaret saw their purpose instantly. Chinese water torture. 'Let's get back!'

'I don't think I can remember the way.'

She turned and watched him. 'What might persuade you to remember?'

Deep eyes almost serious in the darkness, the tiny smile, only half joking. '*Un beso nada más.*'

Margaret felt paralysed, hypnotised by his complete change in attitude. He couldn't get it right, couldn't read a middle line between lust and rejection. She was scarcely aware now of the darkness, or the noise of the water.

'You didn't need to make it a condition,' she said in soft Spanish.

He flicked out the torch and then held her closely, crushing her against him. Margaret went weak. Finito's lips brushed hers first tenderly, then hungrily, as his hand touched her body, respectfully yet longingly, too. Scared suddenly of herself, Margaret dragged her lips away. Her own hunger made her so dangerous, yet she dared not give in.

*   *   *

The horses were anxious to put the Sacromonte behind them. It was late again. 'They'll miss us,' Margaret said edgily.

Contemptuously Finito spat on the trail. 'They won't even know we're gone. That *gringa* has no idea of security, for all her pretty electronic toys. Anyone could walk into the heart of the convent right now and come out with anything from Fight's master plan to the deployment of every guerrilla throughout the world.'

Margaret's heart jumped. 'How d'you mean?'

'The alarms are too easily neutralised in the archives, and once you get in there you can take anything you want. As for the combination, it's simplicity itself.'

'What is it?'

He turned in the saddle. 'It's the geographical co-ordinates for Tequísquepec in degrees and minutes, reversed. I could get in there myself in three minutes in perfect safety.'

Now how would Finito know a thing like that? She said: 'Why don't you?'

He laughed monosyllabically. 'Maybe one day I will. Right now I know which side my bread's buttered.'

One of the Bodyguard, that was how. Late at night in Finito's bedroom.

Anyway, he was bulling: *he* couldn't get in there, or he'd have done so already and been blackmailing Zelaszny to get her precious secrets back. No man could get anywhere near that alarm panel in Zelaszny's study. But a woman might.

*   *   *

177

The afternoon was parachute training, the aircraft the Beech 18 Margaret had seen before at Alameda, and she flew it in the hot sun at 2,000 feet and the others jumped. She landed alone and parked, and phoned Tequísquepec from the deserted bar in reception. Sabina would fly down, they told her, in the Stationair. Maybe when she got back, she thought, she could catch up on the sleep she'd been missing, every siesta time. Margaret hung up, turned.

And Mario Roca was there.

She caught her breath. He smiled at her, deep-eyed, knowing. He had two *refrescos* in front of him but he was alone.

'*Ven*. She won't be here for ten minutes.'

Something in Margaret's throat blocked her answering. She climbed on the stool beside Roca. All the old humour was still in his eyes, the reassuring wisdom. She was very, very pleased to speak to him again.

They clinked glasses. Roca said, smiling: 'It's been a long time since Lima.'

For a moment she didn't believe it. But she recovered, followed the L with an M. 'I must say I didn't expect you in Mexico.'

'In New York you'd have had more cause to be surprised.' An M with an N.

Dear God. All those years, and she'd never even dreamed he'd been working for DI. 'Mario, what is it?'

Concern was in his deep eyes, but Margaret wouldn't have understood it. Roca had talent-spotted this woman, he felt a paternal responsibility towards her; he'd got her into this predicament. He'd also in some measure made her what she was. That twelve-year-old in Lima with her head full of religious precepts and utter ignorance of the way she appeared to boys and men. She *had* been vulnerable; she *had* critically needed his lessons in self-defence. Yet at that same moment she'd been just discovering her own sexuality. So although that combat training, practising with a man, had been release for her aggression, it had linked violence with sex indivisibly in her mind so that from then on, maybe her whole life long, she would be frightened of both.

She was alive, though, which maybe she wouldn't have been otherwise.

'Caine's in San Diego and I'm linking you.' His voice was calm,

178

his face close, and she was aware of the warmth from him, the masculine aura of perspiration and after-shave. 'Can you report?'

Involuntarily she looked at her watch, though she knew Sabina couldn't be there yet. 'I haven't even sorted it into order . . .'

'*No importa.*'

'All right. Tequísquepec is Fight's world headquarters, it's defended by armed guerrillas commanded by Wanda Zelaszny. They've got a young kid up there, too, Giselle Stamm, she was kidnapped from her home and they've brainwashed her. She . . .' Margaret had to swallow.

'Easy.' Roca put his strong hand on her arm.

'They're ruthless. They've got a master plan for hijacking dangerous chemical loads to threaten cities.'

'Which cities?'

'I think I can find out.' She caught the tremor in her voice. The room felt cold but she knew her face was beaded.

'Find out, Margaret.' Roca was gripping her arm. 'Can you get access to any information about who and where Fight's guerrillas are? Film it and bring it to me.' Under the bar counter he was handing her a miniature camera and a cluster of film cassettes. 'You've used this type?'

'I've trained on it.' She thrust it into her flight briefcase. 'Mario, you must take care! They killed a woman last night. Paquita Villegas. She was Cuban, they said she was a spy.'

Their eyes met, Margaret's grey, wide with concern behind her glasses; Roca's deep and dark, wise and glare-wrinkled. But Roca's shifted away, because they'd both heard the engine as Sabina Stamm touched down in the Stationair.

CHAPTER 31

By the time Desatnick's report about Gregorio Tabio and what she'd done with him reached Pasarell, it was late afternoon, Tuesday, April 23, and the investigators at the Paris talks were looking forward to an evening off. Pasarell's news kept them going for some hours. For a start, all existing theories about involvement in Fight by Moscow and Havana had been stood on their heads.

The next question, once they'd all satisfied themselves that Desatnick had drawn the correct conclusions, was what to do about it. Every nation where Fight had been known to be active was represented at the talks – *except* the Communist powers. It took Barrington Yorke to voice the dilemma in plain English: should those present invite the KGB to join them at the Paris talks, or should they risk having two unco-ordinated operations against Fight, one in the West, one behind the Curtain, by which key members of Fight might escape?

Pasarell and Pedragoza threw up their hands in horror; it was almost the first time they'd agreed on anything. Brouzet seemed undecided.

Barrington Yorke was the only one who argued definitely in favour of inviting KGB participation. But in the vote he was overruled.

*   *   *

Pedragoza brought his own piece of news to the conference halfway through discussions on Wednesday, April 24. Paquita Villegas, the Cuban agent, was dead. They'd been talking over the implications of that for half an hour before Pasarell asked how Pedragoza knew: Pasarell should have had that from his own linkage, Desatnick in San Diego, and he'd heard no word.

Well, naturally, Pedragoza explained, Mexico has a covert unit monitoring the actions of Barrington Yorke's Peruvian agent, who made the discovery. 'As we agreed, did we not, Mr Barrington Yorke?'

'Certainly we agreed that Mexico would monitor Britain's linking agent.' Barrington Yorke nodded, bony hands folded. He could read doubt and suspicion in Frank Pasarell's mind.

Barrington Yorke had no such doubts, he knew perfectly well that information hadn't come through Roca. That meant that Mexican intelligence had an agent inside Tequísquepec. That was how they'd managed to send in Pedragoza so quickly: he was probably the deputy in an operation that was running already. It worried Barrington Yorke that Mexico hadn't seen fit to admit it; although the US stance hadn't been calculated to win its neighbour's trust.

But Barrington Yorke knew that Mexico's agent was one of a very small group at Zelaszny's convent: the men. They hadn't got a woman in there. A woman would have been into Fight's archives long ago and blown the whole thing open.

*　　*　　*

It was evening when Carla Desatnick trudged into the house off Mission Valley Road. She looked gloomy.

Richard Caine said: 'How did he take it?'

'How d'ya think?' She dumped her bag and jerked her cigarettes out of it. 'You wanna fix me a drink?'

Caine poured Jim Beam on the rocks. He was glad he hadn't had the task of breaking the news to Gregorio Tabio, cooling his heels in the lock-up at FBI headquarters, that his agent had just been butchered.

They drank; Desatnick threw her bourbon down.

She said: 'He wants us to turn him loose so he can go get revenge.'

'Any excuse.'

'Goddammit, *I*'d want revenge!' Her eyes blazed. 'If we'd let him go first off, if we'd just set tags . . .'

'It'll keep the silly bitches' minds off Rahab.' Steadily Caine made Desatnick another drink.

181

'Richard, that's a woman dead . . .'

He said: 'Radio, you know, that's how they got her.'

'So how come you trust Roca using radio?'

'He's got the new micro unit sending scrambled high-speed groups. Fight isn't going to strip-search him like they can anyone in their own backyard. He isn't transmitting from slap underneath their antennae, either, like Rahab would have to.' He stared Desatnick out. 'Radio sending from Tequísquepec would give Rahab away. Sending from the airport, it won't give Roca away.'

* * *

They were still arguing about it when the phone rang. It was FBI Washington, for Desatnick. Caine heard her going, 'Yeah . . . yeah . . .' with a lot of intervening silences, then she came back, looking sober.

'Cuba's been on to the State Department, demanding the release of an illegally held diplomat by the name of G. Tabio. State told 'em where they could stuff it. So now we have a polite Note from the Soviet embassy saying is it true the US Government has incarcerated this guy without trial, because if so it's against the Helsinki Accord on human rights 'n' all. From the Soviets! Shit!'

'And?' Caine said.

'State denies jailing anyone without trial, which we can prove. Meantime, they have actually spoken with Andreyev, who, surprise surprise, was behind the Soviet Note.'

That impressed Caine. 'What did they say to Andreyev?'

'They said, well, y'know, we have this constant problem with illegal immigration, and we don't know but it is *possible* your guy Tabio *might* be among these seventeen trillion guys we are currently checking out as suspected illegals. If we find he is, howsabout we deport him? But, oh no. Comrade Lieutenant-General Andreyev doesn't want *that* sort of thing on his guy's passport.' She flopped on the sofa and sighed.

* * *

In Paris it was still Wednesday, but only just, when Pasarell got the signal from Desatnick. It wasn't about Andreyev kicking up the dust, they knew about that in Paris already. It was to say that Roca had made contact with Rahab and was standing by to receive the information Paris needed to go ahead with the big strike against Fight.

CHAPTER 32

This evening was warmer. In the starlight Coral Bargellini and someone else were splashing in the pool, while Finito played his guitar again to Sharon Levenson and her Brazilian girlfriend, and Giselle sat at the opposite corner from him and ignored Pham Anh, trying to talk, until the Vietnamese kid gave up and went away. She looked so despondent, Margaret thought. If Sabina had thought bringing the girl here would make her happier, it hadn't worked, at least in the short run.

'Your combat's very good, Giselle, but you must remember you're light, and you mustn't get close in with a heavier opponent.'

Giselle turned, and flicked the long hair. She didn't smile, and Margaret realised she'd tempered the compliment with a criticism. She crossed her knees, in the old jeans, and shifted the Peruvian shawl to keep it from slipping. Giselle was wearing old jeans, too, tight on her hips, with a belled peasant-smock shirt.

'Sometimes I wish . . .' Then she turned her shoulder quickly.

Margaret leaned slightly. Starlight was catching tears on Giselle's cheeks. Margaret waited till Giselle dabbed at them. 'What do you wish?'

'Nothing.' An angry shrug. 'But you're just all on at me, all the time.' She paused. 'I've been in action now. I should have thought that was enough for you all to leave me alone, just for a little while.'

It was true, then, that she'd been there when they shot Paquita. Margaret had wondered, from the despairing way she'd gone at the unarmed-combat training.

'But you seem lonely here.'

'Maybe. But not alone.' Tears again. 'It . . . I . . .' Giselle dabbed her eyes, struggling. 'When I first went away with

184

Sabina, it was . . . it was horrible, but it was exciting, because the police were looking for us. It was almost like a game. When we left Germany to come here, Sabina said it would be just like living in a big family, only properly run, with everyone equal, and no male pig at the top making slaves of the women.'

Margaret waited. 'And is it?'

'No, it isn't, it was never meant to be. We're the spearhead of a guerrilla army. It's just not *like* a family. Things are better than in a male-dominated family, they're fairer, and we're all developing our true potential because without a male slavemaster we're free to do so. But . . . but there isn't much difference between having a man in supreme charge, and a woman.'

And Giselle did miss her family, however much she ranted against it. Sabina wasn't her true family. Her family was her father, who'd had the courage to change his mind, and the woman he'd married, as much for Giselle's sake as his own. Sabina was part of this guerrilla army that never let up the pressure on Giselle.

Scarcely audibly, the kid whispered: 'Sometimes I wish Sabina never had brought me here.'

Margaret swallowed, tried to think of an answer.

Frightened suddenly, Giselle turned, big eyes searching Margaret's face. 'Please, you won't tell anyone I said this?'

*   *   *

Lonely over the desert with the dawn sun low Margaret had the single-seat Mustang at full throttle, climbing, Sharon Levenson forty yards off the starboard tip, when the two black shapes solidified out of the dazzle, boring in fast. 'Falcon Flight, break left, two bandits ten o'clock high.' And the shove on the shoulders as the gravity pulled her deep in her seat, the slight slip of her glasses despite the sticking plaster, clinking more tangibly than audibly against the bridge of the oxygen mask.

Thursday, April 25, air combat training. Playing fighter pilots, with techniques a generation out of date.

Down on the ground with the flying suits half unzipped and the sweat cooling, Finito replayed the moves with his stiffened fingers simulating the Mustangs. 'You, Margarita, you lost a wingtip shot off, and we'd have come and caught you if you hadn't been clever. You, Sharon, Sabina got you. You blew up in mid-air.' They ran through it all. '*Bueno*, we take off again. This time, you bounce us.'

The sun higher now, the cockpit well sweltering, the blare of the engine filling her head, the two Mustangs banking round fast as Margaret led Sharon in. Then it got mixed up and it wasn't Margaret hunting Finito's fighter, it was Sabina Stamm in Margaret's six o'clock the way her father, the Nazi ace, had once hung on the tails of Russian and American and British fighters when Mustangs had been the latest thing in technology.

And Margaret terrified, even in the knowledge that this was a game, because she was throwing every trick in the book and she still couldn't escape.

Noon, and they were exhausted. *Refrescos* in the bar at reception, and the shock-headed barman in his white coat serving them.

Margaret left the alert signal for Mario Roca, the way they'd agreed.

*　　*　　*

She picked the siesta. The combination for the archives door was in Zelaszny's study; she knew because she'd seen it. Michiko Ishida, from the Bodyguard, was hanging round the patio, and would have seen anyone approaching Zelaszny's eyrie through the admin wing. But no one was there to see Margaret go in from the library and try the door at the top of the spiral stair.

Locked. Aware of her danger, Margaret located the electronic warner. She parted its wires and worked on the lock. It took longer than she'd thought. Her ears were straining but all she could hear was her breath, shallow, trembling, and the lub-dub, lub-dub of her heart, crashing like marching feet through the empty library.

The door opened. She stepped in quickly. She hated this task. Loosening tongues was one thing, but she wouldn't talk her way out of this. Alarm panel. She slid the card across the printed circuit the way they'd shown her, she counted the fuses. Four, five, six. Out, all of them.

She breathed again.

Combination. She'd triple-checked. What she hadn't triple-

186

checked was whether Finito had told her the truth in the first place or whether he'd sent her into a trap. 28°55′N, 112°2′W. Reverse it. Fighting to keep her fingers steady, she turned the dials. A strand of hair came loose and tickled.

And Finito hadn't lied. In the centre of the dial, the pearl-coloured disc glowed green.

Library: clear. Margaret went back down the spiral stair and into the archives.

A light was on already in the windowless, vault-like chamber. The combination had turned it on. Dear Lord, keep the library empty, don't let anyone go to Zelaszny's study.

Priority one: master plan. The cities: New York, Chicago, Los Angeles, London, Munich, Tokyo. The types of chemicals, the way they behaved, the way you transported them. Addresses of the plants that made them; addresses of the plants where they carried them. Margaret noticed a couple of hazardous-chemical movement schedules for the London area that bore Mary Abbott's sourceline.

It took a while before it sank in that she wasn't looking at a master plan at all. Fight hadn't got one. What she was looking at was a collection of intelligence reports, of varying degrees of up-to-date-ness and presumably of reliability also, on which one day action *might* be based.

The idea, though, that was nasty enough. Margaret started on deployment.

Once again, disillusionment surprised her. Nadezhda Sokolova's net that was supposedly being built up in the Comecon countries scarcely existed apart from a few cells in Cuba. Miranda Nwokoye's African and Asian net didn't even exist on paper, let alone on the ground.

The Western world, Japan included, was a different matter. The US had the biggest cell structure of all, but in Canada, Mexico, Brazil there were significant numbers. Japan had eighty names. Europe, too: France, Belgium, West Germany, Italy; a hundred-odd guerrillas in the UK. But this was the last file.

She was putting it back when Julie O'Dell's name caught her eye.

She was long past the time she'd allowed herself as safe. But this was something she had to know, and she reached in and took out the file. She didn't bother with the camera, she just read the file, memorised it.

It *had* been Lorraine Easson who'd killed Julie. The knife. She'd already guessed.

But there was more to it, there was background that Margaret hadn't suspected, and something caught in her throat as she read it, something that brought tears to her eyes in a surge of rage and despair.

*   *   *

At the airfield before the late afternoon's flying Margaret muttered that she had to go to the loo first. Sharon Levenson thought that was a good idea, which was a nuisance, and Margaret had to wait in the heavy, foetid shadows, sweat rolling off her, until Sharon was clear. When she timed the wait, Mario Roca was there in the half-light in the ridiculous and malodorous passage that linked the *caballeros* with the *señoras*.

She gave him the camera quickly, and the used and unused cassettes. 'All the names and the chemicals stuff. Mario, listen, the chemicals stuff isn't even a coherent plan yet. If we can stop them collecting details of the movements schedules, they'll be helpless.'

Roca smiled in the half-light. Without a word, he raised Margaret's slim hand to his lips and kissed it. Then they turned their backs and went quickly out, and never saw each other alive again.

CHAPTER 33

Less resentment might have been caused all around, Frank Pasarell caught himself thinking on Thursday, April 25, if, just once, Pedragoza had turned up at half past eight to the Paris conference room with his tie crooked, or looking even slightly hungover. Pasarell's body clock was still on New York time even four days after arriving; he was having trouble getting to sleep at night and even more trouble getting up in the morning. He could forgive Brouzet and Barrington Yorke. Brouzet had garlic breath and baggy eyes as if he always discussed existentialism until four in the morning; and Barrington Yorke, in the sole, shiny suit that he'd brought from London, always looked like a professor from a very obscure university. But Pedragoza always walked in, straight-backed, with his Latin grace and his bright, alert eyes, and not a crease wrong on his immaculate, coffee-coloured suit. Worse than that, though, his brain was always in perfect working order.

He kicked off on Thursday with a request from his bosses in Mexico City – expressed more as an intention – that, when the big strike against Fight took place, Mexican intelligence should detain Rahab for debriefing. Oh, yes, well, with access for certain other interested parties, of course.

Barrington Yorke folded bony hands together and settled his leather elbow patches on the conference table. He didn't like the sound of that. No one who knew Rahab's identity had leaked it at the talks. But Mexico knew about Roca and was monitoring him – by consent – and Roca had made contact maybe twice now with Rahab. It would be naïve to suppose the Mexicans didn't know who she was.

'May I take it that the UK would be one of those "interested parties", who, according to this proposal, would be granted

189

access to Rahab?'

'Certainly, sir.'

'Maybe, Mr Pedragoza, you'd be good enough to provide some more details of the proposal. How long would Mexican intelligence plan to detain Rahab? How would she be treated?'

'We would detain Rahab as long as necessary for full debriefing. The UK's own observers could verify the matter. Rahab would naturally be treated as she deserves.'

At least, Pasarell thought, Pedragoza didn't disguise it when he was making up the script as he went along.

Barrington Yorke leaned a little forward. 'So if the Mexican authorities deemed Rahab to have committed any offence, they might bring her to trial – irrespective of the practical value of whatever intelligence she may have supplied to this operation.'

'Sir, there has been no agreement on immunity from civil charges.'

They could get her on anything, Pasarell recognised. Slap a charge on her, bring her before a court, and hold her as long as they liked. He was starting to dislike Pedragoza a lot. Treating Rahab 'as she deserved' might involve rough handling if she tried to resist. It might involve almost anything.

'What would be the attitude of the Mexican authorities,' Barrington Yorke asked, 'if for any reason Rahab found it necessary to leave unconventionally?'

In her socks, that was what he meant.

'Naturally, sir, we should wish to prevent Rahab from leaving Mexico without consulting us. As you would yourselves in the opposite case.'

Barrington Yorke said: 'Mr Pedragoza, Her Majesty's Government would like a written undertaking from the Mexican authorities agreeing how long Rahab would be detained for questioning, ensuring her immunity from civil charges, and providing certain guarantees regarding her treatment.'

Pedragoza gave him a dubious look. 'I shall pass on your request, sir.'

Someone said what about Gregorio Tabio: he was in the same boat in the States that Rahab might shortly be in Mexico. Tabio, Barrington Yorke pointed out, was much more use to the operation back in Havana and attacking Fight than in an FBI cell in San Diego. Pasarell had to agree, in principle; but in practice,

190

Andreyev was getting on everyone's nerves, and handing Tabio back looked a bit like yielding to Soviet pressure.

But this was a case where the principle of attacking Fight came first.

Pasarell sighed. 'Okay, never mind what it looks like. I'll try and get him sent home to sweep out his backyard while we sweep out ours.'

CHAPTER 34

Visibility was hardest in the burning sky. Yet again Margaret craned her neck, wrenching on the muscles, straining against the harness. And got it, the tiny black razor-edge, coming at her out of the dazzle. Break. And the *g* force, driving her down into the cockpit well as she stood the Mustang on a wingtip and the Mirage came in, *no, much too close, no*! And then slamming the thing level through the slipstream to try for a shot in the camera guns before Sabina vanished into sun again.

Dissimilar air combat. It meant practising against another sort of aircraft. Big Phantoms practising against little F5s, simulating MiG21s, were one thing. Sabina Stamm in a Mirage she seemed determined to use on bisecting your Mustang was another.

And with the radar in the Mirage, Sabina could find a Mustang very quickly and precisely. All you had in the Mustang was a light that flashed on the panel when the little antenna built into your tailcone started picking up pulses from the opposition's search radar.

They landed, evening light bleeding into the sky. Margaret was drained, physically and mentally. Sharon had flown the other Mustang, Charlotte Rondeau the other Mirage; but Sabina had flown deliberately dangerously, deliberately harassing Margaret with risky close flying. And then demonstrated her mastery by deft, split-second evasion.

In the sickly, acrid darkness of the flimsy cubicle Margaret changed out of the sweat-heavy flying overall and into jeans and shirt. In the bar, Rondeau was sitting over tequila with a disdainful Sabina. Sharon hadn't come in yet. Sabina gave Margaret the same hard stare she'd used in the debriefing, determined to psych her out. The Mirage's gun camera had shown only a couple of hits on the Mustang, Margaret's responses prompt, and Sabina hadn't liked that. Maybe she was afraid of Margaret putting subversive ideas into Giselle's head, like loving people.

'Just a *refresco*, thanks.'

The shock-headed barman, face solemn, caught Margaret's eye as he passed her glass. His hand lingered just long enough to show her the slip of paper between two fingers.

She took it fast and tucked it in her sleeve.

Sharon came in. Margaret had finished half her drink, though it hadn't been easy. 'Must go to the loo again,' she mumbled. And slipped out. Round the corner of the building she opened the note. It was in Spanish. *See me urgently*. No signature, but there was only one person who would have sent it.

Margaret trod the note into the dusty earth. She made for the Water Commission offices. Something wasn't right, she knew it.

Purple in the improbable sky was turning to Prussian blue of night. The shadows fell chilly. No lights were on in the offices as Margaret went in. Her eyes probed the shadow, no sound reached her. The building was lifeless. Fright crawled in her scalp.

In the corridor with its lingering aura of cooling-fan grease and coarse tobacco she counted doors. She opened Roca's door but waited on the threshold, wondering what it was that made her nose wrinkle.

Dried blood. She snapped on the light, risk forgotten.

Mario Roca was on his back where they'd dumped him, his tanned face turned aside and his wise eyes sightless, red in his silver hair and drying on his torn, white civil servant's shirt. Vision blurred. When it returned, Margaret was hanging on the door, stomach surging. Her brain wasn't working any more, and it didn't matter if that *was* the reaction of an amateur.

She took one pace into the room and behind her Coral Bargellini said, voice like a cleaver, 'Okay, shithead, don't try anything. You're covered.'

Window, Mustang, scramble. But she was only halfway to the light switch to blind Coral when the shutters swung and Lorraine Easson vaulted through, hard-eyed, an M3 in her hands. Giselle came through behind with another and they spread out, crouched, a well drilled team, guns on Margaret, as Coral walked in with a Smith & Wesson .38, at her shoulder Sharon Levenson and Rondeau and Sabina Stamm with M3s.

Just for a moment it was relief, the end to the long deception. Then Margaret saw the hatred in Coral's multicoloured eyes and knew instantly how she was going to die.

*   *   *

After the rough, angry body search at Tequísquepec they gave Margaret's clothes back. Her glasses weren't with them and that shook her confidence. Tension speared into her stomach, fatigue throbbed in her brain. She was as good as dead. Now.

And therefore they could do what they liked with her, she didn't care, they'd killed Mario Roca and Paquita Villegas and Julie O'Dell and all the others and now Margaret herself, so she would fight them to the last protest of misused nerve endings that put the remains of her brain into terminal shock.

The basement room was cut into the limestone of Tequísquepec. Its chill shocked Margaret, after the heat. Zelaszny was at a desk with Coral beside her, the black Jodie Sadler standing one side of them, Giovanna Piotti the other. They were carrying M3s because, Margaret realised, the slow, heavy 9mm round would enter human tissue and stay there, unlike the 7.62mm that the FAL fired, which was so powerful it would go straight through and then ricochet round the room. Lorraine and Sabina gripped Margaret's arms as she faced Zelaszny, taller than her captors, dry-mouthed, fighting her shivering.

Zelaszny studied her for some moments. Her voice seemed to come from far away. 'I didn't expect this from you, Margaret.'

Margaret took her mind away and saw herself, momentarily, in the old Seneca, going through the updraught at Denham.

'We trusted you. We showed you around, we gave you responsibility. And this is thanks. You certainly know how to put folks' backs up.'

Or maybe those first flying lessons. Clear air over the Andes, the ochre dirt of Cuzco.

'Take a look.'

Cuzco vanished and the camera was on Zelaszny's desk, open; close by, the developed microfilms. Poor Mario, he hadn't even got them out.

'Why Mexico? That's what gets me.' Zelaszny seemed to be

musing rather than interrogating. 'Why operate with a squad of Mexican goons? And then get out away from them where we could get him?'

Guilt sweated from Margaret's temples, the torment worse than any pain. She could see it now. Mario had been in there with Mexican clearance but the Mexicans had sent a team to monitor him. He'd known it. And in striving to keep Margaret's identity from the Mexicans he'd been so slippery with them that they'd got clumsy, they'd given themselves away to Fight. And so him also. And so her. He must have been trying to get the films out from under the Mexicans' noses when the Fight guerrillas took him. But he wouldn't have given them much. Not Mario.

Zelaszny's voice had been soft. But it went hard now. 'Okay, Margaret, now, we don't have time for luxuries like rehabilitation. So we're going to have to kill you.' That's news? Dear Lord, let me hold out till You receive my spirit. 'But first you're going to tell us everything.'

Yes, all you want. About those cloudless days in Cuzco and the mental anguish when the earthquakes mutilated people you loved, good people, people who'd suffered enough already and who still trusted God, for all the pain. All the pain. And the simple people who took it without complaint, silent in their grief. Silent in the torture. Silent, as a malign nature battered their brains with loss no one could bear. Silent in the confidence, rooted in body, that God wouldn't let them down.

* * *

Vision part-returned through the haze of stomach-turning agony and it was no malign nature that had battered Margaret, it was people with heads full of hate. Cold penetrated the pain and in her limp huddle on the stone she shivered, but she knew she'd told nothing.

Distant, Lorraine Easson said: 'More softening-up, that's what the cow needs.'

'We won't get anything out of her tonight.' Tina Zeiss; voice inappropriately concerned. 'Leave her get some breath back.'

'I say we knock the fight out of her now.' Sabina.

Coral said: 'She's conscious again.'

Pause. Pain grinding through the shivering flesh, irrelevant.

195

She was dead already.

'Margaret.' The voice, soft despite the curt tone, close by her head. She didn't trust it yet she couldn't ignore it.

Tina was crouching, with her pointed chin, and concern in her big, slanting eyes mixed with guilt because she was braving the others' disapproval to do this. 'C'm'on.' She had water.

Margaret shifted slightly. The water moistened her lips and thinned the taste of blood in her mouth. Gratitude overwhelmed her and she couldn't speak. But then Tina had gone.

A steel grab fastened in her hair that when it jerked neck-wrenchingly backwards was attached to Sabina, distorted and distant, savage. 'We try some more, Leader, or. . . ?'

In the pause, a creaking sound came from Margaret's throat. Pain tears she hadn't known she'd shed dried tautly on her cheeks.

'No,' Zelaszny said. 'Put her under the Sacromonte and see how she likes the drip treatment.'

CHAPTER 35

It was lunchtime in San Diego when Carla Desatnick got her new orders from the State Department, relayed via FBI Washington. Gregorio Tabio was no longer an illegal immigrant, he wasn't even an undesirable alien. Instead he had diplomatic status, as of now, and would Assistant Special Agent-in-Charge Desatnick kindly go find out what she could do for Señor Tabio.

She went. Within two hours, Tabio was on a flight for Havana, where he intended to do everything necessary to knock the fight out of Fight in Cuba.

The US Justice Department was under pressure from Pasarell now, not just Desatnick, and finally it gave in and approached the air force. The operation was at a crucial phase and they had to have electronic surveillance.

The air force had its first E3A on station, flying from a base outside Phoenix, Arizona, at 1600 Pacific time, running a tightish, racetrack pattern at 42,000 feet and sweeping the Alameda and Tequísquepec areas with its radar. A second was on its way south from Nevada to take over when the first one's crew ran out of coffee.

Five minutes later, at 1605 Pacific time, 1705 at Tequísquepec, Richard Caine's radio receiver bleeped in San Diego. When he unscrambled the signal on the tape, it was from Mario Roca. He'd got Rahab's films, he was on his way out with them.

And then for a long time nothing happened.

Carla Desatnick was staying away from the Jim Beam, she needed her head clear. She wasn't staying away from cigarettes, though. The house off Mission Valley Road was a thick blue haze in the warmth as late afternoon became early evening.

'Sit down and calm down,' Richard Caine said. He was smoking, too, but nothing like so much. 'He's travelling, he's not going to radio in at every crossroads.'

'Well, how come that goddam plane can't pick his car up on its radar?' Desatnick grumbled.

Caine ignored her. She knew as well as he did what sort of definition the E3A had, and it wasn't going to be scanning for individual, private cars.

The E3A wasn't in direct radio contact with San Diego. But it was with its Phoenix base and it had some capability for telemetry: data transmission direct from the computers on the aircraft to terminals on the ground. At Phoenix a USAF major had responsibility for keeping Desatnick up-to-date with the E3A's findings.

He phoned in shortly after seven. 'Airborne radar's reporting aircraft movements, ma'am, looks like a combat training detail. We have two traces at jet speeds and two that could be a high-powered prop type, and we're guessing Mirages for the first and Mustangs for the second.'

Desatnick considered. 'You don't have any sign of one of them breaking away for the north?'

'No, ma'am. But what they are reporting is what they figure to be military vehicles. They can't be entirely sure, as these traces are right on the limit of the radar's range, but they look like they're south of Tequísquepec.'

That got her guessing. 'What are these things doing?'

'Seems like nothing very much, ma'am.'

She hung up. She lit another cigarette, but it didn't help the deductive processes. Caine didn't offer any helpful ideas, either, but he didn't like it. Desatnick could tell, from the sudden way he stopped nagging her.

At 2005 the phone rang again, and again Desatnick grabbed it. 'Hello?'

'Carla? Frank.'

And something was wrong. Wrong enough for Pasarell to be phoning on an open line from Paris. Where it was five in the morning.

'What is it?'

'Pedragoza has just had word from his own local sources that Roca's dead.'

'Oh, Jesus. Oh, no. What about Rahab?'

'No word.' Pasarell sounded deadpan but Desatnick knew he

was just as shocked as she was. 'I'm enciphering what details we know on to telex right now. You should have it, uh, maybe ten minutes.'

They hung up. Desatnick swung round from the phone and for the first time let herself go, let herself screech at Caine the way she'd been building up to for a week.

The telex arrived but it hardly told them more than Pasarell's phone call had.

Caine tapped an unlit cigarette on his case. He was frowning, his voice no more than a mutter. 'We don't even know who that bastard Pedragoza's source is. We don't know how Fight got Roca. We can only guess where this Mexican source is. We can only guess what this electronic stuff on "military vehicles" might mean.'

Desatnick jumped to her feet. 'I'm going to Phoenix. I'm getting on that next E3A when it goes up. You're in charge here.'

Caine stared. 'What the hell for? All you're going to see is a load of little electronic blips that mean bugger-all to you. You'll be cooped up on that plane for God knows how long . . .'

'Eight hours they stay on station.'

'. . . in no position to do anything if the thing blows up in our faces down here.'

'Listen, wise-ass, it blew up already. At least up there I can trace which way the fragments come down.' She picked up the phone.

TEQUÍSQUEPEC
HILL

Sierra Madre Occidental →

Sacromonte

Small-arms range

Pasture

Forestry clearance

'The Convent'

Finito's cottage

Altipuerto

↓ To Alameda

Forest

Low scrub

Roads

Slopes

metres

0   300   600   900

N

MISSION

CHAPTER 36

Without anyone needing to speak, they all halted, involuntarily, on the edge of the underground lake beneath the Sacromonte. This was a ritual, Margaret thought absently. It was as if they'd all become possessed by the spirits of the ancient people who'd come here to perform their own ritual sacrifices.

Partly it was the damp down here, partly the loss of body heat, through pain and exhaustion, partly the way they'd left her stripped to the waist, wearing only jeans. But she felt bitterly cold.

'*Move*!' Coral yelled, the command echoing over the water's rush, and they marched Margaret the length of the lake's edge and under the drip.

Maybe it had been a premonition, her being so scared here with Finito.

Coral said: 'Okay!'

Lorraine Easson grabbed one of Margaret's arms, Sabina Stamm the other, yanking them high, cracking her head into the rock wall so that the vomit almost spilt up from her churning stomach. The stakes were higher than she'd thought, meant for a man, perhaps.

The first drip hit her as they lashed her wrists to the rusty metal. It shattered on the crown of her head like a bullet of ice and the pain swelled slowly into a big, cold globe in her brain, long after the drop had gone. It was a double torture, she realised detachedly. Body weight swung you forward and down, as in crucifixion, and, similarly, death would come when the muscles grew too weary to hold the weight off the lungs. Then you would asphyxiate.

She might even die before morning and maybe that wasn't such a bad thing.

Drip. The ice bullet burst against her skull and the pain speared through her, swelling the cold globe of agony in her brain.

Coral lifted a big handlamp. They were facing her in a semicircle, backed off and below, Lorraine, Sabina, Sharon Levenson, Jodie Sadler, Tina Zeiss, even little Giselle, the same wild light in all their eyes.

Tina gave a shriek of laughter, echoing. It sounded hysterical.

Coral called out: 'Well, it's one helluva way to spend Easter!' Then they were all laughing, the jackal cries mingling away with the water.

The weight dragged on her trapezius muscles. Her breasts hung limp, pathetic. Another drip crashed into her.

'How does it feel, spy?' Giselle shouted. 'You're going to die!'

So vicious in front of the others, Margaret thought; she felt such a need to impress the senior guerrillas. Really trying to please parent figures all the time.

Lorraine sneered: 'You won't look so tough come morning.'

Drip, the pain shivering through her skull. Then her eyes chanced on Tina's. Strangely, there was fright, and, almost, compassion in the wide-eyed gaze.

Coral laughed stonily. 'So long, spy. You won't get down from there, but if you do, don't imagine you'll get away. Find your way out of this rabbit warren and all you'll trip over is the guard on the door. Okay, now hang there and rot!'

Then when they'd gone there was total, almost tangible blackness, filled with the mind-eroding echo of the water and the brain-rending, slow bullets of the drip.

*　　*　　*

Drip. And drip. And drip. And drip.

No wonder it sent you insane; it was impossible not to keep bracing yourself for the next one and yet you always mistimed it. *Drip*, and the lights blazed again in your skull so that the anguish of your torn, chafed wrists on the stakes and the cramp in your neck and stomach and the weight on your shoulders were all trivial irritations compared with the bursting of your brain. In the utter darkness the flashing lights were hallucinations. A bad trip. Maybe it was all a bad trip, a bad drip, a mad drip.

Drip. And drip. And drip. And drip.

*   *   *

Once upon another planet there'd been a girl child in an enchanted valley of copper-skinned people in red ponchos who'd been kind, gentle, and so silent that you didn't know they were suffering.

Drip.

Only when the mountains fell and the water stopped. Then someone with a crushed limb couldn't keep from screaming and the girl child's games of doctors and nurses suddenly meant something, but nothing, because there was nothing you could do but watch them die, your friends.

Drip.

God let it happen. They didn't understand it and nor did you, but God wasn't less real for leaving someone under the drip with the weight of the universe on their lungs, so you resolved to come back one day, come back and save your friends.

Drip.

Medicine and flying so in the midst of death there could be life or at least could once have been. But Julie had died and the menace had been more pressing, and so many more lives you had to save, sooner, more urgently, but now it was all so futile and not just because of the drip, drip, drip, drip.

Drip.

Those whom the gods wish to destroy they first make mad, using Chinese water torture, for instance. But the gods of the ancient priests, they were false gods, the true God was different. Maybe there was some supernatural deal involved, like with Job in the Old Testament; how else could God let them get away with it? But He'd let the earthquakes happen. He could let a woman go mad for the hubris of a project to take life to the midst of death.

Drip.

And dear God, He had, because the light beside the black lake came closer even after she blinked, and for all her disbelieving it there was a man's shape behind it.

*   *   *

Finito grinned up at her, shining the torch. '*Hola, guapa. ¿Qué tal?*'

She was hallucinating. He kept coming and going through the pounding behind her eyes and the drip.

She croaked: 'Take that light out of my eyes.' It swung away. Lips cracked, Margaret said: 'What do you want?'

He chuckled. A whiff of tequila reached her. 'What will you give me if I cut you down?'

She wanted to screech at him but was too weary. There was no call to taunt her. '*Eres loco.*'

He shouted with laughter, the sound bouncing crazy echoes all round the cavern and tangling itself up with the whirl of the water. Then he reached up and sliced through the ropes lashing her to the twin stakes.

Margaret's legs buckled and she collapsed forward and he caught her and then for some seconds she must have blacked out in incredulous relief. Next she knew, he was lifting her bodily, her head on his shoulder, his arms, one round her shoulders, one under her knees, a more powerful man than she'd imagined, his warmth consoling her, close, with the sweetness of tequila on his breath and his voice soft, loving almost, whispering to her. '*Eh, mi pobrecita,* you're frozen, they must be crazy; what have they done to you?' That was when she gave in and the silent sobs came up rackingly out of her, hot tears on Finito's broad chest as he carried her caressingly along the lake's edge.

Something got through from memory, filtered by the mind's self-protective mechanism of unreality.

'Finito . . . g-guard at the . . .'

He chuckled. '*Chito, niña.* They left Lorraine on guard and she's sleeping like a baby. *Mira.*'

They were level with the tunnel mouth. A lamp stood just inside it, battery running down, and in the bubble of light Lorraine had her head on her knees, breathing evenly.

'We can't . . . get p-past . . .'

'We don't need to.'

Round a rock buttress there was another tunnel and Finito carried Margaret into it and after that she took little notice of what was happening until they came out in the clean night air among a jumble of limestone under the cypresses.

Finito swung into the saddle without even releasing Margaret. He made her sip water as they jogged slowly, gently down the moonlit trail. He was rubbing the warmth back into her shivering body and caressing her bare breasts at the same time and she wouldn't have protested, even if it hadn't made her feel so good.

*   *   *

In the low-raftered, white *cortijo* a pine fire smouldered, resiny and warm. Finito lowered Margaret on to a couch and it was so soft that she passed into sleep in the forty-five seconds it took him to come back with a big slug of tequila.

'Sip that. No, sip it.'

You're supposed to drink tequila by tipping back the lot in one go, but if Margaret had tried that, she'd have choked herself. Patiently Finito sat and made her sip it. When she'd finished, he was holding a dressing gown for her.

'*¿Cómo va eso?*'

She felt much more alive. 'What'll happen when they find I've gone?'

Over the wide fireplace, a clock ticked softly. It said 0255.

Finito murmured: 'I'll look after you. They'll never find you here. There's plenty of time, and first you need rest.'

Fatigue weakened her brain function and she believed him. Scented woodsmoke filled her senses and Finito's deep eyes looked kind, concerned.

'*Anda.*' He helped her up and supported her through a door and she gasped, to see a sunken bath of warm bubbles in an elegant, tiled room. She collapsed on a couch, the dressing gown wrapped round her bare shoulders, and let the warmth pervade her body in creeping sleep as Finito slipped the jeans off her and then eased her, naked, into the sensuous luxury of the water. She let her eyes close, her body lying limp among the bubbles as Finito touched her and caressed her, and as the relaxation overtook her, the pain of the drip, the bruises, the chafing, receded. In that moment, she could have given in to the feelings.

But there was still enough edge left to make her check Finito's watch: 0311.

Out and dried, she lay on the couch again and Finito massaged her with oil from a bottle. 'This'll make you feel better. We used

207

to use this when I played football for the air force.'

He was right: the knots of cramp had gone, the pain dulled. If only the weariness could have retreated as far. She squeezed away tears. 'I don't see . . . why you're doing this for me.'

'*Es cosa de honor.*' Anger flashed in his dark eyes; you didn't argue when someone from the Spanish tradition said a thing was a matter of honour. 'I'm responsible, if only partly.' His soft voice was bitter. 'You know about my darkroom and that stuff. The *gringa* came to me to develop the microfilms you passed to Roca.'

He saw the jolt, saw Margaret bite her lip. He wanted to hold her but he knew this wasn't the time.

'Margarita, you know I wasn't there, you know I knew nothing about it.' His murmur was urgent. 'They said he was tough, that *hombre*. He didn't tell them a word. He didn't tell them about you – they'd already seen you rendezvous with him. And he died before they could even hurt him that much. Heart failure.'

Margaret wanted to believe that. But, either way, it didn't alter the fact that she was guilty again, over another death.

'Catalina Sánchez's in trouble,' Finito said. 'Two spies in three days. She's supposed to be in charge of security, over Jo Colwell's head.' Colwell was chief of the Bodyguard. 'And that *gringa* sits up there theorising while Catalina's supporters squabble with Coral Bargellini's supporters over whose fault it was.'

Coral's, by implication, for bringing Margaret with her from New York; Sánchez's for letting her into the convent at all. She realised slowly what Finito was saying. The guerrillas were splitting into at least two camps, possibly even with a threat to Zelaszny's power. Coral, Margaret knew, saw herself as Zelaszny's successor; a big enough bungle at Tequísquepec might suggest to her that her time had come to oust Zelaszny. Fight's HQ had never been weaker.

'Will you forgive me for developing the microfilm?' Finito muttered.

Margaret turned her head, chestnut hair loose, tousled. Her lips wouldn't form the smile and all she saw was the time: 0328.

Determination replaced the plea in Finito's eyes. 'I'll show you why you should forgive me. *Ven.*'

He took her arm, she gathered the dressing gown round her

208

and limped after him.

The darkroom contained the predictable blow-ups of ladies in the skin: one of them Coral, surprisingly; another, a pretty Vietnamese girl Margaret had noticed in the convent. There was a superb study of one of the horses.

And the microcamera, on a workbench beside an OM1 and a Hasselblad.

'The *gringa* made me bring it here,' he said. 'For tests. I could have told her one obvious way to test it.' He turned.

Margaret blinked. 'Are you suggesting. . . ?'

'A deal. I can get the exposed films from the convent.'

Her lip was quivering. 'And is getting out of here included?'

'Depends on the extent of the deal.'

A successful operation. For her body.

Listen, kid, we're not in the nineteenth century now. But the plain, primitive physical contact, it frightened her. *No one still figures it's a fate worse than death.* The idea, though. The terror in relinquishing her mind's restraint over her body. All right, then, Margaret Stubbs, beat your hang-ups.

Finito said: 'Suppose I throw these in, too?' He held out her glasses.

Margaret smiled, slowly, eyes on Finito's face. 'All right. It's a deal.'

*   *   *

She tossed the dressing gown on the chair and climbed between the sheets. The bedroom was dimly lit, cool from the night that was visible as a slender, dark upright between the full-length shutters part-open on to the terraces. The emptiness reminded Margaret of the giddy drop beyond the terrace, deep into the canyon, and she wasn't sure which was more frightening, being out there or being in here. But she was committed now. She wouldn't let herself be afraid.

It was 0351. Finito threw down his clothes. Naked, he had the same tan all over. His broad, powerful build lent him tangible presence, and the muscles in his chest, shoulders, thighs promised gentleness as well as strength. Rich, dark hair covered his chest and legs.

He grinned at her. '*Momento.*'

He slipped on the dressing gown and walked out, belting it. Margaret heard the key turn in the outside door. She wondered, fleetingly, why he should lock the door when the bedroom shutters were open on to the high terrace, but it wasn't important. Not as important as the next few minutes.

When he walked back in, he threw himself full length beside her, tearing the sheet away from her, without even stopping to take off the dressing gown. His lips pressed against hers and opened and as his body stretched against hers she knew he was well roused, and she reached against him, fingertips touching his face as he thrust his hand between their bodies, hard on her breast. Moving her legs subtly against him, Margaret drew her hands down to his jaw.

Then slipped them crosshanded on to his lapels high under the chin.

His grin broadened. He chuckled. '*Tigre-gata*,' he said, 'tigercat.'

Steadily Margaret tightened up the strangle.

'¡*Basta*!' Finito said suddenly. 'That's enough.' She said nothing, just kept her eyes fixed on his and tightened the strangle. He said, 'Lay off right now or I'll hurt you!' She said nothing, just went on reading Finito's eyes.

And was ready for it when he pitched sideways off the bed.

White-knuckled, she clung on, falling out of bed as he went over, refusing to be shaken loose, even if they rolled out on the terrace, and now he knew she meant it and he grabbed at her wrists, jerking against her grip slowly tightening and starting to frighten him now. Still she clung on. With an angry grunt he rolled over, still hoping to shake her off, and with a crash they went into a JVC speaker.

Margaret knew she'd won. Finito wasn't fighting for his life.

He realised now that all he'd done was tighten her grip and with his eyes wide in panic and his breath gone he clutched desperately at her wrists, fighting to break her hold. His mouth was open but no sound came. Then his eyes rolled upwards, he lost consciousness.

Hating herself, Margaret counted five more long seconds and let go. Finito sagged limply. She grabbed his wrist, terrified, but the pulse was still there. She straightened, breathing quickly.

Finito's pruning cutters were on the kitchen table and she

dashed back with them, clipped off a length of flex from the hi-fi and tied his hands and feet firmly. A dishcloth served as a gag.

She was taking away his watch when Lorraine Easson walked in carrying a Smith & Wesson .38 Military Airweight and a personal radio.

* * *

Margaret realised she was facing Lorraine, naked, lips parted, shock drumming in her mind. Through the red starry film of disbelief Lorraine nodded knowingly, hard-eyed, her pistol pointing at Margaret's stomach.

'Bloody brilliant. All mouth, that bloke. Trust him to bugger the whole thing up. "Give her the soft-sell, works wonders." Mother Superior must want her head read for buying that.' She jerked the pistol. 'Okay, cow, grab stratosphere, the orgy's over.'

So that was it. Slowly Margaret raised her hands. Hard-sell, soft-sell, the old, old interrogation technique. What a fool, not to realise. Lorraine never had been asleep; Finito had gone to the door to open it, not lock it.

'Stupid prick,' Lorraine said to Finito's inert body. Legs spaced in her uniform and boots, she kept her eyes on Margaret and fumbled for the transmit switch on the radio in her left hand. For a moment she couldn't find it, and she glanced down.

Margaret swung both feet in a leap that got Lorraine's gun hand with one heel and stomach with the other and as the .38 blasted splinters from a rafter and bounced through on to the terrace Lorraine tumbled backwards. Margaret slammed both arms out, breakfalling, then jack-knifed into a fast follow through. Lorraine caught her shoulders against the wall, knew she was propped, and swung a boot. It hit Margaret glancingly, hard, on one thigh. As Margaret evaded, Lorraine grabbed down to her belt.

She pointed the sheath-knife at Margaret. The one with the notch. The one that had killed Julie O'Dell.

They faced one another, breathing tensely. The radio lay in a corner.

'Right,' Lorraine said, eyes glittering. She grinned. 'Right.'

Margaret looked at the blade and contemplated the classic

counter for a knife attack but reflected that Lorraine knew too much judo for that to work. It would just put Margaret closer to the knife. She never had beaten Lorraine at judo. Fright in her mind rose towards terror.

'Jodie's mob's on their way up from the convent,' Lorraine said, 'but they'll be too late. They want you alive, but sod that. I'm killing you.'

Of all the possible situations Margaret had trained for, the last one she'd have expected was to be unarmed, naked, with a hundred-foot drop at her back and a killer with a knife at her front.

'You killed Julie.'

'You bet I bloody well did. *And* I'll kill you, you cow. Resisting arrest, how about that? Go on, look scared. I mean it. Julie was nice and scared, like a rabbit, paralysed. But she never suffered enough. You'll suffer.'

Margaret was edging backwards. She wasn't ready for it when Lorraine struck like a snake and at once recoiled back out of reach, grinning. But the knife had drawn blood, a nick on Margaret's stomach.

'See what I mean?'

Now Margaret knew. That lunge could have been right into her. *You will win; never forget it; never let them make you doubt it.* But he was dead now and Lorraine had Margaret psyched. She was never going to beat Lorraine's knife unarmed.

But then, she didn't need to.

'I want you to be really scared,' Lorraine said, almost crooning. 'I could cut you to bits with this knife. Much worse than I did with Julie – she got off lightly. Or of course you could fall over the terrace. Nice long drop down there, Maggie.'

The height. It was the main reason why she hadn't yet moved. Lorraine knew Margaret. She knew how scared Margaret was about height.

But Margaret wasn't just going to stand there and get butchered.

She risked it, straight backwards with her eyes on Lorraine, smashing open the full-length shutters with her elbows. Too late, Lorraine remembered the revolver, and she lunged. Margaret scooped up the gun as she swerved along the terrace, groped for the trigger but couldn't find it. Lorraine went after her

212

desperately because as soon as Margaret had the gun Lorraine wouldn't get near her. In her near-panic she closed in too far, the knife thrust out in front of her. Dawn light silvered the blade.

The classic judo counter for a knife attack is a simple move involving leverage on the forearm. It can be applied very quickly, even when you're busy dropping a revolver. Especially when the knife attacker leans their weight as far forward as Lorraine was doing.

The knife clanged free. Margaret saw it fall and started letting go the grip and Lorraine with her balance all gone did the only thing she could. She tipped her weight at Margaret, shoulder to Margaret's chest.

The impact shifted Margaret a yard back and put Lorraine between her and both weapons. But unarmed now. They faced each other, dark shapes in the dawn.

Margaret knew it. She knew she was going to win.

She sprang at Lorraine, ignoring the smarting from the cut on her stomach, grasping for Lorraine's arm, the collar of her uniform shirt. And now it was Lorraine who was scared, Lorraine who wasn't going to face her opponent without a weapon.

She flung herself backwards, not looking at Margaret, not looking behind, looking only down, for the knife or the gun. And caught the low wall behind her ankles, hard.

*   *   *

When Margaret, kneeling, nerved herself to look over, Lorraine was just visible a hundred feet down on the shadowy ledge of prickly-pear and brittlebush. She didn't look dead. She had her knees tucked up and a hand up to her face as if to suck her thumb while she nodded asleep. But she wasn't moving, nor would she.

Margaret went back inside. Inside her mind Lorraine's scream was still echoing.

Finito was stirring, eyelids aflicker, but no more than that. The radio lay where it had fallen. It wasn't transmitting, but Lorraine had certainly radioed before she walked in here. The guerrillas wouldn't be long coming. *So move, Margaret Stubbs.*

Her pants, jeans and boots were in the bathroom. Also in the bathroom she found antiseptic and sticking plaster for the nick

213

on her stomach. On her belt she had one of the webbing pouches that was part of their uniform and she tried to put the packet of plasters in the pouch; she might have further use for them. Then she dropped them, she was shaking so much.

She grabbed a shirt of Finito's from the wardrobe, then found her glasses, in the darkroom. Also the microcamera, the unused film cassettes. They went in the pouch on her belt.

Light was spreading in the sky. It was 0416. Zelaszny's guerrillas might already be dashing to cut off all exits from Tequísquepec, but they wouldn't catch her trying them. Not yet. She began moving in cover back towards the convent.

CHAPTER 37

Mission commander aboard the E3A was a knobbly-faced fifty-year-old with a lieutenant-colonel's badges and an inexhaustible supply of chewing gum. On the big aircraft he gave Carla Desatnick a warmer welcome than she reckoned he intended, and sat her next to him at an aft-facing console with panels for intercom and air-to-ground radio. Also clocks that showed Zulu time – Greenwich Mean – and Paris, Pacific and mountain time. Mountain time was local for Phoenix and for Tequísquepec.

The E3A was on station, on time, at 0130 mountain time and at 0158 they called Desatnick to the screen that had picked up the suspected military vehicles.

On the display they'd thrown up a computer-drawn map of the area they were sweeping: the Gulf of California, Alameda town, Tequísquepec hill. Desatnick couldn't properly see the pale orange traces even when the operator pointed them out.

'This is exactly how we pictured it from the other crew's reports, ma'am. See, there's way too much stuff there for any random gathering of vehicles.'

She leaned over him, holding hair back from her face. 'What do *you* reckon?'

'Well, if I knew there was a military objective here' – he indicated Tequísquepec – 'I'd take a guess and say this might be a military force standing by to go in.'

Desatnick got on the radio. Phoenix would pass on her message to Washington, Washington would pass it to Paris, where it was 1003 and the talks in full swing. Then Pasarell could ask Pedragoza what the Mexican army thought it was doing poised to go into Tequísquepec.

Could ask. Whether he *would* ask was another matter entirely.

An hour and a half went by and the E3A flew round and round

in its racetrack pattern, over the Sonoran Desert, almost on the border but not quite.

Then at 0335 they had it confirmed, the vehicles were moving, closing in on Tequísquepec along the foot of the Sierra Madre. It wasn't civilian stuff. Not in those numbers, not half an hour before dawn. Desatnick got on the radio again.

An hour later the movements all stopped. It wasn't clear why. But what was clear was that now the vehicles were at the foot of Tequísquepec itself. If they had artillery among them it could flatten the convent from where it stood. Desatnick radioed in.

She got an answer back by the same route at 0455 and it wasn't what she'd been expecting. Pedragoza's source inside Tequísquepec had confirmed their worst fears. Fight had captured Rahab, she was in their hands.

*   *   *

No safe way existed of getting inside the convent. Margaret waited in cover in the ragged coca growth under the admin block walls, eyes blurring, head sagging under its weight, and tried to think which way offered least danger. Maybe if she closed her eyes, the answer would come. She tried. Then her mind was saying, *surely it can't be time to get up yet*, and she jerked her eyes open, dismally. She didn't know how long she'd been asleep, minutes or seconds; but even a second might be enough to kill her; and it wasn't even necessary.

Daylight was turning from brown to soft yellow. Margaret tore a lower leaf off the coca and broke it. The aroma wasn't promising, but it might work, just. She tried it. At first it was scarcely perceptible.

Then there was warm numbness in her mouth; and her mind viewed her body from outside and broke through the weariness; and her limbs grew light, no longer part of her. Pain had been gnawing at her head, gnawing at her stomach, hunger, not just the knife wound; but now there was nothing.

She stopped herself, in the act of taking another leaf. She'd had several; any more and she'd be into orbit.

She took handfuls of leaves and stowed them in the pouch on her belt with the microcamera and first-aid kit. If they stayed cool, if the cocaine didn't dry out of them, they might

216

keep their effect.

It was 0515. She'd been here more than half an hour. She'd missed the chance she might have had right at the start because she'd expected to find the whole place swarming. Instead, it hadn't been until almost five that the first search parties had set out. Jodie Sadler – if she, as Lorraine had implied, had been in charge of the squad tasked with re-arresting Margaret – must have dithered after getting Lorraine's last radio signal. Maybe she'd thought Finito and Lorraine between them couldn't possibly let Margaret escape.

Lorraine. Margaret could still hear the scream, in her mind.

She crossed under the coca in a painful belly crawl, the .38 she'd taken from the *cortijo* hard, cruel, on her hip. At the edge of the foliage, she stopped, six feet across the path from an office window. There'd been guards patrolling periodically. One was coming now, dark, square-built, and Margaret shrank under the shadow, thinking: knock one down and they'll *know* you're here. Then she stopped breathing because the guard was García.

His boots crunched on the brittle earth of the path. They stopped a foot from Margaret's nose. She knew she'd had it. García never missed a thing and Margaret was in no stance to bring him down and hide him, unconscious, before he used his radio. Even if she was ever capable of bringing down a brute the size of García.

The boots turned, their backs turned towards Margaret, not polished for parade but dulled to avoid catching sun. There was enough to catch, even now. García was checking the window.

He felt satisfied and he moved on. He went out of sight.

Margaret broke cover. García had checked that window so there was virtually no prospect there but it was the only immediate chance and needed ruling out before she tried something riskier.

And García must have been checking merely that it was as he'd last seen it, because the window was open.

Margaret rolled inside with her breathing shallow and her senses tuned up with the coca. She left the window as she'd found it, to the millimetre, waiting for a tense moment while her eyes adjusted to the shadows inside. Then she went through the office and along the corridor and into the library.

Some guards were around in the patio, she'd heard them

shouting, sending parties out on the hill to hunt for her. They had the patrol round the walls, but no one was expecting her in the middle of the convent. Quite right, too. She'd known the library would be empty. People didn't browse among the propaganda books while there was a crisis on.

She climbed the spiral stair and picked her way into Wanda Zelaszny's study. She neutralised the printed circuits the way she'd done the first time. She'd removed five of the six fuses when the stair creaked and a key went *clunk* in the door.

CHAPTER 38

Any self-respecting Parisian ought to be in his favourite eating place at one in the afternoon, not round a conference table, but the circumstances weren't normal and Brouzet was remaining patient. Pasarell, his heavy shoulders menacing, was asking Pedragoza for clarification of what he described as a 'Pentagon' report, filed from a 'routine' USAF reconnaissance flight, that a collection of military vehicles had moved into striking range of Tequísquepec.

It was true, Pedragoza admitted. Information from within the guerrilla HQ suggested that crimes were being committed, also that attempts to arrest suspects might be resisted; so the army had been brought in to reinforce a police action.

Pasarell pointed out angrily that that meant Mexico's action would be unco-ordinated with the main international action. Pedragoza couldn't confirm or deny: he had no information about timing. Barrington Yorke pointed out that at a time like this, their main concerns should include also Rahab's safety.

But Rahab was beyond their helping now.

At 1320 Pasarell got a new report from Desatnick, via Washington. The military vehicles at the foot of Tequísquepec had deployed, evidently into covert positions, and had stopped moving.

They checked the time, 0520 at Tequísquepec, well after dawn. Something had happened, the army had changed its plans. Something had cropped up to forestall the dawn raid they'd all been expecting.

Pedragoza had been expecting it, too. This got him guessing as much as the others and he went out to the phone. He was back at 1340, but his phone conversation hadn't helped much. As far as he could gather, Mexico City didn't know what was happening,

219

either.

Things quietened down enough for them to get bored and send for lunch. Then at 1430 Pasarell got word again from Desatnick: a small group of military vehicles was making for Tequísquepec along the road, moving quickly. Pedragoza went back to the phone.

He was at the conference table again at 1445. It was true. The army had been ordered in.

Barrington Yorke knew perfectly well that an operation like this hadn't been set up at a week's notice. He knew perfectly well that Pedragoza and his superiors had been less than forthright about their intentions, let alone their sources inside Fight. But this was no time for recriminations.

He folded his bony hands. 'Well, it's obviously too late to save Rahab now. Unfortunately we can't help that. Our chief imperative is to prepare for co-ordinated international action against Fight on the basis of whatever information we can get.'

The big strike. They began setting it up.

*　　*　　*

Coca in Margaret's bloodstream kept the panic from her brain. She backed fast behind the door with Lorraine's .38 in her hand and knew with the heightened perception of the drug that only one person was coming.

Wanda Zelaszny. Margaret saw the grey hair, the blue cotton dress, as Zelaszny turned her back, oblivious, and shut the door. She covered Zelaszny's mouth with her hand and touched her spine with the pistol muzzle. She felt only compassion as the fright jolted the older woman.

'Keep calm. I know where the alarms are, so don't go near them or I'll be compelled to use force.'

Zelaszny was trembling all over. Margaret released her and stepped sideways, across the door. Zelaszny whiplashed round, pale, lips parted, eyes round behind her glasses. So ready to encourage others to use violence, so terrified when she felt its threat against herself.

'What d'you want? How did you get in here?'

'I should have thought the first answer was obvious. No, don't move.'

Zelaszny was edging away, instinctively. It shocked Margaret to see how badly she was shaking. 'You came to kill me.'

Margaret studied the violet eyes. She smiled, amused. 'You'd be dead by now if I had. And why assume that? It's you who believe in killing, not me.'

Zelaszny's lip twitched. 'But men, Margaret, not other women.'

'Men are people, too, Wanda.' She'd never heard anyone use Zelaszny's first name, they called her Leader; yet it seemed right, now; and Margaret wanted to convince this person. Maybe just in wanting that she was under the Zelaszny effect. 'And what about Julie O'Dell, Paquita Villegas?'

'What about Lorraine Easson? She's dead, Margaret, you broke nearly every bone in her body.'

If only she knew how it had been. 'Lorraine would have killed me.' Sunlight on the desk and the armchairs, shadow of the shutters and her awful feeling of guilt. That scream. It was 0605.

'Possibly. And if we'd let O'Dell and Villegas live, many women would have died. It's force to fight force, you just said so yourself.'

'Don't oversimplify, Wanda. You're making war on all men, and in your fight, thousands of women will die as well. I'm fighting to save those people before your philosophy kills them.'

'You are begging the question. However many thousands may die in women's struggle against tyranny, millions more will be saved to live better lives, to live at all!'

'They'd be saved anyway by a peaceful women's movement. Maybe what I've done *is* as evil as what you do, but I don't think so, because intentions must count for something. If someone attacks me, I'm entitled to defend myself. But you have no telling how many women and children will die along with their men when you start releasing chlorine and igniting toluene.'

Distant shouting below, the drub of boots, slam of a rifle butt on flagstones. Up here the real fighting was going on, yet the spartan office lay peaceful. 0608. Zelaszny's face, her whole body, pleaded. 'Margaret, I wish I understood you. You seemed so sincere. I thought you believed in women's fight.'

'I believe in it completely, but I believe in people. Your books are tremendous – no one could disagree with you about the way to survival. But as soon as you take arms against people, of course people will fight you, and then women as well as men will die.'

'You still don't understand. We women *have* to fight, because our interests go so diametrically against male, established interests that there's no other way we'll achieve our objects.'

'It's you who don't understand, Wanda. Revolutions might speed progress, but society only ever changes organically, when people as a whole are ready. You can't impose progress on people by an armed dictatorship, or by kidnapping them from their homes and then brainwashing them. You can't change society from a closed, island community, you can only change it by being part of society. And whether you're here at Tequís-quepec or on Guerrillera Island, you're just *not* part.'

Zelaszny shook her head. 'That kind of change has to be measured geologically. We need an end to tyranny *now*.'

Rifle grease: that was the smell that didn't belong in an ordinary office: the HK53 and the Mondragón in their rack on the wall. Margaret could smell her own sweat, too; and Wanda Zelaszny's fear. But she only ever fooled around with those guns, Sharon had told Margaret, she'd never fought with them. She let other women do that. 0611.

'You've never seen a place where women really do suffer tyranny, Wanda. I could take you to places I know in the remote Andes where you'd be surprised. No armed invasion will liberate women like that overnight, it takes education, conditioning, it takes open-minded women from outside tackling traditional masculine tasks, and vice versa, and it takes the whole community's acceptance of that. Sometimes I wonder whether you've ever known real tyranny, whether, in terms of what women like that put up with, you aren't simply spoilt.'

'You're the one who's spoilt, Margaret. You're the one who's going to be a doctor, who's taking a pilot's licence, who has the whole world at her feet. And what d'you do? Side with men so that other women don't get the chances you got.'

0612.

'That's simply not true. I want to see more women get opportunities like mine—but women in Peru and Bolivia, not women in the West who've hardly got a thing to fight for.'

'Then the way to do it is to join me.' Zelaszny was pleading again. A stray hair tickled Margaret's cheek and Finito's shirt was softer than her jeans and she felt the compulsion, the hypnotic urge to do as this woman begged her. But they'd killed Julie, they'd killed Mario Roca, they'd killed all the love inside little Giselle. 'Margaret, you have so much you could bring to our fight – brains, talent, character, sensitivity. I *like* you. Don't you see, we see eye to eye on so much?'

'Yes, we do.' It was odd; she liked Zelaszny, too, despite the battle of wills between them. 'It's only the crux of the matter that we'll never agree on.'

'But we *can* agree, Margaret.' Zelaszny took off her glasses, and the intimacy had the effect of drawing the women together as Zelaszny moved to the desk to set them down. 'Stay with us. You'll see my ideas are right. I understand what you've done, and I do see why, but all that can be forgotten.' 0613. 'Please.' She held out her hand. 'Put down the gun and come back to us.'

Margaret lifted her chin and laughed.

Zelaszny stabbed for the alarm panel and hit one with the fuse gone so nothing happened as Margaret dived at her and Zelaszny's finger caught the card and flicked it out from the printed circuit. Margaret wrenched her away and in that instant Zelaszny got the one live alarm. With the savagery of panic Margaret chopped Zelaszny on the side of the head but already the sound was jangling out right through the convent. Zelaszny slumped. Margaret grabbed for the combination.

22115582. Green light on. She dived for the stairs.

The nearest Bodyguard might take a full minute getting to the office but Margaret had used twelve seconds dialling so call it forty-five seconds, optimistically. Not enough time therefore something had to go and that was the so-called master plan. She rejected the idea of simply tearing pages out of the files, she hadn't room for them in the pouch on her belt and besides, this way the Mexican authorities couldn't accuse her of removing evidence, should *that* question arise. Deployment details. They'd do for a worldwide strike against Fight, and if that happened there'd be no master plan to counter. She was filming fast. The coca that had betrayed her in absurd overconfidence now kept her hands steady for a sharp image on the microfilm.

Frame 46. Frame 47. Frame 48.

Slam, clunk, thud above and they'd got there. One minute four seconds, plus the twelve dialling, sixteen, and still more files to film. Scream, *Leader*, what a typically feminine reaction, total blind flap. Frame 52, frame 53, frame 54. But would they see the green light in the dial, and if they did, would they connect it? Frame 59, frame 60, frame 61. Dear Lord, close their eyes and blunt their wits. She reloaded the camera.

More banging and thumping above and now someone shrilling orders in near-hysterical Spanish which can sound hysterical even at calm discussion level. But someone else was arguing, anxious to look after Zelaszny, so therefore at least she was still unconscious and now frame 96, frame 97, frame 98 and finish. Margaret gulped a breath.

No one had come down the spiral stair because it rattled so much you'd have to be stone deaf to miss it. Perfect.

She walked softly out on to the cantilevered platform with the camera in the pouch and the .38 in her hand. Into the lean, black barrel of Giselle Stamm's FAL.

CHAPTER 39

No scream, because she fought it. Giselle was silent, small hands on the big rifle, big blue troubled eyes watching Margaret. Margaret was holding the .38 and telling herself that with things in this state she would *have* to use it. But she couldn't. Not on a child. Margaret's eyes filled with despair.

But Giselle should have been yelling blue murder by now.

Giselle took one hand from the rifle and it drooped, too heavy for her. She took Margaret's gun hand and pushed gently until the .38 pointed down. Eyes on Margaret's, she pointed upstairs, then touched her lips. She nodded downwards, a flick of the long hair. She whispered: 'This way.'

The long hair lifted on her thin shoulders as she went down silently with the rifle. Margaret stole after her, down the steps to the library's basement. Behind a rack of feminist newsletters Giselle opened a door and Margaret went through after her. Further steps led down. Somewhere among these limestone tunnels, Margaret recalled, they'd had the Sokolova-Kuhr lecture about dangerous chemicals. Giselle glanced about, head cocked, listening. She halted, slung the rifle on her shoulder, and turned.

'*Gott sei Dank*. We're safe. Did you get the pictures?'

In the gloom Margaret was staring, mouth open, utterly baffled. 'How did you know?'

'García told me. He warned . . .'

'*García?*'

Giselle said: 'He's a Mexican government agent.'

*　　*　　*

Cold in the tunnel turned Margaret gooseflesh as the sweat dried

225

on her. She couldn't take her eyes off the little shadowy figure with the rifle as big as herself. Then as the shock wore off Margaret started to see how it fitted.

García *had* seen her, hiding in the coca. Totonaco he might be, halfwit he wasn't: he knew what she'd come back for. He'd *opened* that window, just for her to get in and get her films. Knowing that a woman might do it but a man never could.

'But . . . but what's happening? Why did García tell *you* I was there?'

'I was called out on search. They said Lorraine Easson was dead and Finito was under arrest and you were trying to escape. I drew my rifle from the armoury just before six and they set me on patrolling the HQ area – they wouldn't let me out on the hill, I . . . I was in trouble.'

'Trouble?'

'Catalina was sent to her quarters last night, because of . . . because of the spying. They were going to put someone else in command of security. When I came back from . . . from the Sacromonte, I went to see her. Well, I wasn't supposed to, so they confined me to my quarters, too. Until they needed everyone out on search. It's been awful. Everybody's been meeting in little groups and talking secretly. And nobody's had any sleep, hardly.'

As Finito had hinted. The camp had been breaking up, Zelaszny's authority starting to disintegrate. She'd managed to keep her command structure intact, though.

Soft as they were, their voices were echoing in the chilly, dark, limestone corridor. 'What happened then?' Margaret murmured.

Giselle was glancing about, unsure whether to expect hunting guerrillas to run out from somewhere. 'I started my patrol and García caught me and took me aside. It was just after six.'

And Margaret in Zelaszny's study, arguing it out, or trying to. García had known. He'd known Margaret would need help to get out.

'He said he was a Mexican agent. He said we had to watch out, because there was going to be trouble here. He told me you were here in the convent, and where to find you.'

'Did he say what sort of trouble?' Her voice had gone sharp.

Giselle shook her head, in the shadows. 'He just said there was

226

danger and we had to get away.'

'We?'

'You and me.'

'Why you?'

'Because . . . well, he said because he knew I'd been kidnapped here, sort of. He knew I didn't want to be here any more, even though I'd wanted to at first, when Sabina made me believe . . .' Giselle's voice caught. 'I believed it was right. But I can't . . . I don't understand any more.'

Margaret reached and gripped Giselle's arm. It seemed thin, even compared with her own. Giselle had to swallow. She said: 'García said you were a very brave woman and you'd help me to escape.'

Pity. It hadn't been perverted lust on that flat, expressionless face when she'd seen him looking at Giselle. It had been a man taking pity on a kid in trouble. All this time, Margaret thought, having to be hard, going against her nature, she herself had lost the capacity for pity that she'd once had and prized.

'I know the way,' Giselle said. 'This is the old Oraboca mine. There's a network of tunnels that goes down through the hill and comes out in a limestone cave in the olive groves down below.'

'How do you know that?' Margaret's voice was sharp again.

Even in the half-dark she saw Giselle's eyes go round. 'García told me. Look, he gave me a map.' Giselle flashed a torch at the roughly sketched sheet, the rifle propped precariously at her side.

Margaret disliked that, on instinct. She couldn't help it if people spotted her present movements and made accurate guesses at her future ones. But placing herself somewhere someone was expecting her was asking for trouble.

'Did García tell you I'm *not* a Mexican agent?' Giselle simply stared. Margaret grasped her arm. 'García's helped both of us, he's got us out of danger. But what he wants is the films I've just taken, for his own government to use. He'll have set people waiting for us down there at the cave mouth. We'll get out of here some other way.'

'But, Margaret . . .' Fear rang in her voice.

'Listen, how did you get into Mexico? Legally?' She paused. 'Whoever's waiting down there will be perfectly polite and civilised, not like this lot.' She jerked her head towards Fight's

227

HQ. 'But they'll have the law on their side and they'll have the power to put you and me in prison. You and I are going to Alameda airport, taking an aircraft, and flying to the United States. We'll be safer there.'

Giselle went on staring. 'How will we get there?'

'Any way we can find once we get out on Tequísquepec hill.' Margaret started leading off towards the stairs. It was 0632.

*　　*　　*

Margaret didn't know the tunnel system under the convent. Giselle did. They needed to come up in the transport park, Margaret said; then maybe they could steal a vehicle and drive down to Alameda. Giselle took Margaret up and down steps, round corners, along corridors; all deserted. At one point she pointed upwards and said: 'That's the pool.' Presently they climbed a flight of steps, cut into the stone, that ended at a door. Giselle hung back.

'This is the generator room.'

Margaret could hear the machinery running. The generator was in a building adjoining the block that housed the sauna and the radio tower, the opposite end of the pool from Zelaszny's eyrie, and with a door leading into the transport park.

'Give me the rifle,' Margaret murmured. 'It's too big for you if we have to run for it.'

She gave Giselle the .38. Even for Margaret, the FAL was heavy. There was no purpose in subtlety. She shoved the door open and strode into the generator room, Giselle behind her. The building was deserted, the outer door open, giving a glimpse of the transport park. It was 0640. Margaret led Giselle to the outer door.

They heard the shooting before they came out into daylight.

*　　*　　*

It was the radio tower. Someone was up there snapping single shots out of a full-bore rifle like the one Margaret was holding, and in the transport park and elsewhere, Fight guerrillas were using every scrap of cover they could find to shoot back and try to blast whoever it was out of it again. Margaret, heart in her throat, tried for a moment to guess whether this was factional fighting or whether some outside force had taken over the radio tower, but she couldn't have told. Distant at the far end of the park she saw guerrillas dashing in and out of the armoury. Closer, in the middle of the transport park, a heap of rags wasn't a heap of rags but a dead guerrilla. In shock Margaret recognised Tina Zeiss. The kindhearted one, the one who'd brought her water.

Giselle stifled a scream. Margaret seized her arm.

'Forget the transport. If we can make it across to the trees we can get down to the *altipuerto*. There are two aircraft there.'

It was a good sixty yards: ten to the transport park gate; fifty across the open ground where the guerrillas played football. There was no one on the gate. Whether anyone was in cover beyond the wall was something they'd simply have to find out.

'Go!'

They ran.

If anyone fired at them, Margaret wasn't aware of it. Through the open gate she swung round with the FAL across her hip. But no one was there. She swung back. Giselle was wide-eyed, face flushed, unhurt.

'Okay!'

Fifty yards had never seemed longer. On her long legs Margaret could run, but she'd never tried sprinting with a nine-pound rifle in her hands. Giselle kept pace easily, the .38 in her hand and her hair flying back. If she'd got nothing else out of her spell in the convent, at least she was fit.

In the edge of the trees they stopped, chests heaving. They got their breath back. Margaret said: 'We can't hang around here. Can you jog down to the *altipuerto*?'

Giselle nodded.

Margaret jerked her head and started loping off, Giselle at her heels, and in that same moment she heard the growl of an aircraft engine. Alarmed, she bobbed her head around, peering through the trees, and glimpsed the Stationair, airborne and turning away down for Alameda. She thought: too bad, we'll have the Mustang if that's there. Then from behind came the deep sound of armoured vehicles' engines.

She twisted, on the run. Giselle stumbled into her. They both stared.

Two armoured personnel carriers came round the corner of

the complex. They drove into the open space Margaret and Giselle had just crossed. They weren't tracked, they had four tyred wheels. They had turrets with a big barrel sticking out but they weren't doing any shooting.

Fight was. Margaret heard the clang of ricochets against the armour plating and then saw four guerrillas tumble over the wall. There was virtually no cover. Margaret recognised Cathy Latta as the one who sprinted ahead of the others with her rifle slung, jerked back an arm, and then hurled what she'd been holding. The grenade took out a wheel and axle assembly on the first APC.

Then the guerrillas were scattering into whatever cover they could find and the men in the APCs were retaliating. This was the danger García had meant when he'd warned Giselle, Margaret realised. He'd known the army was coming in. He'd probably played a big part in controlling the operation.

But Margaret and Giselle weren't staying to watch. Margaret hit Giselle on the arm and then loped off again, moving now faster than before.

* * *

The Mustang was still there, under the awning. Margaret had hardly dared hope it would be. But getting it airborne might not be an easy matter. There'd been parties out searching for Margaret for a couple of hours; some of them were still on their way back to the convent to find out what was happening; periodically Margaret and Giselle had glimpsed movements through the trees. If one of the search parties spotted them, there'd be trouble.

'Help me, Giselle.' She was pulling up the trolley-acc to start the Merlin.

They positioned it, Giselle straining. Hands shaking, glasses misting, Margaret plugged in the leads and then set the thing running. This was all taking so long.

'Stand guard.'

Giselle caught the rifle as Margaret chucked it. Margaret swung into the front cockpit. She skipped half the checklist items. The main thing to know was whether it still had petrol in the tanks and whether the engine would start. Margaret tried it.

It caught thunderously.

Margaret set the throttle. She levered herself out. She unplugged the trolley-acc, the awning bellying in the gale from the propellor, and nudged Giselle's shoulder. They shoved the trolley clear of the wing and then ran back, Giselle's hair blowing, tossing. Margaret put her lips to Giselle's ear.

'You first. In the back.'

Giselle climbed up. Margaret glanced round as she followed Giselle on to the wing root, but there still wasn't anyone near. Somebody *must* come before long, though, to see who was making all the noise. Giselle hadn't been in anything like this before. Margaret had to fix the seat harness for her. She hunted round the cockpit, irritable now in her impatience. But there wasn't a helmet or an oxygen mask, just an intercom headset. And the flight Margaret had in mind would be well above oxygen height.

She took out the flimsy headset, reached into the front cockpit, and took out the helmet and mask she'd already seen there. She got them on Giselle's head and plugged in. And too bad about herself. She'd spent long enough living at high altitude to manage without. She dropped into the front cockpit, slapped a plaster on the bridge of her nose, put on the flimsy headset, and strapped in. She started the checks: full and free movement on the flying controls; full and part extension on the flaps. Power check. A bit of a drop on the left magneto when the revs came back, but too bad, this was a fighter scramble or something very like it.

Margaret prodded the brakes and let the Mustang roll, swinging the long nose to find the ramp down to the short, sloping runway, flicking the cooling shutters with the other hand as she steered.

She was tail-up and full throttle on the runway before she realised someone *had* turned up to see who was making all the noise. She felt more than heard the bullet strikes, she glimpsed guerrillas with rifles, somewhere beside the runway, she sensed a missed beat in the blaring engine, though it might have been imagination.

But the Merlin kept running. Margaret hit the undercarriage lever and dipped the long nose and felt the drumming as the wheels came into the wells, still spinning, and then she was

231

banking left and down, round the hillside, clear of the rifles.

She tried the intercom. 'Giselle, can you hear me? Are you all right?'

'Yes. I'm okay. Are you?'

'Fine.'

She rolled the Mustang back to the right and trimmed into the climb. Then realised that the cockpit was starting to fill up with a smell of unburnt petrol.

CHAPTER 40

At seven in the morning, mountain time, Carla Desatnick's E3A still wasn't due off station for two and a half hours and Desatnick had had all the coffee she could take, not to say all the avuncular bonhomie she could take from the knobbly-faced mission commander.

From the displays, fighting was obviously taking place at Tequísquepec. But the displays couldn't tell them who was winning, they could barely make at all clear what was happening.

Then at 0703 one of the operators called on the intercom. He'd got a trace for an aircraft that had taken off from Tequísquepec, settled on a heading of 320°, and started climbing. It wasn't the same flight pattern as the light aircraft that had gone up at 0645: that one had simply landed at Alameda. This one was flying north, towards the border, and it didn't care who knew about it. Any pilot hoping to hide his course or destination would have been on the deck.

They watched it. They didn't know what to make of it. They were still making wild guesses about it when at 0710 a similar trace came up from Alameda.

The guesses got wilder.

They had height information. Trace A, the first one, had settled at 20,000 feet, moving at 345mph. The speed suggested one of the rebuilt Mustangs; although the knobbly-faced mission commander reckoned a Mustang should have been moving faster. More like the 415mph of Trace B, flying north now at 25,000 feet.

Then at 0719:30 a third trace came up from Alameda, went straight to 25,000 feet, and started moving far faster than either of the others, 570mph. Again flying north.

Desatnick said suddenly: 'They're moving Zelaszny. That first

233

trace, at six forty-five – they were flying her down to Alameda. Now they're getting her someplace safe, out of the battle. We'd better stand by to intercept.'

The commander said: 'Would they move her at that height? In full radar view?'

It was 0725. Another operator came through, voice urgent. 'We have radar, we have search radar pulses from Trace C. It's transmitting right now.'

A rapid glance passed between Desatnick and the commander. Then the radio fizzed.

They knew the Cadal frequency and they'd had one receiver tuned in and listening-out, but they'd had nothing off it so far. Now they got voice, a woman, the accent North American, maybe Canadian. 'Witch Hunter from Witch Eagle, negative so far on scan. You have sighting?' A pause. Another woman, the accent distinctly German. 'Witch Hunter. Negative.' And then nothing.

Desatnick looked at the commander, her eyes narrow. 'Rahab. That's who it is in Trace A. The other two traces must be Fight planes. What in hell are they *doing*?'

The commander's eyes held Desatnick's steadily. He was still chewing gum. 'What that jet's doing is exactly what we're doing.' He watched her, making her guess. 'It's operating as an AWACS – airborne warning and control system. It's gonna find something with that radar, and my guess is that's Trace A. Then it's gonna steer a fighter on to what it finds, and my guess is the fighter's Trace B.'

There hadn't been a lot of colour in Desatnick's cheeks, not after jumping time zones again and missing a night's sleep. But what there had been drained out altogether.

'Shit, man. We can't let them do that. We better do something, we better call up the . . .'

He put the avuncular, infuriating hand on her arm. 'Easy, lady. Those aircraft are just as visible on Mexican radar as they are on ours, and they're way deep inside Mexico. If anybody's gonna break it up, it's the Mexicans.'

'But we don't even *want* . . .'

'Those two in pursuit won't even hack it. You know what the combat radius of a Mirage is at that speed? It might not even get Trace A on its radar before it runs out of fuel.' He chewed gum a moment, watching her. 'But I'll tell you what I will do. I'll call up a fighter CAP – uh, combat air patrol – and have 'em stand by on our pattern.'

It was 0727.

*   *   *

Something *was* wrong with that Merlin. The Mustang wasn't climbing as it should have been and there was periodic backfiring. Margaret saw the flames, sometimes, at the exhaust stubs.

Then, urging the thing laboriously through 10,000 feet, she checked all the dials again and got it. Manifold pressure was down. One of the rifle bullets must have holed the manifold somewhere. That would explain the reek of petrol.

Suddenly she was trembling, and it wasn't from the temperature, dropping as they climbed higher. That engine bay must be full of unburnt mixture by now, just waiting to warm up to flashpoint. And they weren't even wearing parachutes.

Any other day of her life this would be a case for immediate force-landing. You didn't play with fire. Most of all you didn't play with fire in the air.

But if she came down now, she'd be in the middle of the Sonoran Desert, and it wouldn't even be a case of Mexican security getting to her first and getting her films. Fight would catch her first. She hadn't got far enough from Tequísquepec.

Besides, if all that mixture hadn't caught fire yet, it was probably because it was blowing out too fast through the bulletholes in the cowling. The engine had been quite warm enough to ignite it when the damage happened in the first place.

She settled the Mustang heading 320° at 20,000 feet and juggled the throttle and mixture until the Merlin ran mostly without backfiring. It was a long way up if the engine did catch fire but she needed the height, to be sure of showing up on US radar.

'Giselle, are you all right?'

'I'm cold.' On the intercom Margaret could hear Giselle's teeth chattering.

They had hot-weather clothes on. Sea-level temperature was 75° Fahrenheit, up here at 20,000 feet it was 9°, way below

235

freezing.

'I'm afraid you will be, Giselle. But we've got to stay this high up. Is your oxygen working properly?'

'Yes.'

Margaret was taking big, deep lungfuls. There wasn't a lot of oxygen at 20,000 feet. But she'd manage, she'd lived longer at high altitude than low, and she still had her system full of coca.

But the coca wasn't damping out the shivering in her hands, it wasn't stopping the very slow darkening round the edges of her vision that she'd been watching for, the first symptoms of anoxia. Coca wouldn't get this aircraft down if she lost consciousness.

When the voices came in the headset at 0725 she was shocked, suddenly. She hadn't thought they might use the Mirage and the Mustang Finito had said were on permanent readiness at Alameda. And she recognised them. Sabina Stamm, flying Witch Hunter. Charlotte Rondeau, the radar expert, flying Witch Eagle.

Tautly Margaret reached to the avionics panel. She switched on the radar receiver.

0730. They were managing a true airspeed of 345mph. It should have been nearer 390mph for the two-seater, but even so they'd covered almost 170 miles. Ninety miles to go and they'd be in US airspace. No flashing lights yet, no radar pulses in the six o'clock. They'd outfly the other two yet. 0731.

On the radio, Rondeau's voice said: 'Witch Hunter, squawk Fox Fox.' Automatically Margaret glanced at the avionics panel. Thinking was growing progressively harder as more of her concentration went into operating her lungs. But she wouldn't have known the transponder code Rondeau and Sabina had agreed to identify friend from foe anyway. 'Roger, Witch Hunter.' Rondeau had seen Sabina's squawk.

'Giselle.'

'I'm okay.' But on the intercom her voice came strained. She was a tough kid, she was game. But spend long enough at this temperature and anyone would go under. How long before they showed up on US radar?

0733. They'd flown 184 miles. Say seventy-six to the border. Less than twenty more minutes of this. Giselle had heard the transmissions but she didn't know what they meant. Nevertheless, very soon Margaret was going to have to tell her. 0734. On the avionics panel a light started flashing and Margaret's stomach went empty.

She heard Rondeau's voice, on the radio. 'Witch Hunter from Witch Eagle. Target locked in, stand by for guidance to killing range.'

*   *   *

At the E3A's radar display the knobbly-faced commander was pointing when the blip of light that was Witch Hunter, Sabina Stamm's Mustang, went suddenly big and bright, then shrank back to normal size.

Desatnick snapped: 'What happened?'

'She did like the AWACS pilot said, she squawked IFF. Identification Friend and Foe uses a thing called a transponder that receives a radar wave and modifies it. You saw what happened on the return.'

Desatnick flicked her eyes at the clocks on the console. 0732 local time, 1532 in Paris. Not that anyone in Paris was in much position to do anything.

'Have we seen *nothing* coming up outa the Mexican air bases?'

'Nope.' It was one of the operators. 'Looks like they spotted them too late, if at all. They're too far north now for anything to reach them from the fighter bases. Only base left now between them and the border is Tijuana, and all they have there is a couple of Grumman rescue amphibians.'

It was 0733:30. The commander nudged Desatnick's elbow. 'Take a look outside, lady.'

She'd forgotten the portholes even existed, she'd been so engrossed in the radar displays. She ducked her head and peered out, and saw four Phantoms formating on them, fifty yards off the wingtip. The fighter CAP. Then there was voice again off the Cadal frequency, stronger, getting closer.

'Steer three three five and buster. Your target is headed three two zero, speed 345mph, range one seven miles.'

'Witch Hunter.'

'Witch Eagle, your course is converging now. Stand by for course correction. Do you see any contrail yet?'

'Witch Hunter, negative.'

'Witch Eagle. Start left turn on to three two zero. Okay, hold

237

it, hold it. You are now in her six o'clock. Range one six miles.'

Desatnick realised she was trying to light a cigarette but not succeeding. A crewman reached with a lighter. Desatnick said: 'We have to confirm it, we have to have an identity for Trace A. If that's Rahab, we have to keep that fighter off her. C'm'on, man, let's get on that radio.'

'Trace A's gonna make it, lady.' Desatnick wished the commander would stop calling her 'lady'. 'That Mirage is hot-danged close to its combat radius, and without its radar guidance, Trace B isn't too likely to catch Trace A.'

'What if B picks up A's contrail?' Red-eyed, Desatnick stared him out, the cigarette smoke rising between them. She said: 'Listen, colonel, I don't want to have to pull rank. But *my* department's picking up the check for this flight.'

He sighed. 'Okay, lady.' He opened the radio.

CHAPTER 41

Nine degrees Fahrenheit was twenty-three below freezing and it felt like it, coca in the bloodstream or not. But Giselle had no coca in the bloodstream, just the light bush shirt and trousers on that she'd worn at Tequísquepec. 0737. Margaret wondered whether Giselle was still conscious. Her own vision was blurring and every time she worked her lungs it was more effort than before and the flashing light of the radar warner mesmerised her. No feeling remained in her fingertips or her feet. Maybe it didn't matter if she passed out at the controls. Maybe it didn't matter if Sabina caught her. 0738. The voice in her headset shook her, so sudden.

'US airborne radar, unidentified aircraft over Sonoran Desert, speed 345mph, track three two zero, approaching US airspace, identify yourself, identify yourself.'

It took a moment before she realised they were speaking to her. When she did, she could barely manage to press the transmit button.

'Hallo, US airborne radar, this is Rahab.' She had to gulp, that had taken a lot of breath. 'I'm requesting clearance on course into the US.'

Again the voice came on the flimsy headset. 'Roger, Rahab, you're cleared as requested.'

She felt so tired. She kept struggling to keep her teeth from chattering. Even the sun on the cockpit seemed to make no difference, although it had at first. She switched to intercom and said: 'Giselle?' and heard a shivery 'Hullo?' in reply. Still conscious, then. The Americans were still on at her, she realised.

'Rahab, Rahab, do you read?' She recognised the urgency in the voice, and she knew this wasn't the one she'd heard before. This was a woman. 'You have pursuit, looks like a Mustang at

239

one three miles' range, it's being guided on by a jet but it just found your contrail. Get down out of contrail height right now. Just hit the border, honey, we have Phantom CAP right here to cover you.'

'Roger, US radar.'

She was trying to take it in. It was all getting so dark in here, that was the trouble. Maybe if she stopped pumping her lungs she'd remember how to start letting down. Then the urgency got to her and she was scared, and her numbed fingers were changing the elevator trim as she put the nose down, and she was scanning the engine dials as she eased back the throttle and re-adjusted the mixture. 0741. The light on the avionics panel wasn't flashing any more and it dawned on Margaret why not. Rondeau's Mirage had run out of range. She'd turned back.

But Sabina wouldn't have turned back.

Giselle's voice came in the headset, teeth chattering. 'What's wrong?'

Laboriously Margaret answered: 'We're being followed. We might have to jig around a bit.'

Flame spat from the exhaust stubs as the engine started backfiring, protesting against the new throttle and mixture settings. That woke her. She grabbed for the levers by her left hand.

Sabina's voice came on the radio: 'I've got you, Stubbs, I can see you. Don't start thinking you've got away from us. You won't even make the border at the speed I'm catching you.'

She was seven miles behind. And Margaret had an engine that was getting sicker by the minute.

*   *   *

Desatnick wasn't sure which was worse, the uncomprehending nonchalance of the gum-chewing mission commander or her own hair, falling round her eyes with a grip gone. 'Get those Phantoms off station! Get 'em the hell down there and blast that second Mustang! Jesus, they'll be there and back inside seconds, the Mexicans won't even know about them!'

'Don't you bet on that, lady.' He was imperturbable, infuriating. 'They're still in Mexico and we're staying the legal side of the border. Anyhow, Rahab is gonna make it. She's only eighteen miles short of the border right now, she'll have it in sight any minute.'

* * *

The backfiring had stopped but the power was down. Whether that mattered Margaret wasn't sure. She was coming down at 3,000 feet a minute and she wouldn't be making a contrail now. Eleven thousand. It didn't seem any warmer yet. And the landscape didn't look friendlier as it came closer, clearer.

She radioed. 'US radar, Rahab, can you give me a QNH?'

QNH meant sea-level air pressure. She needed to know that to relate her altitude to that of the terrain. So far, she'd had the altimeter on standard setting, 1013.2 millibars.

'Roger, Rahab, your QNH is one zero two one decimal five. You better work out your own safety height. You're over meseta averaging 1,000 feet altitude and the peaks go up to 2,300.'

She acknowledged. She was going through 5,000 feet, feeling the sun at last, feeling also a stab of fear in knowing that that 5,000 feet gave her less than 3,000 feet clearance over the terrain. She could see the brown rocks from this distance, she could pick out the individual saguaros with their huge branches reaching upwards. 0744. She'd flown 248 miles since takeoff. Twelve to the border.

But Sabina Stamm was in her six o'clock at two miles, and her engine wasn't spluttering and hiccuping like Margaret's was. She got the voice in the headset.

'Put it down, Stubbs, you may as well give up now. You aren't going to make it.'

Margaret thought about answering. In the hesitation, Carla Desatnick's voice came on. 'Pay no mind to her, honey, you're almost on the border! We have those Phantoms waiting for you!'

Engine. Temperatures and pressures anything but normal, coolant getting hot, oil pressure low, manifold pressure down. She could smell oil starting to burn, sickly sweet. That engine was dying slowly. Deliberately, Margaret thumbed the radio button.

'Sabina, I've got Giselle with me. You mustn't hurt Giselle.'

Her fingers should have been warming up faster than this. Instead they were just aching, cruelly, they were scarcely even less numb. 0745. She was down to 2,000 feet on the QNH setting

241

and she levelled the Mustang. This was as low as she dared go. Sabina hadn't radioed back, so maybe it had worked. At least down here she could breathe properly, and things didn't look all dark. Even so, it wasn't easy, the desert all hazed with dust and heat-shimmer as the day warmed up.

Sabina's voice, taut, very angry, said: 'Prove it!'

Margaret twisted, against the harness. The transmission had sounded very strong. She searched a moment, past Giselle, wide-eyed over the oxygen mask, past the tall tail. And got it, the flash of sun on the other Mustang's canopy, the little dark cross-shape against the burning sky. Five hundred yards. Too far to fire accurately. But closing.

She told Giselle: 'Talk to Sabina.' Then just listened out.

'Sabina!' Fear in the kid's voice. '*Sabina, was willst du denn mit uns machen*?'

Damn. She should have known they'd use German. Sabina came back equally unintelligibly and the only word Margaret picked up was *Notlandung*, forced landing. Then Giselle again. '*Sabina, du kannst nicht, du kannst uns nicht abschiessen*!' Margaret didn't follow the words but she knew the girl was begging for mercy.

'All right, I say it in English.' Her voice harsh, the Mustang closing in, Margaret weaving the nose around a huge outcrop as it reached up for her out of the desert floor. 'You hear, Stubbs? You put that Mustang down immediately or you'll get shot down.'

Five miles to the border. Sabina's Mustang inside four hundred yards off the six o'clock, not far outside shooting distance.

Margaret answered. 'Sabina, you're mad, it's your own daughter!'

'And how did *you* get her away from me? What lies have *you* told her?'

On a rise in the ground a group of saguaros reached up almost to the Mustang's belly. Giselle answered before Margaret had a chance to.

'You were the one who told me lies, you and our so-called Leader! I'm leaving because I want to! There's only evil back there! If you go back to it, you're taking part in evil, too!'

That had torn it. Margaret glanced back, and saw Giselle

242

twisting over her shoulder to look at Sabina's Mustang, less than two hundred yards astern now.

Sabina said: 'This is your last chance. You've got a count of five to line up for your force-landing, or I'll shoot. *Eins. Zwei.*'

In the aft cockpit Giselle whipped round, facing forward again. 'Margaret, *please*! Get us out of here!'

* * *

Aboard the E3A it had gone very quiet, and the background noise of the four jets and the pressurisation were things no one was noticing. The radar was showing a lot of ground return from the broken terrain immediately south of the border. They could pick out the traces for the two Mustangs, but only just. Enough, though. Enough to tell that they were barely a hundred yards apart and three miles the wrong side of the line.

* * *

In the headset Sabina's voice said: *'Fünf.'* Then nothing. Margaret timed maybe two fifths of a second.

Then switched up the nose and gave it full left rudder and saw the tracer from Sabina's burst go wide. You had to use tracer. You couldn't tell where you were shooting, otherwise. Sabina was the chief flying instructor, the dogfight expert, daughter of the Nazi fighter ace. And Margaret's mouth had gone dry.

She rolled hard right, saw in the same moment that Sabina was rolling left, and rolled fast left again as Sabina went right. Barrel cactus on a hillock slammed past the cockpit. The scissors, they called this, because it was a constant series of crossovers. Each pilot striving to get into the other one's six o'clock for a burst from the cannon or a radar lock so the missiles could be launched. The first one to break out was usually the one who died.

Hard left, hard right, hard left again. The flimsy headset down round her neck and dangling, *g* force wrenching on her glasses so she had to wonder when the frame would snap. Usually you started a scissors from four or five thousand feet and took it down to the deck, but this time they were on the deck already and flying it horizontally. Hard left, hard right, a glimpse of tracer.

243

Had she been late with the break or was it just Sabina trying to psych her into making a mistake? Backfiring again on the Merlin, worse than before, and this time as she broke left it was round the sheer cliff of a red mesa. This was what would defeat her. So many obstructions down here, limiting the scope and time for the manoeuvring. The buttes, the rocky hillsides, the great green saguaros; even, briefly glimpsed, a group of roofless walls that must have been derelict mine buildings. Hard right, hard left, backfiring.

And straight ahead, a massive clump of organ-pipe cactus, unavoidable if she kept up the turn.

It wasn't a choice. Margaret broke out of the scissors. She was shocked, battered by the *g* forces, terrified because of what she'd just done and of what she'd laid them both open to.

Sabina came round the other side of the cactus fast and low in a shallow bank and as Margaret rolled back into the turn Sabina's wing lit up. The burst got them.

Flying glass, metal shards, and the Mustang swaying jolting in the impacts. Wind stormed in wildly and Margaret's hair lashed around, forward and back, and she couldn't see and something punched her in the face and now something else on the chest. She was fighting for breath again. But she'd reacted, she was still flying the aeroplane or maybe it was flying her. She'd throttled back, risking the backfires, and tightened the turn.

Now she could see again. Sabina's faster turn had run her wide. Retrim. Assess.

Pain on one cheek, thick warmth trickling down the rib cage, blood; ignore. Altimeter smashed, turn-and-slip smashed, a nuisance, no more: she'd manage with the horizon and VSI when the surviving gyros settled down. She couldn't free a hand to get the headset back on and ask if Giselle was all right, so she threw a glance aft. The wide eyes were shocked but alive. They'd been lucky, all that armour plating round the cockpits. The fierce blasting was coming from the left-hand front windscreen panel, not starred but shot out altogether. And the petrol smell was more pungent than ever.

Margaret looked up from the cockpit and out. Sabina wasn't quite back in the six o'clock, coming in now to finish them off.

Somewhere down by her jawbone the headset was wittering away distantly. 'Rahab, Rahab, turn north three five zero, you're one mile from the border! Rahab, do you read?' She thought:

244

buzz off. She had enough on her hands with Sabina behind her and a sick engine in front. She eased back the throttle and the stubs hiccuped flame but it was Sabina she was after, and she found her. Turning tightly, but not quite tightly enough. This was going to be risky. But it was the only chance Margaret could see.

Out of the left bank she rolled fully right and stood the Mustang on its starboard wingtip. She should have put in top rudder to keep the line true but she didn't. Close as they were to the desert floor, she let the height slip off and put them closer in the moment before she rolled fully back left. And she'd beaten Sabina, beaten her on sheer nerve or maybe desperation.

Sabina lifted her nose, wary of getting down where Margaret was at the speeds they were flying. She'd turned right. She'd had to, anything else would have put Margaret into her six o'clock.

She crossed over Margaret's Mustang with a *whoomp* of noise, close enough to show Margaret the smoke streaks under her wing where she'd fired. Margaret had the long nose up again and even Giselle saw it was a potential deflection shot and Margaret, shocked, heard the voice in the headphones at her neck: 'Shoot her, shoot her!' But Margaret had other ideas.

As Sabina wrenched away into what she obviously thought was going to be an action replay of the last scissors, Margaret gave her Mustang full throttle and swung the nose due north.

She didn't feel so cold any more. The directional gyro was toppled but she found her heading on the magnetic compass. Sunlight gleamed, maybe 6,000 feet, out to the east, and Margaret looked quickly. She saw the smoke trails first, the Phantom CAP coming down to cover her. She twisted back and looked for Sabina; she realised Giselle was looking, too.

Parallax drifted the fighter away from them but didn't hide Sabina's ferocious turn. She'd seen what Margaret had done, seen how she'd tricked her. Margaret was still turning but now Sabina had lined up to cut the corner. And she was going to do it, going to catch them after all. Because Margaret's engine was banging, coughing, missing, hardly turning out power at all now.

A hill came up and Margaret tried to lift the Mustang over it but it wouldn't climb and instead she banked round the edge. So much to do and so little time. She needed to know where the flat patches were but she needed to know where Sabina was, too.

Sabina came over the top of the hill, found Margaret, and lined up. Margaret broke right, towards the hill. Sabina was firing already and in her fury she kept the gun button down and steered savagely round after Margaret as Margaret rolled back the other way to miss the sharp rise of the slope. Sabina wasn't so quick. She was turning, trying to get Margaret back in her sights, when her wingtip clipped the slope. She was flying at 400mph.

One minute she was there. The next there was just a huge, long plume of dirt boiling and bellying and trailing in the wind, deep in its cartwheeling heart something blazing red, incandescent. You couldn't have told it was an aircraft.

But Margaret had overdone it as well. Her engine had finally caught fire.

*   *   *

You never had enough hands. Mixture, fully lean. Fuel, off. Mags, off. Generator, on. Radio. *Blast* that lousy headset, still dangling round her neck. She was unpowered at 250mph, skimming the desert, feathery brown smoke streaming back from the exhaust stubs, both sides. She took both hands off the controls and pulled the headset back on. It was all right, with so much speed left she wouldn't lose height.

'US airborne radar, Rahab.'

'Go ahead, Rahab.'

'I'm low down with an engine fire that I think is under control. I'm standing by to force-land. This is to fix my position. Do you want me to keep transmitting or will you see where I come down?' She was exhausted, though, not even sure whether the fire *was* under control. Something blurred her vision which she realised was blood running into her eye. That wasn't going to help in judging the first wheels-up approach she'd ever flown.

'We have you locked in right here on the radar, Rahab. You save your hands for the landing. And God grant it's a safe one.' She'd never met that man who was speaking, maybe never would, but by the sudden shake in his voice she could tell that he knew exactly what she had on her hands. A very dangerous manoeuvre with no certainty at all of success.

'Thanks, US radar. Rahab, out.'

Speed, down to 180mph. The engine still pouring smoke. Somewhere in the bay she still had a CO_2 canister for precisely this situation. She found the button. The engine went on smoking but the smoke turned from brown to black. She didn't know whether that was good or bad.

'Giselle. Are you all right?' Was she all right? She'd just seen her mother incinerated. Was she all right?

'Yes.'

'We're going to force-land. If we're lucky, we won't turn over, but it'll be rough. Get out as soon as we stop moving and get well away from the aircraft. Don't worry about me.'

'Okay.'

Speed, 150mph. They came over a sharp rim like a crater and over a lava bed, brownish-black, pebble-strewn, flat for miles. Perfect. She thought she could tell where the wind was. She turned into it, lowered the flaps, retrimmed nose-up, watching as the speed came back. 110mph, 100mph.

'Giselle! Hold tight!'

Flecks of flame at the stubs. That blasted thing was still burning. Margaret trimmed the nose further back, increasing the drag. Full flap.

The rear fuselage tore into the lava bed. Pebbles smashed up under the wing and the nose slammed down and pitched Margaret forward into the instrument panel with barely time to swing up an arm to shield her face.

*   *   *

Noise was ringing in Margaret's brain. Mixed in with it, very distant, she thought she could hear Lorraine's scream. In her aural balance mechanism something tried to convince her that she was hurtling forwards, but her vision, blurred from the impact, told her she wasn't. She remembered the fire. Her hands were shaking and she could barely undo the seat harness. Nothing had happened yet that might have put that fire out.

'Margaret. Margaret.'

It surprised her to realise Giselle was trying to help her out. Giselle had been quicker getting out of the cockpit. Margaret fumbled, got the harness off, levered herself out.

Giselle was supporting Margaret now, moving her away from the Mustang. Margaret discovered that she was staggering. Noise made her look up, and she saw a Phantom, circling. They'd made it, they'd crossed the border.

Giselle was saying, 'I'm glad . . . I'm glad,' over and over, and Margaret realised it was because Sabina was dead.

247

CHAPTER 42

Data from the films they processed as soon as the helicopters brought them in started running on the computer terminals in Paris at 1750 local. By 1840 it was all in, all the names, locations, roles, ranks. It had been a bit of a day for the investigators sitting round their conference table. But no one disagreed about the moves.

At 1900 Paris time the police and security forces internally got clearance to go. Most of them had their plans ready, but, even so, it took about an hour, on average, to get the officers into position.

In Cuba that made it 1400 local time when Gregorio Tabio sent his crews in. They had a mobile operations van in Havana and Tabio was in it, making sure things ran the way he wanted them to. They did. Tabio's crews outnumbered the Fight cell members two or three to one, and there wasn't much bother. It was a big operation and the most conspicuous absentee was Lieutenant-General Vassily Andreyev. Andreyev was keeping an even lower profile than usual.

New York time was also 1400 when the FBI agents moved. They found Poppy O'Quinn delivering Marlena Kuhr to a board meeting in Manhattan, and they let them separate, Poppy still in the Silver Spur, Kuhr in the huge building's flower-bedecked, first-floor foyer, before they took them. Kuhr went quietly, dangerously, reeling off the names of all the lawyers she wanted. Poppy saw them coming. She grabbed for the Colt in the glove locker but she didn't get a chance to use it because an officer she hadn't seen caught her from behind and twisted the gun free.

The Japanese police had what should have been one of the easiest tasks because there it was 0500 when they went in. They seized most cell members individually, still in bed. But in Tokyo, one cell turned an attempted arrest into a bloody siege that had four streets cordoned between the Kabuki-za Theatre and the Sumida River for seven hours.

The West German Grenzschutzgruppen started their big operation at 2000. Mostly they crushed the Fight cells quickly, but in Heidelberg a commander gave the game away, and the resulting running gun battle through the straggling town centre left six guerrillas, two Grenzschutz officers and one bystander dead.

The French acted marginally sooner and generally more efficiently. One of those arrested was Thérèse Boucher, Fight's European flying expert and Command Cell member. They found her at her aero club and she was too astonished to resist.

Detective Chief Inspector Eve McKnight commanded the nationwide operation in the UK. It went smoothly. Only in Glasgow did a single cell resist, and a police officer was hurt, although not seriously. Mary Abbott was alone at home, making supper, when the police arrived at 1935; she gave herself up contemptuously. Renata Vernon was setting out from her commune with a group of other young people, mostly women, when the police arrived at 1950. The resulting scene led to eight commune members, most of them connected with Fight's agitprop, getting charged with obstruction or assaults on police; but their most serious offensive weapon had been a satchel full of books. Renata made for the rally-tuned Celica. She was still having visions of a rip-roaring car chase through the streets of London when she tripped on her granny dress and they caught her.

Mexico was the one that had jumped the gun. Doña Alma Múñoz was arrested at her luxury villa on the edge of Mexico City at 0705 local time, but she wasn't the only one, and police were still clearing up the debris eighteen hours later. But by then it was all over.

*   *   *

That was the first message that Richard Caine had for Margaret Stubbs when at 1600 mountain time he flew into the USAF base outside Phoenix where the rescue helicopter had landed her and Giselle. He was shocked to see how pale she was. When he asked if she was hurt she wouldn't tell him, she was too tired, too edgy;

but he found out later that she'd been bleeding from half a dozen splinter wounds on the head and chest when they flew her in, quite apart from the nick on her stomach, which had opened up again. Giselle had suffered splinter wounds, too, and Margaret had seemed much more concerned about her than about Caine. But Giselle wasn't even there when Caine arrived. The Americans, with a fine disregard for red tape that Margaret couldn't help admiring, had packed the kid straight off on a Military Airlift Command flight to West Germany, where her father and stepmother were waiting.

Margaret looked at Caine over their coffee cups, both people haggard, white-faced, baggy-eyed. Margaret glanced at her watch, actually Finito's. 'Apparently I'm supposed to present myself to the embassy in Washington to collect travel documents. My passport's still at Tequísquepec. There's a flight out, shortly.'

'I must say I'm bloody relieved you got out,' Caine said. 'You've done marvellously.'

She looked at him. She could still see Mario Roca's sightless eyes, still hear Lorraine's scream. She said nothing. Through the big window she could see the E3A that had tracked her, standing in the sun with its radar dish looking menacing; in the corridor, boots thudded, and an NCO shouted, with the broad vowels of New Orleans.

Caine said: 'I've been talking to someone who wants to recommend you for the OBE.'

Margaret turned, sharply, in the lightweight, utilitarian chair, and screwed her eyes up into the dazzle, staring at the E3A. After a moment she said: 'What did happen at Tequísquepec?'

'I was hoping you'd tell me that.'

She swung back to him, the grey eyes angry now behind her glasses. Her hair felt heavy, gritty on her neck, and she wished she'd had time to wash it. 'You know what I mean.'

'Oh, the closing scores?'

'Don't be so callous, Richard!'

He grinned at her, half mischievous, half something else. He was dying for a cigarette but he knew of old that at a time like this the smoke would annoy her. He went serious again. 'The whole thing was in García's hands. Mexican intelligence sent García in there in the first place, months ago, because they suspected

250

something funny was going on but they couldn't run a proper investigation. And the reason they couldn't run an open investigation was doña Alma Múñoz. She had so many top politicians and civil servants eating out of her hand, not to say taking pesos out of her handbag, that it was never permitted; in the same way that no investigation was ever permitted into Cadal.'

Margaret nodded. She'd met that situation before in Latin America.

'That was also why Pedragoza's people didn't dare admit, even at the Paris talks, that they had a source in there. They were as scared of word getting back to their own ministries as they were of it getting back to Fight.'

'Sounds as if it might have amounted to the same thing.'

'Right. What happened in the end was that, about the time you arrived at Tequísquepec, García and his team reckoned they had enough on Fight – and Múñoz – to go ahead. García was as surprised as anyone about Paquita Villegas, but he decided that, with Fight command at odds with itself over that, *then* was the time to mop the whole place up with an army raid. Villegas got killed in the early hours of Wednesday, and García got on to his team to go in at dawn on Friday. Only, on Thursday evening, *you* got caught.

'García got a message out, delaying the operation. He'd seen the way things were going, he'd seen the way Sánchez had been disciplined and Bargellini was seriously contemplating taking over from Zelaszny. He reckoned if they timed it right, Fight would save the army a lot of trouble, by splitting itself up without artificial help. He was partly right.

'His difficulty, though, was the same as Villegas's: he didn't dare use radio, except very sparingly and in extreme circumstances, for fear of having Fight's highly skilful radio operators intercept and trace his signals.'

On the runway, distant, Margaret saw two Phantoms land. Somewhere out of sight, a civilian turbofan was running, maybe another MAC flight. She felt so tired, but every time she closed her eyes she saw the Mustang, with half the instruments shot out and flame spitting from the engine.

'By the time the army was in position at the foot of Tequísquepec hill, García hadn't been able to come across with a

251

situation update, because of the crisis in the convent. All those paranoid bitches were ready to shoot everything that even thought about moving. After two spies in three days, they were really busy suspecting one another.

'That, incidentally, was another reason why García was so concerned about Giselle Stamm. He'd sussed out her mother well enough to know that if Sabina ever thought she was under suspicion, the first thing she'd do would be throw Giselle to the wolves.'

And Margaret had despised him so much. Guilt pricked behind her eyes.

'So the army sent a foot patrol up to recce the place while they waited. So there's García, waiting for the convent to fall apart, and there's this foot squad creeping through the sagebrush or whatever they've got down there, when all of a sudden it transpires that this filthy British agent has escaped from the trap Finito & Co lured her into. García naturally recognised his moment.'

'All right. So he spotted me, he got word to Giselle, we got out. What was happening during that time?'

'Finito had been slapped in the cells at the convent for letting you go. García first got word to Giselle, then went to Finito. García, of course, had had duplicate keys for ages for every area of the convent that he could get at – which included the cells but didn't include Zelaszny's block. He offered Finito a choice: either he could stay in the cells and be out of harm's way when the balloon went up, and then face every criminal charge in the book; or he could fight beside García to soften the place up for the army attack. You can guess which one he chose.'

Margaret's eyes narrowed. 'When Giselle and I came out of the tunnels, there was a fire fight going on, evidently around the radio tower.'

'Right. García and Finito shot their way in there and held it until the army arrived – one, because it was easy to defend; and, two, because as long as they held it, Zelaszny couldn't warn the world network of what was happening. That was how come we were able to clean them all up with so little trouble.'

She went on watching him. She'd borrowed a cardigan but she was still wearing the boots and battered jeans she'd worn to make her breakout, with Finito's shirt. She saw Caine's eyes flicker over her. The reason she wasn't wearing a bra was that she hadn't happened to lay hands on one, not to make a bloke look like that.

Caine added: 'Bargellini had actually used the outbreak of fighting, plus Zelaszny's rather concussed condition after your contretemps up there, for a pretty shrewd attempt to take over the organisation. She sent Zelaszny down to Alameda in the Stationair with Levenson, Rondeau and Sabina Stamm so that at least one of Fight's pilots could get Zelaszny out of the danger zone – leaving Bargellini, legitimately enough, in actual command. If they'd beaten off the army, Zelaszny would never have resumed the leadership. As it was, someone down at the *altipuerto* recognised you in the Mustang and radioed Bargellini. Bargellini concluded that you were a bigger threat than the Mexican army, and so sent Rondeau and Sabina Stamm after you.'

'And was my guess right about García having someone waiting for Giselle and me at the exit from the cave system?'

'Dead right.' That thinking had impressed Caine.

'So why didn't the Mexican air force try to intercept us? We took almost an hour getting to the border.'

'Very simple. They hadn't got the right sort of planes in the right sort of places. Even if they'd twigged it the moment you took off, they could never have done it.'

Margaret waited, thinking bitterly, a little longer. She kept her eyes away from Caine and his film-star looks; though she knew he wasn't keeping his eyes away from her.

'And what about the people? The guerrillas?'

'Margaret – don't flagellate yourself.'

She turned, eyes blazing again. 'Rot you, Richard, I've a right to know!'

He sighed. 'All right. Out of about a hundred and ten up there, twenty-five were killed and eighteen wounded, for eight soldiers killed and eleven wounded. Quite honestly, those women put up a sod of a fight. The head of the Bodyguard, Jo Colwell, was killed; both the Piotti sisters; Tina Zeiss, from New York; a Bodyguard called Annabel Hardy. Levenson won't fly helicopters again, she lost a leg in a shoot-out down at Alameda, in which, incidentally, they got Zelaszny alive and unhurt. Bargellini's on a milk diet from now on, she got a bullet in the stomach. Jodie Sadler was also badly hurt, they aren't sure whether she'll live.'

'What about Charlotte Rondeau? Cathy Latta? Or that Vietnamese kid, Pham Anh?'

'Rondeau landed safely at Alameda and walked straight into the arms of the law. Both the Lattas were arrested unhurt, so was Pham Anh.'

Someone knocked at the door. A USAF lieutenant walked in, an olive-skinned man about Margaret's age. 'Ma'am, your flight's boarding.'

*　　*　　*

From the door of the office block they could see the tail of the Boeing 737 VIP transport. The lieutenant had gone. In the afternoon sun Richard Caine halted, and took both Margaret's hands.

'You've done incredibly. I know, it's been bloody tough on you, Margaret darling. But it's honestly been fantastic working with you. You've done a hell of a good job and I'll see the right people know about it. I know you've got yourself screwed up over it, it's hardly surprising. But you'll see it differently when you've had some time to think about it.'

She smiled, privately, watching Caine's eyes. He amused her when he tried to go serious on her, he always sounded so trite. Her hands didn't respond to his.

'I've got ends to tie up here, I'll be in England in about a week.' He smiled. 'Margaret, my love, it's over now. We can start where we left off, before.'

'No,' Margaret said.

He answered quickly: 'Now, you know you don't mean that.'

Hammering echoed from a hangar. Bleakly Margaret smiled. 'Richard, you've conned me for long enough. I'm not having it any more.'

'What the hell does that mean?' It came out so slickly.

'If you teach people to spy,' she said, 'make sure *you* have no secrets.'

His face had gone still. 'Margaret, what d'you mean?'

'I mean Julie. You don't know everything I found in Zelaszny's archives. I didn't even film all of it.'

He tilted his head. 'What about Julie?'

She pulled her hands away, though he tried to grasp them. 'You killed Julie, Richard. Lorraine used the knife, but you killed her. And you did it to hook me, and that was your worst insolence, because you made *me* responsible, even knowing nothing about it.'

His head was wagging. 'You're crazy.'

'I was, once. Or at least, unbelievably obtuse. You remember that car I helped build? When they used it to try and kill you I thought I'd been blown. I never realised how it was that they knew who you were and needed to kill you. It was because of Julie.'

His lips were parted. The New Orleans NCO was shouting again, unseen.

'Then even later, when Marlena Kuhr told me officially that I was in Fight for the wrong reasons, and why they'd killed Julie, I still didn't connect it. But it was all there in black and white in Zelaszny's files.'

'You'd believe . . .'

'Yes, I would believe, because it fits!' Anger radiated from her. 'It fits the events, it fits your character, Richard. You wanted me to infiltrate Fight. You knew it would take a massive personal shock to make me do it. Zelaszny's account was explicit. First, Julie was asking the right questions in the right places. Then she was seen contacting a man. Then the man was found to be a DI agent. Therefore Julie was a potential DI infiltrator and had to be killed. The man just happened to be Richard Caine and Julie's death just happened to be the one thing that would shake me into the Fight operation. And don't give me the "routine inquiries" line. Professional intelligence operators don't get seen with contacts unless they intend to, and they don't leak their identity unless they intend to, either.'

'You're talking nonsense.'

'I'm talking absolute truth and you know it! Lives may mean nothing to you, Richard, but they mean a great deal to me. You made me a killer, right from the start. It wasn't me holding the knife when Julie died, it wasn't me beating Mario Roca to the point of heart failure. But it was always me, causing it, whether I even knew about it or not. That's despicable to me. It's even worse than being an outright killer like Lorraine.' She laughed bitterly. 'But I'm that as well now. It even ended up with me

255

killing her with my bare hands.'

Angrily Caine said: 'For Christ's sake stop getting hysterical.'

'You've forced me to destroy life, Richard. Well, in doing so you've succeeded in destroying almost everything I've lived for. Except one thing: I can still say this. I don't want to see you, or hear of or from you or your department, ever again. I'm not interested in the bribe you once offered me. If I ever take a commercial flying test, it'll be in my own right. There won't be you or anyone else working a fraud.' She started to turn.

Caine grabbed her arm. 'Calm down, Margaret, for God's sake . . .'

She pulled free. 'Goodbye, Richard.'

'Margaret, you can't go like this.'

'That's all, Richard. Goodbye.'

She turned her back and went. Caine opened his mouth, but any words he might have spoken were lost in the noise of a takeoff. He was staring as she walked evenly round the corner.

*   *   *

Through the mental exhaustion of the long, attritive days of tension, the sun-hot tarmac was claustrophobic, even before she reached the 737. Weariness pervaded Margaret's movements and the wounds on her chest and head smarted as she climbed the airstairs. The quiet inside the jet emphasised her loneliness.

The man who showed her to a seat was just an ordinary air force steward on an ordinary air force flight. He spoke sympathetically to her. He'd noted her white face, and he was used to people who were scared of flying.